Here There Were Dragons
AFV Defender, Book 2

Michelle L. Levigne

www.YeOldeDragonBooks.com

Ye Olde Dragon Books
P.O. Box 30802
Middleburg Hts., OH 44130

www.YeOldeDragonBooks.com

2OldeDragons@gmail.com

Chapter One

Chief of Talents M'kar arrived late for the morning briefing session, and entered the captain's ready room snickering, her gaze fixed on her tablet. Her little brown drac, Barroo, leaned so far forward from his perch on her shoulder he was about to fall off, and he was also snickering. Rather, the drac equivalent.

"This had better be good," Captain Genys Arroyan said, looking up from the stack of message disks that had just been delivered by the courier ship, *Proximity*.

"Incredibly good. You do know about the feud my father has with the Maniterri ambassador?" M'kar's gaze shifted to the disks sitting on Genys' desk. "I don't suppose it'll help your mood at all to know that among all that drek you have to wade through, there's some entertainment?"

"Entertainment at the expense of anyone from Maniterr?" Head Sociologist Maora raised her head from her ever-present knotwork, this time royal blue threads and silver beads. "I'd wade through a lava flow for that." She held out her hand for the tablet.

"What feud?" Security Chief Decker said. His hot pink drac, Spitfire, let out a chortle, and rose up in the air to fly intersecting circles with Barroo and Genys' black Battleaxe. "I'm getting images from the brat ... someone was trying to capture dracs?" He snorted and his perpetual scowl turned into a grin. "With nets? What kind of idiots ... oh, right, you did say Maniterri."

"Background explanation first." Genys pushed aside the disks and held out her hand for the tablet. A sigh escaped her when M'kar clutched the tablet to her chest and sat down in the conversation pit facing her desk. "Basically, when Maniterr first made contact with the Alliance, they made the mistake of thinking Nisandros would be an ally, assuming they were total misogynists."

"That's just the head of the world-destroying comet," M'kar muttered. "Ambassador Vitiarre at that time was just a very junior diplomat. My father and Uncle Asvreel were guides for the diplomatic party. It didn't take long for the Maniterri to start giving advice for 'improving' Nisandrian culture. Clothes, jewelry, layers of makeup, ritual manners, and smothering protocol."

"You've read Ashrock's series about the scouting ship that runs into one ridiculous culture after another?" Genys took back the tale. "That hilarious episode about the people so obsessed with fashion they didn't notice when they set off a nuclear bomb? Entirely based on the Maniterri."

"They don't like being mocked, do they?" Maora said, eyes sparkling with malicious delight.

"That's all our clan did," M'kar continued, "until the diplomats left in a snit. Vitiarre deliberately runs into Po'pa every time he comes to Le'anka for meetings, to make more demands for recompense for bad manners all those years ago. So of course, when the Maniterri tried to claim all authority over Draxonis, Po'pa was in the front row, like a judicial reporter, catching every detail."

"What's Draxonis?" Decker asked.

"Oh. Sorry." M'kar pointed downward at the deck. "That's the new official name for Drac World. Rammed through at hyper-speed just to irritate Vitiarre."

"Lovely," Genys murmured, and glanced at the index printed on the sleeve that protected the disks. She found the one covering the naming of the planet the *Defender* currently orbited.

They were into their fifth dec supporting and overseeing the survey teams doing a full-spectrum study of the home planet of the dracs: biological, geological, bacteriological, moving from one continent to another. The teams had just finished surveying the main continent where the *Defender*'s landing party had encountered the tribe led by Granny, the conniving silver drac matriarch currently (to Genys' relief) making life miserable for the personnel of Anwesta Medical Station. The first survey drones had been sent across a strait to the small continent to the east, and had run into trouble. For this morning's briefing session, the fate of four dying probes had just been upstaged by the representatives of a fashion-obsessed, lawsuit-waiting-to-happen culture.

If they had a chance to laugh first thing in the morning, maybe that wasn't such a bad thing?

M'kar gestured at her tablet, indicating she was ready to link whatever she had received from her father to the main screen beside Genys' desk. The lower level door of the ready room slid open, allowing Jasper Lore, Chief Engineer, into the room. The malfunctioning probes made his technical and creative genius a necessary part of the briefing.

Genys caught up Jasper on what had been discussed so far. He had several choice comments about his own unpleasant encounters with the Maniterri. Their legalistic culture allowed them to include relatives into any debt owed or any contract made with them. One of his foster-siblings had contracted to work for the ambassador several years ago. Vitiarre had then sent a demand to Fleet and to Jasper, ordering him to report to the ambassador's ship to become chief engineer. Fleet immediately responded that while Jasper and the other children found on the derelict ship forty-some years ago regarded each other as siblings, there were no legal bonds between them. Vitiarre argued that since Maniterr was not yet a member of the Alliance, he didn't have to accept their "inferior" legal reasoning. At the same time, he insisted the Alliance had to enforce Maniterri law. Fleet ignored him, and not for the first time.

"Ready for some fun? Vitiarre wasn't involved, too far below his dignity, but … well, you'll see." M'kar tapped her tablet screen.

On the desk screen, six Maniterri men crept down a long corridor, from one doorway to another. The coding next to each door indicated they were on board Anwesta Medical Station.

"How did they get permission to come on board?" Decker blurted.

Obviously, no one had taught the Maniterri the concept of dressing for stealth. The loud, clashing colors of their flowing, multi-layered robes, most definitely not uniforms, must have triggered the security system. The sight of the young men, wearing enough jewelry to jingle like a junk cart, carrying and tripping over nets, would have alerted even a half-asleep guard. Someone, Genys decided, must have realized there was comic potential right from the start and didn't do anything to stop the young men.

"This was less than four hours after Vitiarre's nephew publicly humiliated himself. He's had it in for Master Reydon since his application for private studies was denied. No Maniterri have psionic powers," M'kar added with a smirk. "The big *no'a'chic'ska* has been mocking Thyal as a weakling hypochondriac."

Decker laughed. "Just got an image from Spitfire. Infrenx went after the idiot, didn't she?"

As they talked, they watched the six Maniterri wander the

corridors, turning and fleeing five times when they came close to encountering someone in uniform. Genys muffled a chuckle when she saw the same security personnel in three of those near misses. Her general familiarity with the multiple decks of the medical station gave her a good idea of what access tubes those guards had to slide down to get from one section to another ahead of the intruders. Security was playing with them.

"Claws ready to rip his fancy clothes to shreds. Terrified him into wetting himself. Made a public spectacle in his hurry to get away. His loss of decorum earned him a reprimand from quite a few of his uncle's party," M'kar added.

"Oh, I see where this is going," Genys said. "Running into Infrenx let the Maniterri know dracs existed, and they found some way to try to claim authority over Drac -- sorry, Draxonis?"

"First Vitiarre wanted Thyal to hand over Infrenx, insisting he was at fault in the incident. He claimed her colors would perfectly compliment his wardrobe for this session of the Congress."

Jasper muttered under his breath. His words were garbled from his increasingly wide grin as the Maniterri on the screen fell over themselves again, to avoid the same security personnel. Genys did catch a few words: "deranged wannabe fashion demi-gods," and "send them into a burping Chute without life-support gear."

"Is there more to this?" Maora asked.

"Wait for it." M'kar settled back more comfortably on the couch. Barroo chirped to the other two dracs, and they all settled down on their adopted parents' shoulders.

"Did they at least catch the mental defectives who ferried those nitzicks up to the station and got them through security?" Decker said.

M'kar grinned, baring her teeth. He barked a few chuckles and settled back to watch.

A silver blur appeared in the corner of the image on the screen. Genys sat up, knowing that irritating, troublemaking blur. Granny. Probably the Maniterri had made enough noise the matriarch of the station's dracs had come to investigate.

"And in three," M'kar murmured. "Two. One."

A swirling kaleidoscope of colors and wings and claws popped into the corridor, in front of, behind, and over the heads of the Maniterri. Four of the six immediately dropped to their knees, wrapped the flowing sleeves of their gaudy robes over their heads, and wailed. Most of Anwesta's drac population shrieked and trilled. They swooped down, battering the heads and backs of the intruders. But didn't claw them, Genys realized after only a few seconds. The blue and green and purple sparks in the dracs' eyes meant they were having fun.

The two Maniterri who stayed on their feet pivoted, mouths dropping open, staring at the dracs. Genys could have sworn one of them drooled. The other one attempted to swing a net around and snag a lavender drac. The drac teleported out and the net fell, catching the man kneeling next to him.

After nearly two minutes of blinding swirls of color and the dracs trilling and clearly having a good time, three Maniterri got to their feet and swung their nets at them. Every time a net wrapped around a drac, a split second later the prey popped out and the net fell limp. Then the drac popped back in, above the head of the one holding the net, slapped the fool's head with each wing, and returned to the swirling, teasing mid-air dance.

One Maniterri slammed his net down to the deck and stomped on it. Decker burst out laughing. Another swung his net around and instead of catching a drac, he entangled the man next to him. He yanked hard enough to pull him off his feet, knocking down both men. Maora laughed.

Then a lime green drac swooped in, and instead of slapping the man who had just failed to capture her, she snagged a bracelet right off his wrist. He let out a shriek, leaped to take it back, and tripped over the two men who had fallen down next to him. They yelled and punched at him. He struggled to his feet and kicked one of them. The dracs dove like one body and swarmed the Maniterri so they vanished entirely from sight for twenty-two heartbeats. Genys counted.

Then the dracs popped out of sight, leaving the six men sprawled on the deck, breathless, wide-eyed and visibly stunned. Their clothes were shredded, all their jewelry was gone, and their thick, stylized makeup had run with sweat. M'kar raised her tablet, tapped a control, and the video closed.

"Think we can teach our dracs that trick?" Decker said, giving Genys a wide-eyed look of entirely false innocence.

She grinned and shook her head. Although, come to think of it, she wouldn't be surprised if the teacher dracs, the adults assigned to guide and oversee the young dracs who had adopted the crew, wouldn't do something like that on their own. Just give them enough provocation to swarm and attack. Miniature dragons indeed!

"Knowing how those indiferps think," Jasper said, "they tried to sue for full ownership of Anwesta, in recompense?"

"You'd expect that, wouldn't you?" M'kar hooked her thumb at the stack of disks on Genys' desk. "My father warned me about the dec's worth of argument and data searches and claims and counterclaims. Draxonis was chosen as the name, instead of honoring the *Corona* crew, to cut off claims in the future. Because we all know how the Maniterri never give up."

"They just manufacture new reasons for claims to reinforce their demands," he said, smile fading. "How do they justify trying to claim Drac World? Okay, Draxonis," he added, giving a slightly irritated look at Barro and Spitfire, who trilled at him.

"Give us the abbreviated version, preferably with some of the Poet Prime's humor?" Genys said.

"All the arguing and days of rapid legislation on Maniterr boils down to this." M'kar put her tablet on the couch and leaned forward, elbows on her knees. "The newest member of the *Corona*'s crew is the granddaughter of a woman who fled Maniterr in her childhood. Her presence, according to the Maniterri, gives them claim to authority over the planet. Everyone else on the ship comes from a planet that belongs to the Alliance, which cancels, in favor of the Alliance, any claim their homeworlds would make."

"But Maniterri women have no legal rights, no ability to inherit," Maora said. "They are the property of their husbands, meaning their birth clans have no claim to them and their descendants. Any offspring of that Maniterri woman belong to her husband's family. They have no claim on that woman's descendants, by their own law."

Barroo crooned sadly. Battleaxe echoed him.

"Okay, what do the brats know?" Decker said.

M'kar pointed at the disks again. "Metric tons of legislation, with a lot of string-pulling and bribery and threats and calling in debts of honor from centuries ago. Females now have just enough citizenship standing to give Maniterri authorities control over anything they accomplish off-planet. The children they produce, profitable inventions, and most notably, scientific discoveries. Plus, they warped it all into a matter of honor, to take legal action against anyone who harms a Maniterri woman."

"So not only are they claiming all authority over Draxonis," Genys said slowly, as the idea settled into her head. "They're also suing the *Corona*'s crew and their families because of what happened to the ship. So they want all the *Corona*'s dracs handed over to them."

"Got it in one. And that's why you're captain."

"But the Alliance doesn't have to enforce Maniterri law, so all their arguing is … No. Please tell me I'm delusional."

"Even if they become members of the Alliance tomorrow, there's no way Maniterr will be given authority over Draxonis," Maora said, her mouth twisting like she wanted to smile and make it all a joke.

"Considering all the legal and political wrangling they consider a necessary part of any contract, I wouldn't expect to see Maniterr become part of the Alliance for … ten years," Jasper said. "We've got time."

"Time for what, exactly?" Decker said.

"Survey the planet, for one thing. And for another, figure out how to royally insult and hack off all of Maniterr, so they'll pick up their toys and go home and refuse to join the Alliance." He shrugged and held out his tablet. "By the way, I think I figured out what hinked those probes."

Genys laughed. It was just like Jasper to have looked at the data that came in overnight from the survey teams and chew on the problem over his breakfast. Then, come up with a solution in the time it took to walk from his quarters to her ready room.

"How?" she said. "What is it? There's no technology down there."

"Well, there has to be. My guess is some signal, traveling on a frequency we don't use. If you don't know what to look for --"

"-- you don't see it, even though it's jumping up and down in front of you, flashing lights in your eyes," Decker finished for him. The two men exchanged grins.

"Care to tell us what the inside joke is?" Maora drawled.

"It's a training program we're devising for the kids. That Pace boy is a prodigy. Instinctive. He knows how to think outside the parameters and figure out what's missing from the manuals, so to speak." The security chief shook his head. "We're training them to look for what isn't there. That was on your mind when you got this, wasn't it?"

Jasper nodded. "Micro-bursts on extremely low-intensity carrier beams. I sent some test parameters to the probe team. That's why I was late. They reported finding several blips already. We're going to need to catch a pattern before we can triangulate and home in on the frequency. Once we find the frequency and unravel the coding, we can devise a shut-down command for whatever is attacking the probes."

"That simple?" Genys said.

Jasper shrugged, nodded. "Need me for anything else?" He waited for Genys to shake her head, then glanced to M'kar. "Send me a copy of that recording?"

"Already in your personal feed." She got up when he did, and Decker followed them out of the ready room.

Genys watched them go and repressed a sigh, anticipating all the hours, and hours, of reading and catching up on reports and analyzing the ruckus taking place in the Alliance Congress. All thanks to a spoiled brat diplomat's determination to have whatever he wanted. She looked to Maora, who was already tapping away at her tablet. Probably sending for her underlings who were best suited to studying the mounds of data compressed into the disks sitting on her desk.

"I think we're going to be grateful we're on this side of the Chute, out of reach of the Maniterri for the next few decs," Genys said with a sigh. "Take this to the conference room?"

"We should pray we're stuck here for the next few luns," Maora said. "I have this awful feeling that I might be grateful I don't have a drac just yet."

Genys wished she could make a joke that Maora had just jinxed them, but suddenly she was too tired and felt the first harbingers of a massive paperwork headache.

> *Captain's Log*
> ***Draxonis Survey Mission: Day 45***
> *Chief Engineer Lore has discovered nanites at the core of the*

probe malfunctions. As theorized, once he located the proper frequency, he sent the shut-down command. The probes can now carry out their functions.

Addendums Drax-31-101, -102, -104, -106, and -111 contain all the scientific analyses and sociological theorizing resulting from the cascade of discoveries once our teams were able to cross the strait and set foot on Continent Drax-02.

This required half a day of negotiations between Chief of Talents Lt. M'kar and the local drac population. It appears several tribes of dracs have the task of keeping all life forms from crossing the strait to the next continent. After condensing the impressions received, the continent is now called Forbidden Island. Special commendation to Lt. M'kar for the physical strain from being overwhelmed by forty-some-odd infuriated, panicking dracs.

Base theory: there was once an advanced civilization on Draxonis. Whether they were limited to Forbidden Island, or they retreated there as their civilization decayed, we have yet to determine. The nanites appear to have just one function: to kill all technology. Destroy programming, then take apart any synthesized or processed materials. This explains why preliminary scans of the planet's surface revealed no signs of civilization. No manufactured compounds. No machines of any kind. No signs Humans ever lived here, other than caches of ceramic plates, unofficially labeled libraries by the sociologists.

We are fortunate, protected by Enlo, that it appears no nanites migrated off of Forbidden Island. Otherwise the Corona might have been infected and brought the nanites back to the Alliance on their first trip, and spread who knows where or how long, until someone came up with a solution.

Lt. Cmdr. Sociologist Maora theorizes the civilization knew what was happening to them, and they recorded what they could in a material not targeted by the nanites. Whether this was in the hope they could rebuild their civilization someday, or as a warning for their descendants, we can only theorize.

~~~~~

Far too many images to process had spilled from the sentinel dracs into M'kar's brain. She was grateful to team with Celeste Coltray, because sharing the overwhelming load of impressions with the talented artist helped relieve the pressure and aided in finding some sense in what the dracs tried to communicate.
~~~~~

"So far it backs up the foundation theory. A civilization disintegrated here." M'kar studied the holographic projection of Forbidden Island, covering the conference table, and narrowed her eyes as she looked from one blinking yellow light to another, marking the caches of plates discovered so far. The entire command crew sat around the table to hear her report, and more than half the sociologists, historians, and psychologists in the crew. "The dracs didn't like them. We're lucky we met Granny's tribe first. They convinced the coastal dracs we're trustworthy."

"Good for us," Genys murmured. "Any explanation why they didn't like the people of Forbidden Island?"

"Bad people. I get that impression repeatedly. They hurt the dracs." She reached up and stroked Barroo, who hunkered down on her shoulder and crooned softly, sharing her unease over that knowledge. "They made machines, ships, and ... I get the impression of someone taking dracs apart, down to the cellular level. How could dracs understand genetic engineering? But that's the impression I'm getting."

"To hurt the big ones," Treinna whispered. A soft crooning answered her words, and M'kar turned enough to see the ship's linguist. Moonrise was cuddled in her arms, her head rubbing Treinna's breastbone. "They wanted to use the dracs to hurt ... an image in my head of ... bigger dracs?"

"This?" Celeste turned her sketchpad around, to show a rough outline of a classical rendering of a dragon. The drac perched on the dragon's foreleg indicated the difference in scale between the two.

"We are in so much trouble," Genys said.

"No, the people who were trying to use the dracs to destroy the dragons got themselves into trouble," Brea said. Her lemon-yellow drac, Boomer, perched on her shoulder and rubbed her cheek with his head.

Celeste's thick stack of sketches were simplistic, but clear enough in what they represented. She copied the images to the tablets of everyone in the room. M'kar watched their reactions, widening eyes, suddenly straightened shoulders, grunts or heads shaking. One image certainly looked like an artist's sketch of a Chute, opening into another galaxy, showing one planet.

Taking the drac impressions and Celeste's sketches into consideration, those gathered around the conference table came up with a preliminary hypothesis to include in their next report. At some time, people living on Draxonis were at war with a planet on the other end of the Chute. They seemed to be trying to genetically engineer the dracs to fight the dragon-like creatures on the other planet. Someone created the nanites, which then destroyed their civilization.

One large hiccup in the theory: there was no planet, for several days in any direction, on the other end of the Chute leading to Draxonis. So who were the Draxonans fighting?

~~~~~

"Captain to the bridge." Gate Team Head Taggert broke into Genys' morning workout in the simulator. "Ma'am, I'd like to report a spatial anomaly."

She barely refrained from asking, "How can there be *another* spatial anomaly with a Chute so close?" What she understood of Gates and Chutes, it was impossible for any other anomalies to form close enough to the Draxonis Chute for the *Defender*'s sensors to catch it. Simply put, Chutes sucked up all the energies for several light years around and in a sense yanked all the tangled energy lines straight, preventing other anomalies.

"What kind? Where?" she said, after pausing a few seconds to consider different questions that wouldn't imply Taggert had just suffered a lapse of some kind. She mentally shrugged and chose to head for the bridge in her workout clothes.

"Haven't exactly located it yet. I'm just getting readings."

"On my way."

The bridge was quiet, everyone focused on their stations, when Genys hurried through the lift doors ten minutes later.

"Update?" she said, crossing over to Taggert's station.

"Can't exactly pinpoint it." Taggert's nose gave the characteristic rabbit-like twitch that indicated excitement, not fear. One good point Genys was glad to note. "Readings put it almost equally distant from Draxonis, on the other side of the planet, nearly on a straight line …" He shook his shaved, ebony head three times before looking up from his station. "It's something out of legend."

"Legend." Genys fought a dropping-twisting-nauseated sensation. She always associated the word "legend" with Captain Shryne of the *Inquest*. Granted, the woman was a hero to a large
~~~~~

portion of the Fleet and the Alliance, but "legend" now also implied darker, dangerous tendencies that quite frankly verged on insane and suicidal, thanks to Captain Shryne and her adventures.

"Does somebody up there want to tell me why we're getting a nascent Gate alert down here?" Jasper called from Engineering.

Genys shook her head, never breaking eye contact with Taggert. She swallowed hard and sorted through several dozen responses. Just the fact Jasper was calling up to her was startling. Jasper never called her with a question or problem. He dealt with it, and she never knew there was a problem until after the fact. After he lectured whoever of his engineering geniuses hadn't been genius enough to deal with it before he had to deal with it.

"What exactly is a nascent Gate alert?" she said, after discarding several responses that would have impugned Jasper's experience and intelligence.

Taggert slowly raised his hand. "It's experimental. Something we cobbled together after a really long Brain Blast tournament," he said with a shrug. "We're getting some spatial anomaly readings up here, Jasper. I've been doing a search backward, and it appears to have started maybe four days ago, but the changes haven't been strong enough to register or trigger any warnings until now. The flux shifted, progressing a dozen degrees in an hour, when it was taking two days for each degree until now. Something is developing out in space, with Draxonis between it and the Chute."

"How come the teams down on the planet haven't noticed it or alerted us to it?" Genys said.

Chapter Two

"That's easy," Jasper said, after only a few seconds of silence.

Meanwhile, Taggert consulted his station and Genys listened for any emergencies or problems coming from the rest of the ship. She silently thanked Enlo for the efficiency of her crew, so they didn't need her to deal with trouble right now.

"They're looking down, focusing on the planet. They're not watching over their heads, and they aren't expecting anything. Kind of stupid, if you think about it," he added, his voice softening.

Taggert grinned and one eyebrow cocked upward so high it would have vanished into his hair, if he had any.

"And we noticed it because?" she prompted.

"We're constantly looking," Taggert said.

"Why a nascent Gate?" she had to know. "Nobody knows what a nascent Gate would look or sound like or the energies it would give off. We don't know what an actual, functioning Gate sounds or looks or feels or tastes like." She had to fight to keep her voice down at the end of that statement.

"Stories," Jasper said with a chuckle. "We set up our criteria based on all the legends of Gates and all the theorizing over the years. Even if it isn't a Gate, and even if the Gatekeepers aren't about to burst out and tell us it's about time we showed up ... something is happening out there."

"Oh, joy..." Genys whispered.

~~~~~

The various survey teams gave the equivalent of a shrug when Genys reported what the *Defender* had sensed and theorized out in space on the other side of the planet. They focused on two things. Finding more caches of plates. Or finding the now-dead nanites, to unravel the alien technology to determine if the destruction of their civilization had been an idiotic accident, a result of hubris, or inflicted on them by the planet Draxonis had been fighting. If the images and impressions from the dracs were interpreted correctly.

A new cache of plates found just that morning was generating excitement with Maora's team. The drawings of plants and animals
~~~~~

and theoretical genetic code had been replaced by what might be a written language, along with diagrams of machines. Hopefully that would include the nanites. More proof of Maora's theory, that the Draxonans knew their impending doom, and the ceramic plates were their effort to preserve their knowledge.

Among the plates were more theorized genetic code and intricate, finely detailed renderings of creatures that the life sciences team could only, with caution, label dragons.

"Five species," Boran, chief xenobiologist reported two days later. With a tap on his tablet, the file of his report appeared on the tablets of all the officers and section heads in the conference room. "We've studied them every way we know how and compared with the sketches Celeste and M'kar got from the dracs' memories. Because of the size differential, we can't determine if they are precursors of dracs, if dracs came from them, or they are two different species. Dracs share characteristics with all five species but are not direct copies of any one of them."

Asking the coastal dracs proved fruitless. They refused to have anything to do with anyone who went to Forbidden Island. They caught on that the pictures M'kar asked them about came from Forbidden Island, and refused to look. Barroo and the other dracs on the *Defender* spent a large portion of their time on the planet either giving their Humans sorrowful looks, or driving away the dracs who shrieked and scolded. The uninvited visitors from Draxonis had stopped popping onto the ship. The prohibition against Forbidden Island and what it contained was that strong.

When the teacher dracs on the *Defender* and the remnants of Granny's tribe on Draxonis were asked about Forbidden Island and the existence of the "big ones," they knew nothing. M'kar and Brea estimated they were all young adults and adolescents. Anyone who might have knowledge gathered from other drac tribes had gone with Granny when they stowed away aboard the *Defender*, and were now tending cocoons on Anwesta Medical Station. M'kar and Genys did not look forward to interrogating Granny about what she might know of Forbidden Island and the "big ones." On a positive note, they had been overseeing the study of Draxonis for nearly six decs now and might never leave.

Taggert's team was happily employed studying the growing spatial phenomenon on the far side of Draxonis. Most of their work involved taking measurements and researching records and the oldest fables about travel around the universe after the Gatekeepers scattered the Human race. They theorized and argued to the point that friendships were threatened. Genys feared her entire Gate team and astrogation department had never been happier being so frustrated.

A breakthrough came at the end of dec six of the mission, with the discovery of a cache of ceramic plates containing possible star charts. Unfortunately, several shelves had broken from weight and age. Several caches found so far had lost as much as two-thirds of their stored ceramic plates. There was some duplication from one cache to the next, but not enough to soothe the scientists trying to piece together understanding of this lost culture. In the case of the star chart cache, water had penetrated the underground chambers and caused wood rot. A gap the width of twenty ceramic plates hung open like a missing tooth, over a pile of shards, covered with debris from the eroded ceiling and fragments of shelving. Five plates on the shelf below it were broken, from the ones above falling on them. One team devoted itself to trying to reassemble the broken plates while the others got to work interpreting.

When the plates were laid out in the order they had been filed on the shelves, they told a story of an encroaching phenomenon in space. The broken plates covered what Taggert theorized could be anywhere from three luns to five years in the approach of the phenomenon.

"It's a time-lock Chute," he said, his voice thick and tight with restrained emotions, as he made his report in the conference room. He touched his tablet and the entire tabletop became one screen, showing the plates lined up, with colored highlights changing to mark each item he discussed. "We thought it was only theory, fable."

He gestured at the rounded engraving filling the center of the image. It was eerily close to images M'kar and Celeste had picked up from the dracs before they stopped communicating.

The image seemed to pulsate as Genys stared at it. Rounded, with wavy lines, probably meant to indicate energy enclosing the edges. In the center of the opening in space, one planet, with stars reaching into the distance. Someone had put a glaze of colors on this plate, differentiating between the star system seen through the theorized representation of a Chute and the stars and space supposedly seen in the night sky of Draxonis.

"These plates seem to indicate the passage of time, theoretically how long the time-lock Chute stays open," Taggert continued. Highlights moved from one plate to another. "Note the position of the smallest of Draxonis' four moons. It's far enough away it could almost be considered an asteroid, and its perceived orbit of the other three moons is a clear, calculable measure of time passing."

In the progression of images, the smallest moon, little more than a dot, appeared on top of the other three moons, then traveled to the left around the circle, to end up underneath them, and continue its travel back up to the top of the formation.

"We calculate it takes two years for this particular formation to go through one complete shift and return to the original formation. Maybe it also indicates that the time-lock Chute won't open until the smallest moon is at the top of the formation."

"How long does this theoretical Chute stay open?" Genys asked, gesturing at the array of changing moon formations. Even before Taggert said he couldn't estimate, she knew that. There were too many open gaps in the images, where the broken plates should have been.

He went on to explain what a time-lock Chute was, saving Genys having to ask. She was familiar with the term, but only as a side note in two classes during her time at the Fleet Academy. Something that was mostly theory and fable wasn't generally given much serious thought by those in the command track.

Time-lock Chutes were a variant of burping Chutes, relying on an alignment of spatial phenomena on both ends of the Chute before they would open. How long they stayed open depended on the conditions and energy fluctuations on either end.

"So any indication of how long it takes for this Chute to open? I assume the spatial changes you've detected mean it is preparing to open?" Executive Officer Veylen said.

"We assume the broken plates contain that information. We'll need a far longer period of observation to correctly calculate the buildup of energies in the spatial phenomenon we're monitoring, to have any idea when it will open."

"Since Draxonis is pretty much our discovery ... does that

mean we get to wait for the Chute to open, and head through?"

The speaker cringed as groans, expressions of dismay, and some wry amusement escaped a handful of senior officers around the table. Genys felt sorry for the young man. How could he know he had just invoked the misfit luck of the *Defender* by asking such a pointed question? He was new, a very junior member of Taggert's team, and the kind of brilliant that meant he was awkward in so many other levels of ship society.

"Show some mercy, please," Genys said, looking around the table. "We all have experience with how Fleet operates. Besides, common sense says there are more qualified teams who get the honor of sitting and waiting for the door to open. E&D ships don't sit still. That's the nature of our duty. We go where we're sent. With minimal argument on our part."

She nodded to Taggert, and he nodded back, with a tip of his head toward the crewman. He would explain in private how just speaking the longing of everyone at the table, to stay and explore, meant the *Defender* would not get the assignment.

She was right. Less than a dec after sending a messenger probe back through the Chute with Taggert's report and theory, she received a message that the science vessel *Dandridge* would be taking over the *Defender*'s duties supporting the planetary survey teams. The patience and discipline of Taggert and his team was sorely tested by the time the *Dandridge* showed up to change places with the *Defender* and wait for the Chute to open. The spatial phenomenon had grown by nearly fifteen percent, in size and energy emissions. There were no precedents, no hard data to use as a basis for calculations, but Taggert theorized the Chute would open in less than a Standard year. And the *Defender* wouldn't be there to share in the adventure.

The *Defender* left Draxonis after eight decs on duty, and headed back through the Chute. Genys had her in-depth report ready to send off to Fleet and the Academy as soon as they emerged from the Chute. The influx of newsfeeds that hadn't been sent through the Chute in all that time distracted her, so she barely registered an addendum report from the botany department. A vine discovered on Forbidden Island appeared to be a variant of the vine the dracs chewed to allow them to breathe fire or spit firebombs. Preliminary investigation determined the vine lacked several compounds that young dracs found repellant. Genys wrote a memo requesting the botany department keep that vine out of reach of the ship's dracs, but never sent it. What was the use, when dracs could teleport anywhere they wanted to go? Instead, she sent a memo to Jasper, asking if he had made any progress on creating a theoretical drac-proof fence, to keep dracs out of sensitive areas of the ship, or at need, keep them restrained in one place. She had the awful feeling that might be a necessary piece of equipment someday.

~~~~~

M'kar had the choice of waiting until Thyal contacted her, once the ship came through the Chute and their psionic link resumed, or contacting him to discuss the discoveries on Draxonis. She needed to question Granny and the older dracs on Anwesta about Forbidden Island, and any shared memories about the people who had once lived there. The chance of eliciting a furious firestorm from Granny was good enough reason to present the questions and images to Thyal and have him act as go-between. Get the initial uproar out of the way before the *Defender* reached Anwesta.

Sometimes, she was grateful for this link between their minds that seemed to defy all distances, even jump gates. Everything but Chutes. Let Thyal deal with Granny. He was certainly better equipped to handle stubborn, domineering creatures of all races, as a Le'ankan Master with all the attendant discipline training. And a healthy dose of serenity. That had certainly helped him endure his two-years-and-counting of recovering the use of his own body.

As soon as her duties for post-Chute transition status checks finished, M'kar made her way up to the observation dome for some enforced quiet and solitude, and exhaled a long, cleansing breath in the chilly, dark silence. On her shoulder, Barroo let out a soft trilling coo and nuzzled her cheek.

"Are you mad at me for asking these questions?" She found the empty equipment pedestal and settled down on the floor with her back against it.

Barroo crawled down the front of her jacket and settled on her lap, then looked up at her, big eyes blinking and glowing yellow and green. Curiosity and a little confusion. He tipped his head to the right, then to the left, let out a deep sigh, and curled up, those big eyes focused on her.

M'kar braced herself and called up some of the images she had
~~~~~

gathered from the coastal dracs in their fury, and the images Celeste had drawn.

Barroo shuddered and rose up to clutch at the front of her jacket with all four paws. His eyes shifted to mostly yellow, with streaks of red. Fear. M'kar couldn't repress a partial smile. At least her brown baby wasn't angry with her. If anything … she thought he was afraid *for* her. She cuddled Barroo to comfort him.

"Face it, Junior, your mommy is a coward."

Barroo let out an indignant snort and reared back, bracing his forepaws high on her chest, so he could look her in the eyes. M'kar tried to meet his unblinking gaze, but as usual, he always won the stare-off. Laughing quietly, she scratched down his back to the base of his tail, then from under his chin to the center of his chest. Purring, he settled down, eyes half-lidded, and gave her that sleepy, adoring look that melted her heart. She silently thanked Enlo that Barroo couldn't speak, because then she might never be able to say no to anything he wanted to have or do.

Thyal … we have a problem. Pull out all your diplomatic skills and experience handling difficult students and their triply difficult parents.

Give me a moment. His chuckle came through their link, crossing multiple star systems and jump gates without a heartbeat of delay. *You're leaking a little bit –*

I do not leak! Immediately, tension eased out of her shoulders. Leave it to Thyal to know exactly what to say.

Then how do you explain all the blurry images I'm getting before you even start talking?

She had a flash of an image of him sending his hoverchair out into the sprawl of formal gardens behind his parents' home on Le'anka.

Fine. I'm just frazzled enough to admit to leaking. This once.

Barroo chirped and an image of him playing tag in the air with Infrenx came through their bond.

Troublemaker wants to say hello to Infrenx.

Thyal's chuckle felt deeper this time, wrapping around her like a hug. *She says hello back. You need to convince your captain to bring the ship back here before Infrenx drives me to the breaking point, wanting to see Barroo. Visiting with the dracs up on Anwesta isn't enough for her.*

You could apply to join my ship as a consultant, she offered. A moment later, M'kar nearly slapped her hand over her own mouth.

Where had that idea come from and why had she let it mentally vocalize to him?

I might do that, just to avoid all the not-so-subtle hints from some of the Masters who want to study our bond. Warning, some theorize all the tweaking your ancestors did to your Nisandrian genetics is part of why our part of the team mind-circle stayed open. I've already warned your father to make himself scarce, so they don't put a mental whammy on him and get him to agree to all sorts of tests. All right, I'm out where we won't be interrupted. What's the problem?

M'kar tried to make her sigh of relief entirely physical. She gathered up the images and thoughts and impressions she had semi-organized on her walk to the observation dome. Focusing, she imagined it compressed, then sent everything to Thyal. Then she settled herself to be as comfortable as she could to wait for however long was necessary.

Fascinating, he responded after only a few breaths. *This negates the hoped-for proof of racial memory locked in the genetics.*

Is that all you got out of my latest drac-based headache?

No. Just the first layer. I wonder if I can claim the physical and mental health of my drac as reason enough to come out there to join – Uh, sorry. Firestorm alert.

Then he was gone, entirely gone from the link.

M'kar winced, feeling a single throb of psionic ache that she suspected had come from Thyal to her. A blurry silver image flashed in her mind's eye and she knew what had happened. Not how, but what. Or more accurately, who.

Granny somehow knew what M'kar had been showing Thyal, and she teleported in from Anwesta to scold and lecture.

By the time Thyal reopened their link, M'kar had her theory. Infrenx had probably picked up the images from Thyal as M'kar gave them to him. She didn't understand anything except that it had to do with other dracs. Being exposed to the hierarchy of the Academy in action every day, she had done the logical thing and went to the highest authority to explain the matter. Meaning she had gone straight to Granny, on Anwesta Medical Station, and shared the images picked up from Thyal.

Judging from the nearly fifteen minutes of silence from Thyal, M'kar guessed he had needed help calming Granny, and probably had had to make some promises to her.

Please tell me you aren't heading for the nearest available ship to take you and her to Draxonis, she said, when she felt Thyal's mind-call.

Nearly. I had to promise you would report regularly. She'll have to wait for you to come back to Anwesta.

And she agreed to it?

She did. At least, as much as I can understand. How can someone with no language manage to mutter under her breath?

M'kar laughed and slouched a little against the pedestal.

I'm sure she's planning something. If the distance weren't so great, I'd be half-afraid she'd focus on all the dracs on the Defender *and find some way to teleport herself and join you.*

Please, Thyal, convince her to wait. M'kar shuddered at the mental image of Granny killing herself with the effort. Moving dozens of eggs up from Draxonis to hide them on the *Defender* had worn her out, and she had had help from most of her tribe. If the distance from the planet to a ship in high orbit had done that to her, the distance of numerous galaxies, with four intervening jump gates, would do more than wear out the little silver drac. It could erase her from all existence. Granny's spirit and determination were a force to be reckoned with, but her body was frail. M'kar could only hope Granny was smart enough to realize her limits and not do something that would result in suicide.

Thyal planned to confer with Dulit and Flinders, two drac parents acting as liaisons between the drac population and the medical personnel tending the cocoons. Hopefully with the help of their dracs they could work with the older dracs on Anwesta and find some understanding of the situation with Forbidden Island. That was the best they could do.

M'kar said a quick prayer that Granny would have calmed down by the time the *Defender* returned to Anwesta. Then she went to her duty station to put together a formal report to send with the next message burst Genys was ready to transmit. Sometimes she wished she and Thyal didn't have to pretend they didn't have their mental link, because pretending to communicate by slower methods could sometimes be a problem and a pain. Her parents and Thyal's parents knew, and Dulit, and the Masters at the Academy, of course. The more people who knew, the greater her chances of being transferred off the *Defender* and turning into a long-term scientific study. She swore if that day ever came, she might just steal a ship and turn pirate, to stay free.

~~~~~

Captain's Log

The Defender *has been granted shore leave as a reward for major leaps forward in understanding of the planet Draxonis. We have stopped at Space Station Maqaffree for some well-earned rest and relaxation.*

Personal log

I'm all for delaying our return to Anwesta and facing down Granny. According to Dr. Garion Dulit, the scheming old biddy wasn't happy when we managed to leave the station without her. Until Jasper comes up with the drac-proof fence, I don't want to risk her sneaking on board and then never getting her off again.

Personal log

On a positive note, I think the Defender *has lost the horrendous nickname of* The Nanny Ship.

On a negative note ... to be honest, there really isn't a negative side to this incident that is already being called "The Fried Ankuar Incident." Any day we manage to humiliate and frustrate Ankuar, with plenty of evidence they brought it on themselves, is a good day.

Some Ankuar spotted several of our ship's children at a local entertainment venue. They had fun intimidating and frightening our children, until the ship's dracs, all eighteen, caught their psionic emanations and went teleporting to the rescue.

Enough said.

Except to put it on the record that I never actually told the Ankuar captain we had full-sized dragons on board. He was free to interpret my comment any way he wished.

~~~~~

The *Defender* was half a day out from reporting to Anwesta Station when Battleaxe got twitchy. The drac couldn't sit still for more than ten minutes at a time. She was constantly popping out and back onto the bridge. Genys couldn't coax an explanation out of her. She only knew Battleaxe was distracted and nervous and either couldn't or wouldn't communicate what it was, so she could do something about it.

Sitting in the command chair on the bridge as the *Defender* approached Anwesta grew increasingly uncomfortable. Like someone had slipped itching powder into her bio-liner before she got dressed that morning. Getting up and pacing would help, but she didn't want to transmit her own case of the twitches to the rest of the crew. Tradition kept her in the command chair until the *Defender* settled into orbit around the medical station. Her drac's fidgets gave Genys an awful suspicion she tried to ignore. She simply had too much to deal with right now to take the chance of being paralyzed with dread if she let that thought into her brain.

Usually Battleaxe sat on the perch attached to the command chair when she was on the bridge. Or she flitted from station to station, hovering at the perfect position to see what every officer was doing without getting in the way or being a distraction. The only bump in the road, besides getting official permission to have dracs on the bridge at all, had been convincing the bridge crew not to bring treats for Battleaxe when they came on duty. A fat drac just didn't go with the "look" Genys needed to portray. Lean equaled mean, and if she ever needed Battleaxe on her shoulder during a ship-to-ship real-time video conference, fat would ruin the effect.

The twitches increased as Anwesta grew larger in the front viewscreen, until Axe hadn't come to rest on her perch for more than ten seconds at a time. Genys had counted, which just revealed to her how twitchy she was getting. She wanted to call down to the ship's "drac wrangler" and find out if she knew what the nethers was going on. She suspected that was a conversation that had to be carried on privately, and tradition held her in her command chair until they settled into orbit.

"She's just as twitchy as Moonrise," Treinna murmured from Genys' right, and slightly behind her.

Genys turned sharply, grateful she didn't make a sound. Another sign she had let Battleaxe's mood get to her: she hadn't heard the lift doors open or Treinna come onto the bridge. Moonrise huddled on Treinna's shoulder, tail wrapped around her neck, forepaws clutching at the shoulder seam of her uniform. Usually when Moonrise came onto the bridge, she and Battleaxe did a little aerial dance, as if they hadn't seen each other in luns.

"That does it," Genys muttered, and tapped the short-cut icon on the communication screen on the left arm of her chair. The short-cut had become a necessity since becoming a drac parent. It kept track of M'kar everywhere she went on the ship, and allowed

Genys to break in and establish communication, no matter what her chief drac wrangler might be doing.

"Good," M'kar said, before Genys could do more than open her mouth. "I was going to check on you. Do you need to know where Axe is, too?"

"What do you mean, too?" Treinna stepped to the chair, and kept her voice lowered. It didn't really provide privacy, just the illusion of it. Nothing was private on the bridge.

"Are your dracs with you?"

"Axe and Moon are up here," Genys said. "Whose is missing?" Her gaze flicked to the forward view screen. Instinct had her expecting to see a tiny silver drac come arrowing at them through the dusty, radioactive vacuum of space.

"The first I knew, Boomer and Ha'ess were out of contact, then before I started scanning, they came back, and Decker called down to find out what made Spitfire vanish in the middle of their morning target practice."

"I don't even want to know," Treinna whispered, and grinned.

"Now Barroo and Boomer and Ha'ess are all playing hide'n'seek and sounding very guilty when I make contact." M'kar sighed. "None of the teacher dracs are anywhere to be found, and I'm getting a strong impression from Barroo that he doesn't want to lie to me. Can you interrogate yours?"

"Axe?" Genys held out her hand.

Battleaxe paused near the apex of the domed ceiling with all the sensor equipment jutting out. The black drac started to drop, wings spread, then let out a strangled *cheep*. Moonrise whistled and jumped up with enough force to make Treinna hiss and press a hand against her shoulder. Both dracs vanished in mid-flap.

"Does anybody happen to have solid numbers on just how far ..." Genys shook her head, and eyed Anwesta. "Forget that. If she can teleport between a planet and a ship multiple times in one night, what's to stop her from popping out here to check up on the kids?"

Chapter Three

"Her?" Treinna's eyes widened.

"Demented minds think alike," M'kar said. "I have a good idea where Granny will be holding a debriefing session. I'll let you know when I find them."

"I think we need to spend some time impressing on all the dracs that they're in the Fleet now." Treinna leaned on the arm of the command chair. "They need to learn to ask permission and wait their turn."

"Yeah? And who's brave enough to get in Granny's face and tell her she's being rude?" Genys grinned, though.

Someone with the ability to teleport out of danger in a heartbeat shouldn't have reason to be twitchy or nervous about anything. Then again, there was Granny, the domineering, diminutive silver matriarch of the drac race. There were some things against which even the ability to teleport couldn't shield.

~~~~~

M'kar reported that Granny had actually been affectionate toward her, after more than an hour of huddling with the *Defender's* dracs. After that, she led them to Anwesta, to the massive domed environment created to simulate the conditions on Draxonis. Supposedly they were having a family reunion festival. Genys found it a little funny, a little sad, that her shoulder felt a little bare without Battleaxe perched there

In a reflective mood, she wandered the upper levels of Anwesta Station, and ended up on an observation deck overlooking one of the greenhouses where cocoons and their prisoners in living death were housed and tended, in the hopes of being able to awaken the victims someday. Dracs had provided the first hope for release in decades. She knew an instant cure and a massive awakening were an unrealistic hope, but there was something depressing about knowing no one had awakened yet. Increasing brain activity in every cocoon that a drac had chosen for its focus point, yes. Growing life signs, yes. Those life signs rising noticeably and regularly above the level of a healing trance ... no.
~~~~~

Still, even though the improvement was gradual, almost hard to track, there *was* improvement. It might take a few years before someone awoke from the living death and broke free of their cocoons, but that was years, not lifetimes, or generations. The growing staff of healers gathering around the cocoons had determined the next step in healing was making telepathic contact, to give the victims extensive counseling while they were still comatose. The group mind of the *Corona*'s dracs and Dulit's bond with his drac, Poki, showed him the victims knew what was happening to them as the cocoons pulled them down into sleeping death. No matter how much they were aware before or after the fact, the victims would need emotional and psychological healing and guidance to recover from their luns or years or decades of a coma existence.

Genys checked the chrono in her wristband, wondering if M'kar was finally free of guiding the ship's complement of dracs through assessments. Numerous specialists in different areas were interested in seeing how the *Defender*'s dracs developed, surrounded by Humans. She sent a thought out for Battleaxe, checking if she was free. A moment later the little black drac popped in and trilled happily as she settled onto Genys' shoulder.

"So everything's good again, huh?" she murmured.

Axe chirped and extended one paw. Clasped in her talons was a tiny, much-folded packet of message film. Genys took it and unfolded it and started walking. Just as she expected, it was a note from M'kar:

Ready whenever you are.

~~~~~

Tahl and Brea were busy with their own tasks in the drac-cocoon research project and couldn't join them in Genys' ready room. Whatever M'kar had to report, they had already heard it, being involved in some of the testing.

"So?" Treinna said, stepping into the ready room just steps ahead of Decker. Genys and M'kar were already seated.

Moonrise and Spitfire hopped down off their parents' shoulders and curled up together on the table in the center of the conversation pit. Battleaxe let out a chirp that certainly sounded relieved to Genys, and joined them. They helped themselves to the plates of refreshments. Genys found some amusement in seeing the
~~~~~

little dracs preferred the cheese and meat provided for their parents, rather than the nuts and grains native to Draxonis. Barroo, however, stayed curled up on M'kar's shoulder. The little brown drac looked more somber than usual. Not a good sign.

"Good news, and bad news." M'kar rubbed her eyes with her palms for a moment. "As far as anyone can tell, our dracs are further along in development than the dracs from the *Corona*."

"How is that -- no, wait, I'm not that dense." Decker offered them a crooked grin. "It's weird that our dracs are more developed, since they were hatched *after* the *Corona*'s. So something makes them different. Is that good or bad?"

"Good, if the theory is correct, and all the mental stimulation we give them, all the attention, the travel, contributes to their growth. The growth is physical as well as mental. Dulit theorizes the exposure to children also makes a difference. We have a larger, more active community on the *Defender* than the dracs can access on Anwesta. Most dracs spend their days sitting vigil on cocoons."

"Less stimulation." Genys nodded, turning that information over in her mind. "So … are they proposing we stay in orbit to provide stimulation to the *Corona*'s dracs, and bring them up to speed?" Now that the gauntlet of Granny throwing a hissy had been avoided, she wouldn't mind a lun or two of orbit around Le'anka. Maybe she could catch up with former teachers, indulge in some personal academic research.

"I hope not." M'kar shuddered once. "Enlo, be merciful …" She sighed. Her eyes looked tired. "Status report. The cocoons showing the most brainwave activity are, no surprise, the crew of the *Corona*. Either because they already had a bond with the dracs, or they were the most recent to be cocooned. Both answers have negative aspects. If the amount of time in the cocoon is a factor, that could mean the longer someone has been cocooned, the harder it will be to make contact, stimulate brainwave activity, and bring them out, eventually. If the pre-existing bond with the dracs is a factor, it could mean no matter how long a drac sits on a cocoon, they won't get a strong enough bond to awaken the sleeper. Ever."

"So what do we do?" Treinna asked softly.

"Besides spend more time in the chapel, thanking Enlo for protecting us so far?" Genys fought down a cold, exhausted sensation washing through her, from her chest outward. Battleaxe let out a sad croon, leaped up from the table, and glided over to land and clutch at the front of her jacket. She tucked her head under Genys' chin, crooning. "Thanks, baby. I love you too."

"I think it's a good idea to spend more time in contemplation and prayer, period," Treinna said.

M'kar stayed seated when Treinna and Decker got up to go back to their duties. Genys slumped in the seat opposite her. How hard would it be to just tip over and let herself fall asleep? Her body ached momentarily with exhaustion that wasn't entirely physical.

"Anything you feel free to share with your commanding officer?"

"Can I share it with my friend, first?" M'kar asked. "Then you can decide if this is something my commanding officer can fix."

"Break out the high-intensity chocolate?"

"Ginger, to settle my stomach." She picked up a bottle of chilled water and pressed it to her temples, one side and then the other. "You know about the whole dymcrait encounter, back at the Academy."

"When half your class ..." Genys opened her palm and tapped it, referencing the infrenx tattoo on M'kar's hand.

"We were in our mind-circle during the battle. When Thyal was stung by the dymcrait, the bond stayed open. His parents theorize that protected him from the mind-draining or paralyzing effects of the venom. When I woke up from my healing trance, the link was still there. You should have seen us, Dulit and me, scrambling to get to Thyal's house to stop them from turning off the life-support equipment and performing the ceremony to release his soul to Enlo's care. We're not sure if that would have killed him, or snapped the link with me or ..." She shrugged.

"You might have kept him alive, or you might have been dragged down with him, if they encouraged the end, to save him suffering," Genys murmured.

"Doesn't matter now. Anyway ..." She let out a long sigh. "The link ... is still open. The only thing that interrupted it was when we went down the Chute to Draxonis."

"Still open? Like ... you and Thyal are constantly in contact?"

"Oh, we can turn it on and off. Privacy and all that. Polite and proper, my hearth-brother." She grinned and her eyes took on a distant light for a moment.

Suddenly, all the cryptic comments M'kar made from time to time, when she seemed to be responding to a different conversation, made sense now.

"So why are you telling me this? What's changed, what's happened, that I might need to know as your commander?" Genys shuddered, her mind tired enough to immediately think of all the negatives, such as possible breaches of security.

Not that she would ever accuse Thyal, son of the revered Master Reydon, of ever threatening the security of a starship. Still, there was always the possibility that something he heard or saw through M'kar's senses might slip out at the worst possible moment, heard by the worst possible person, able to use that information to do the worst possible thing to harm the Fleet, the Academy, or the Alliance.

"When we realized the Hivers were dymcraits, Thyal had to tell his parents, to explain where he was getting all that really scary, critical information long before you could file your reports. And of course, key Fleet and Academy personnel had to be told about our little …" she shrugged, "… secret, so the information I passed along could be shared." A long, somewhat rattling sigh. "Now there are rumblings about keeping me on Le'anka for extensive study, to figure out what brought on the link. Thyal and I are both hoping you can keep the wrong strings from being pulled. Like apply for a really long-term mission that will take us to another universe entirely for the next ten years?"

"Hah, you wish," Genys muttered. They shared crooked grins for a few seconds.

"Thyal has pointed out several times that they would need to send me far away, to test the limits of the bond, but there's no guarantee I would stay on the *Defender*. Then there are the Chute researchers, who want to find out what happens during Chute travel that cuts off our link. It might be final proof that Chutes go to other dimensions of reality."

"I don't know off the top of my head what to do. I'll have to think about it, what strings to pull."

"And it's late and you're even more dead tired than me."

"That too."

"Sorry for dumping it on you."

"No, don't be. I worry when things seem to be going too

smoothly and peacefully. It usually means we're going to get hit with something that'll have our eyeballs rattling from the impact." Genys nearly smiled, but the heavy load of new data and considerations made the muscles in her face ache.

Like Treinna said, she needed to do more praying. It was only smart to go to Enlo for guidance and protection *before* they needed it. Usually when disaster struck, there was no time for coherent requests to the All-Maker.

~~~~~

"Kill me now," M'kar muttered.

She and Genys and Veylen were crossing the wide, sunlit plaza of the spaceport that sat equidistant between the Academy, the capital of Le'anka, and the Alliance Congress complex. Genys and Veylen had come down to Le'anka for debriefing meetings. M'kar hitched a ride on the shuttle to spend some leave time visiting her parents before their next assignment: taking twenty Anwesta dracs to the colony world Boorhees. The plan was to pair them with animal-focused Talents training there, to establish better communication and partnership in the effort to free the cocooned Hiver victims. Taking the dracs wouldn't be so difficult, because all the dracs liked and trusted M'kar.

The difficult part was getting them off Anwesta without Granny insisting on coming along. She had made it painfully clear that she wanted to get out and explore the universe. Her mission in life now was to find the "big ones," after the discovery of the plates on Draxonis. No amount of bribery or reasoning could persuade her that her most important role was to lead the dracs on Anwesta. So working around her, keeping her ignorant of plans, was the only viable tactic. Besides, it avoided hours of scolding and spying on her part. That drac-proof fence Jasper kept alternately promising and threatening to invent seemed to be more vital to sanity as the decs went by.

M'kar also needed to consult with Thyal in person, not using their psionic link, to avoid certain interfering dracs overhearing. He had had far more experience dealing with Granny than anyone besides Dulit and Flinders. They couldn't tell Dulit and Flinders about the Boorhees mission because those two men weren't able to hold their thoughts private from Granny's prying.

Barroo had already flown ahead to meet with Infrenx. Thyal
~~~~~

and his parents, Master Reydon and Lady Healer Thean, would be joining them for dinner at the home of Ashrock and Dr. Jeyn.

Now, Genys followed M'kar's line of sight, and saw the massive man stalking toward them from the archway leading onto Academy grounds. She laughed and couldn't quite succeed in choking back the sound when M'kar scowled at her.

"What's the problem?" she asked, and didn't even try to sound innocent.

Quite a few problems could result from Chieftain Ashrock of Nisandros coming to greet them. Judging by the big grin splitting his broad-boned, scarred and tattooed face, and the way he spread his huge, muscled arms, he was going to embarrass his daughter with a loud, public display of affection. Ashrock enjoyed "stretching the expectations and stereotypes of others," as he put it. Usually, he "stretched" people's minds until their brains took on the consistency and pliability of balls of tree sap, and then bounced around the room at dizzying speeds.

"Have you met my father?" M'kar said instead, turning to Veylen.

"I've never had the pleasure. I look forward to it," the *Defender*'s Exo said, somehow managing not to stare or burst out laughing.

Ashrock had come close enough for them to see the designs printed on his knee-length overshirt that hung open, without a belt to hold it in place. The images, in primary colors, were the cover art and interior illustrations from the many children's books Ashrock had published in the years since fleeing Nisandros. Most were anthropomorphic creatures or outright fantasy characters he had adapted from Alliance folklore.

He waited until he was only four or five meters away from them, then shouted something in high Nisandrian. At least, Genys thought it was high Nisandrian. It might have been battle language, for all she knew. The clicks and gutturals contrasted strangely with the cartoon illustrations covering his clothes, which clashed with the tattoos on his face and half-bared arms – and the tattoos that peered through the curly black hair on his half-bared legs. Each tattoo highlighted the scars Ashrock had earned in contests of honor and testing and simple stupid, semi-suicidal adventures (according to M'kar) that were a "normal" part of growing up among the high nobility of Nisandros.

He did it on purpose, making a display and guaranteeing an audience that could not look away when he did what Genys realized M'kar had been dreading.

"Give your Po'pa a hug, *mi'sho'ki!*"

M'kar didn't even try to run. She turned to Genys and mouthed something, pointing to the right. Then her father dove at her from a good four steps away and snatched her up in his enormous, bulging, muscled arms. He swung her around while he planted big, sloppy kisses on her forehead and cheeks. He finished with a kiss on the end of her nose before he put her down with surprising gentleness on the pavement of the plaza.

Genys glanced away for two seconds. Enough time to see the cluster of garishly bright, flowing robes in eye-watering combinations of colors. The word M'kar had mouthed: Maniterri.

That explained everything. Ashrock was making a scene to provoke them.

M'kar's feet were barely solid on the ground when she flexed, bent down hard and snapped upright again, catching Ashrock solid in his breastbone with her left shoulder. She knocked him off balance perfectly, and finished the movement by leaping up, spinning in mid-air, and clocking the side of his head with her knee as he staggered backwards. Down they went, with M'kar snatching at the front of that garishly bright robe, riding her father's chest to the ground. He *oophed* when both her knees hit him in the chest right under his rib cage. Then while he roared laughter, M'kar kissed his forehead and cheeks, and bit the tip of his nose. She shifted to sitting on his chest with one smooth twisting motion, bounced twice, and leaped to her feet.

The silence in the rest of the plaza extended a good hundred meters in all directions, as most onlookers fled in all directions. All but the Maniterri, of course.

"Usually they're not this … exuberant," Genys muttered to Veylen. He tried to smile, but a totally understandable dazed look had his eyes wide.

Then Ashrock was on his feet, his roar toned down to deep chuckles. He wrapped an arm hard around M'kar to hold her to his side, demanding introductions. Genys barely remembered in time to offer a fist-bumping greeting that had her fighting not to wince.

It was far preferable to being swept off her feet in a sideways hug with his free arm. Ashrock had declared after her second visit that as an honored battle-mate and fellow explorer with his daughter, she should consider herself a daughter of his house. Fortunately, that didn't mean she had to participate in wrestling matches and various other demonstrations of athletic suicidal tendencies.

Veylen showed his high intelligence by opting for full formal Le'ankan greetings. He bowed deeply, with the proper hand gestures indicating respect and admiration, placing himself in a subservient position to Ashrock. Despite his boisterous temperament, Ashrock was an incredibly perceptive man, and he had a positive delight in learning to perfection the rituals and courtesies and manners of every world belonging to the Alliance. Once Veylen had set the standard for their interaction, he wouldn't deviate or stretch the boundaries of politeness. At least, as Genys knew from experience, until Veylen did something that Ashrock would insist meant honor required a much closer relationship.

"Are you happy now?" M'kar tipped her head in the direction of the Maniterri, now stalking toward them.

"Not yet," Ashrock said, with a dismissive glance their way. "I owe them for several unpleasant *do'a'zaq* visits from those eye-bleeders. And people say Nisandrians don't know how to dress like civilized beings?" he ended on a growl.

"What did they want?"

Genys muffled a chuckle, after interpreting the Nisandrian word that meant rotting-stinky-putrid-gag-worthy or depending on the context, painful social necessity. With the Maniterri, he probably meant both. Sometimes she really loved the multiple, descriptive meanings bound up in Nisandrian language.

"My grand-monster, of course," Ashrock growled.

Genys glanced at M'kar, who tapped her shoulder. Of course. They wanted Barroo. Vitiarre renewed his complaints against Ashrock, to force M'kar to hand over her drac.

"You are the superior officer to this mentally defective creature?" the Maniterri diplomat said, flicking his fingers at M'kar and directing his words to Veylen.

A single snort of laughter escaped the Exo as he moved back and sideways one step each, putting himself partially behind Genys. The momentary confusion and dawning dismay on the man's arrogantly narrow, painted face, was almost worth the headache Genys anticipated. Misogyny at its worst, on display.

"I am the superior officer," Genys said. "As for the rest of your statement, I see no mentally defective creatures. Academy and Le'ankan security forces would not allow any personnel, dangerous to themselves or to others, to come near the spaceport. Perhaps you are mistaken?"

"Mistaken?" His dismayed look iced over and his face narrowed more, if that was possible. Now she recognized him. This was another of Vitiarre's many nephews. The day just kept getting better and better. And she hadn't even gotten to the debriefing.

"Delusional. The victim of badly written fiction," Ashrock said, stepping over in front of Genys. He planted his big fists in his hips and leaned forward, somehow managing to tower over the entire Maniterri party. "Fiction, as in a polite word for lies. And before you open your mouth to foul the air and our ears, I insist again you desist from including my heir and her fellow officers in your uncle's long-standing, demented feud with me and my household."

"You are an ill-mannered barbarian and we have registered new complaints with your overlords and clan leaders!" someone shrilled from the back of the group, while the diplomat's mouth flapped multiple times with no sound coming out. Judging from the creeping bluish tint under his mask of makeup, probably no air was getting in, either.

Genys hadn't enjoyed herself this much at a dramatic production in a long time. This most certainly deserved to be classed as a farce mocking social interactions.

"Oh, yes, I have already discussed such complaints with my father and uncles and the spiritual leaders of our clan and the council of clan masters. They were quite amused. You should be happy to know," Ashrock continued, vicious mischief lighting up his eyes, "that they have chosen to take your complaints in the spirit in which they were lodged. We are discussing the proper mode of honor combat with which to respond. Honor demands, you know, that the battle be between equals. My father and uncles are considering whether to accept you, as intermediary for your uncle, or demand his presence to settle the matter."

"Combat?" Vitiarre's nephew squeaked. His gaze slid over

Ashrock, head to toe and then from one massive arm to the other. He backed up a step, running into several of his sycophants who were pressed up against him, visibly trying to hide.

"Unacceptable," the same voice squeaked, several notes higher, and still from hiding. Genys guessed that was why he had the courage and breath to speak.

"Nonsense. An honor challenge has been issued by you and yours, and Nisandrian honor demands we respond. Run along and inform your superiors that they'll be hearing from my clan heads to discuss terms of combat. Unless you'd like to apologize right now, and on record?" Ashrock tipped his head slightly to the left, watching as the Maniterri party swung around and made a partially dignified retreat across the plaza. "Is that a no? When can I hear from you on setting a date and time and location for combat?" His voice grew a little louder with every word.

"Po'pa," M'kar said, her voice cracking with the effort not to laugh. "You are my hero."

"Ah, Forefathers, take me home. I can die a happy man." Deep, rumbling laughter that threatened to loosen the tiles of the plaza pavement rolled out of Ashrock. He offered an arm to her, then to Genys, and the four of them started across the plaza.

"Liar, liar, hair on fire," she sang under her breath, once they were nearly to the archway leading to the residential portion of the Academy grounds.

"Me? A liar?" Ashrock sighed. "And thus I fall from grace."

"You should understand," Genys said, turning to Veylen, who only looked amused by the exchange. "Scholar Ashrock has not contacted Nisandros since the day he and Dr. Jeyn and M'kar … expanded their citizenship to the Alliance."

"That's the polite way of saying my love and I had reached our limit of political stupidity and scheming and attempts to either murder or kidnap our child. We fled for the sake of our sanity." Ashrock nodded, looking a little tired.

"The captain neglected to say that Nisandros – and yes, I mean the entire planet, representatives from all levels of society and all divisions, political and bloodline and spiritual and academic and warrior and a dozen others you don't need to hear about." M'kar leaned forward slightly to see around her father's massive chest. "The entire planet contacts my parents regularly. To draw them into taking sides of one sort or another. Making regular demands and threats and pleas and offering bribes, and a few even asking for help in taking asylum in the Alliance."

"I need two secretaries just to handle that harassment and keep telling them to leave me alone. No other response. How am I to write more of my lovely books and do all my research, with nattering idiots taking up my time?" He shook his head.

They were all laughing as they turned down the path paved with green and silver swirls of sand, leading through the trees to the wide double doors of Ashrock and Dr. Jeyn's home.

Chapter Four

The colony world of Boorhees played a vital role in the Academy's mission to train and protect Talents. That meant communications were a high priority. That meant while they were on mission at Boorhees, the *Defender* could keep updated on all developments at Draxonis, especially every change in the spatial anomaly. Genys wavered between gratitude and irritation, because Taggert and his team were nearly in agony at not being on hand for every change.

He was on the bridge when a courier ship arrived at Boorhees. It transmitted a communication burst to the *Defender*. Mykels, on duty in communications that shift, distributed all the messages immediately. Taggert received a report and went perfectly still as he read. Then he inhaled sharply and gripped the edge of the console in front of him. He was silent so long, Genys thought he had stopped breathing.

"Taggert? Something wrong?" she asked, and peripherally saw several people turn from their stations to watch him.

"It's a Chute. And it's open," Taggert nearly wailed. "It seems to be locked open. We've only heard about it in fables and speculated on the science. No wonder we couldn't make any sense from those readings we were getting before we left Draxonis. The *Dandridge* has caught images from the galaxy on the other end. It should be impossible to see the other end of a Chute." He turned away from the message still scrolling up his screen, eyes shining and wide with wonder. Genys was proud of him that he didn't burst into tears, because she knew how disappointed he had to be right that moment. "But that's what the plates showed us, isn't it? We thought they were cramming too much information into drawings. Or they didn't know what they were trying to record. But it was real. It was true. People wrote about this kind of thing in stories and they were laughed at for bad science, but it's real!"

Genys felt like the ship tried to spin around out from underneath her for a moment. The concept was stunning, the implications took her breath away. A Chute stable enough to allow sensors and simple visual recorders to reach to the galaxy on the other end could theoretically offer massive advancements in understanding Gates. The chance to go through that Chute first would be both dangerous and a bright spot on a captain's and ship's records.

However, the *Dandridge* would claim that notation in history.

The only consolation for Taggert and his team was that their vital role in detecting the anomaly so it could be watched meant they had priority in receiving updates. There was a chance they would hear about developments before most scientists in the Alliance.

Yet Genys knew hearing first wasn't good enough. Didn't her crew have the right to be there, on the cutting edge, theorizing with each new bit of data?

"Well, look on the bright side," Taggert said, when the command crew met in the *Defender*'s conference room to discuss the news. "Shryne and the *Inquest* didn't get there ahead of everyone else. Someone else gets to have the glory and the fun."

"You're forgetting something important," Maora said. "Those plates we found certainly indicate a war with another planet on the other end of that Chute. Anyone the *Dandridge* runs into on the other side might not be in a good mood, or friendly toward strangers."

<div align="center">~~~~~</div>

Captain's Log
Second report from the **Dandridge:**
A planet has been found on the other side of the Chute from Draxonis. Why are we not surprised?

One benefit from the characteristics of this Chute that break all the known rules: communication bursts can traverse the Chute. No need to send messenger drones or courier ships. Data pods sent by the Dandridge *still have to be loaded on a courier and sent through the Draxonis Chute, but the delay is cut in half.*

Third report from the **Dandridge:**
The planet has very little visible industry, yet based on the signals received so far, they have an amazingly sophisticated communication network. The low level of technology has activated several Fleet regulations requiring at least two Standard years of

observation before agents will be sent to infiltrate, absorb the culture, establish a foothold, and then make contact.

The planet is surrounded by a network of satellites, yet sensors have not traced any communication between the satellites and the planet. There is a regular pulse of energy transmitted to the satellites from geothermal taps located in areas of past volcanic activity. The theory is those taps syphon geothermal energy directly to the satellites, to keep them functioning. Yet the satellites appear to be separate from the communications network. No use for the satellites has been discovered yet. Perhaps they are left over from a period of much higher technology. Perhaps the same disaster that struck the people of Draxonis crippled the people of this world, and they have lost all their technology.

The Dandridge *has verified that all signs of civilization are limited to one continent. No theories have been formulated at this time. Further study is required.*

The Dandridge's *linguists have gathered enough material from the planetary communications system to begin to learn their language, which has four distinct dialects that do not appear to be limited geographically. The people call their world Castitarus.*

Sixth report from the Dandridge:

Massive amounts of information go through Castitarus' communication system, including education programs at all levels. History and folklore education units have provided information many members of my crew will find fascinating. I'm just grateful Granny isn't here, or on the Dandridge, *because keeping her on the ship would be impossible.*

Castitarus believes in dragons. The images and fables broadcast through the education channels match the images of dragons found on Draxonis. They are called numenjax. They apparently no longer exist, but when they did they were judges and lawgivers and intermediaries between the people and their deity, Praestantaes. No determination yet if Praestantaes is the Castitaran name for Enlo, since basic precepts of their theology are as yet unknown.

Everything relating to the numanjax is in past tense, with indications they vanished more than two hundred Castitaran years ago.

Ninth report from the Dandridge:

Examples of the written language of Castitarus have shown enough similarities with the language found on the Draxonan plates to support a theory that the two planets and cultures did have contact the last time the Chute was open. Treinna and her team have done enough work on the Draxonan language, they are being consulted regularly on interpreting the Castitaran language, which means daily report pods reaching the Defender.

Personal Log

Ashrock has sent M'kar many amusing clips from meetings where Vitiarre has again humiliated himself. He regularly leaps to disagree with every report from the Dandridge's sociologists. The latest humiliation came when Academy sociologists agreed with the conclusion that Castitarus is an entirely matriarchal society. He insists only women appear in the material taken from the communications channels because women are the workers, the laborers, the servants. The males on Castitarus, he insists, are the leaders, the intellectuals. Too refined to deal with commerce, overseeing education, and other mundane details.

Vitiarre has accused the women scientists on the Dandridge *of contaminating the information they glean from the communications channels. He has demanded they be removed from the mission, the ship, and have their scientific credentials revoked. He was ordered by President Aeolian to apologize. In response, he demanded an apology from the crew of the* Dandridge, *their families, and their planets. When many attendees laughed, he had a screaming fit, laced with profanity. Maniterr has withdrawn him from Le'anka. No apologies offered. Vitiarre insists that he has resigned in protest, he has not been withdrawn.*

We can only hope the next ambassador from Maniterr will have more self-control, and maybe better taste in color combinations.

~~~~~

The mission on Boorhees kept M'kar so busy she had to skip many of the regular training sessions with the ship's children. As the resident drac expert, the success of the mission rested on her. She knew that, but instinct told her to pay careful attention to her students. The changes in the shipboard community were still occurring, from the additions to the ship and crew. Several students needed extra monitoring. Starting with Tress Lore, thanks to her father's unknown genetic background and her awakening Talent.
~~~~~

M'kar knew from experience how a Talent could awaken without warning. She could only speculate and imagine how different her life would be now if her Talent had awakened on Nisandros. Maybe the assassination attempts would have stopped, once her relatives and the pure-blood fanatics realized her power and potential. The political and religious power-mongers would have stepped up their schemes to get control over her. However, the quality of training to establish a proper foundation for psionic Talent was questionable on Nisandros.

M'kar called on E'bett and Maenta, the primary schoolteachers on the *Defender*, and confided in them. About the changes she had been sensing among the children. The factors that had changed and shifted in the many different layers of *Defender* society, emotionally and physically.

Both women agreed with her. In more planet-bound childhoods, most of the ship's children might never have awakened to Talents, their psionic potential low, out of the impact range. E'bett and Maenta recommended Genys file a request for a Master from the Academy to join the *Defender* as part of the teaching team. Specifically, a Master with training in guiding new Talents and experience in anomalous Talents. Logic said to assume any Talents developing among the *Defender*'s children would be anomalous in some way.

Genys, M'kar, E'bett and Maenta met with the parents of the children who were showing signs of awakening psionic Talent. They gave the parents the option to request transfer to a less "influential" environment for their children, with no negative marks on their records. Every parent chose to stay on the *Defender* and trust the teachers to know the best tactics to nurture whatever psionic potential their children possessed.

Later, Genys wondered if they were all being just a little too optimistic. Psionics didn't always have a positive aspect. Some Talents were more like a curse on the ones possessing them, rather than a gift. When that happened, staying alert, trying to prepare to handle the results of that awakening, was even more vital to everyone involved.

~~~~~

Genys felt somewhat left out when the *Defender* returned to Anwesta with the new drac-Talent pairings. M'kar, Tahl and Brea
~~~~~

were busy. Treinna and her team were having a field day with the Academy specialists decoding the Castitaran language. Taggert and his team were just as occupied and nearly giddy with the gathered information on the stable Chute. Genys had nothing to do but file reports.

Granted, Granny had a long-lasting temper tantrum when they returned, but that was becoming old hat. The impression Genys got through Battleaxe was that they had left without Granny's blessing, and they hadn't learned their lesson the last time.

Genys hadn't meant to complain of her boredom, and she didn't do so vocally, but the quixotic luck of the *Defender* kicked in within two decs of returning from Boorhees. Their new assignment: *pretend* to go on shore leave.

Mendax was a world currently procrastinating on deciding to join the Alliance. In the meantime, it had submitted to massive, in-depth investigations and had earned probationary status as open to Alliance members. No Fleet ship would come for shore leave until the *Defender* had given its assessment.

Genys had the awful feeling the higher-ups in the Fleet were depending on the misfit luck of the *Defender* to work out the "bugs," or maybe uncover something that someone, somewhere, sensed wasn't quite right.

~~~~~

"You know they're using us for test rodents, don't you?" Genys muttered, standing in the hatch of the shuttle that had just landed and opened to the lush, sweet-sour air of Mendax. Only the two women directly behind her could have heard her.

"And that's a problem because?" Treinna took a deep breath and let it out in a rush. "I know the air on the ship is cleaner and safer. Depending on your definition, a whole lot fresher than air that's been breathed by a thousand lifeforms we haven't even read about yet, but ... gotta love being dirtside all the same."

Maora let out a sigh, of that particular tone that conveyed a patient smile. In a lot of ways, she was the ship's mother. Genys preferred to think of herself as the ship's big sister. The pessimistic one who looked for everything that could possibly go wrong and made sure it didn't happen to all her little brothers and sisters. That was what a captain did.

Maora nudged Genys between her shoulder blades. "Are you
~~~~~

going to pose for the cover of the Fleet quarterly briefing all day, or are you going to let us down onto actual dirt?"

"Nag, nag, nag." Genys grinned. "What do you think, Axe?" She tipped her head back.

Battleaxe popped into sight, warbling with delight, and dive-bombed onto Genys' shoulder. A moment later, Moonrise streaked around from the right side of the shuttle and turned somersaults before coming to a more sedate landing on Treinna's shoulder. She bobbed her head and flicked her forepaws.

"Please, please don't tell me you've been teaching her sign language?" Genys chose discretion over valor by stepping down out of the shuttle and making it official: the crew of the *AFV Defender* had started shore leave on Mendax.

"All right, I won't." Treinna chuckled and held up her hands in mocking fear of a punch that all three women knew would never come.

A querulous rasp came from behind them. They turned to see Spitfire clutching the side of the hatch, sticking only her head outside, and flicking her tongue fast enough to be nearly invisible. Her scowl clearly conveyed a message of, "Get a move on."

"I heard they offered the *Inquest* the chance to be first to have shore leave here," Decker called from the cockpit of the shuttle. "Any shore leave planet that Shryne declines to be the first to officially visit has to have something wrong with it."

"I should think the prohibition on almost all technology would delight her," Maora said. "The woman was born to scramble every partially aware computer and cripple every doomsday device ever devised."

"She just doesn't want to go somewhere she doesn't have a challenge. Even when she's supposed to be relaxing," Treinna offered. She grinned and twiddled her fingers at something Moonrise signaled to her. "So, are we free to relax now?"

"The sooner we get the test run over with, the sooner everybody else can start taking their turns," Genys said with a sigh. "The kids seem to think everything's green." She turned her head enough to see Battleaxe, perched on her shoulder, head turning from side to side rapidly enough to make Genys' neck ache. "Oh, yeah, they're excited and don't sense any trouble."

"Except what they plan on making themselves," Decker said,

stepping into the hatch now. He twitched his shoulder and Spitfire leaped from the hatch to her preferred perch, tail wrapped securely around his throat and sprawled across his shoulder in a semi-recline. He snorted. "The sacrifices we make for our crew."

"Onward," Genys said.

Across the stretch of what she considered a far too short landing field, she made out the low, single-story sprawl of the spaceport administration building. It served as the welcoming center, the supply hub for the guest housing, and information depot for those visiting the planet. Jungle rose up behind the long stretch of building, climbing the gradual ascent of rolling mountains that ringed the flat river plain where the first Human settlement had taken root. The rest of Mendax was allowed to exist as it had been since creation, except for the scattered settlements that were reached by skyships – essentially, vast bags of buoyant gas suspending gondolas holding passengers and freight. The gas jets and air pumps that moved the skyships were apparently the height of the technology permitted outside the administration area.

"The children are going to love all that wilderness out there," Treinna commented, once the first-in team had settled into their quarters and looked over the multi-page visitors' guide, printed rather than displayed on a tablet.

"How do you figure?" Genys let the guide drop onto the table in the courtyard where they sat.

Their quarters consisted of a dozen quaint huts surrounding an open-air courtyard that took advantage of the constantly balmy weather of Mendax. The guide made a soft *crack-splat* as the old-fashioned paper coated in plastic hit the table. With nearly one hundred pages, one-third of them covering prohibitions, it had quite a heft to it.

"They've been itching to get out of the rec deck and the testing mods, and see just how good they really are with all the hunting and tracking tricks M'kar has been teaching them."

"Little monsters'll probably scare the ..." Decker looked around at the three women and grinned before choosing his next words. "... the fewmets out of whatever nasty critters this planet might offer. Might have to go pretty far out into the untamed wildlands of this place before they get to anything that'll stand up against them."

"That's what I don't want to have happen." Genys couldn't help a grin at the thought of the efficient, fearless little fighting corps of the ship's children. The children who had left the *Defender* to go on to the Academy were making quite a name for themselves and adding to the reputation of the ship. She had stopped cringing when she got personal communications from friends who were instructors at the Academy, commenting on the cadets. Someday the news might be bad, but she had learned to enjoy the present moment without letting possible disasters intrude.

Most of the time, anyway.

Captains were trained to worry a full lun ahead of the present moment. If they could handle the strain, they worried two luns ahead. That was how they kept their ships in one piece around themselves and held onto their crew.

Which was why she couldn't shake the awful feeling Fleet suspected Mendax was too good to be true, and they had sent the *Defender* to uncover what was wrong.

Test rodents stay alive by remembering they're being tested, she told herself. She shared that thought with her command crew when her team sent back its report half a day later. Then gave permission for rotating shifts of crew and families to come dirtside.

~~~~~

The wide plaza of the administration center was dotted with information-and-registration cubicles. Ten meters away from M'kar, a handful of *Defender* crew studied the two-meter-by-ten-meter displays of recreational activities available for those on shore leave. They were handily color-coded by intensity of effort required, danger levels, and maturity and skill required.

"Just how much trouble can you get into on a planet where tech is basically outlawed?" a loudmouth with an otherwise gorgeous baritone voice asked.

There's one in every group, M'kar thought. *But why do we always have to have at least twenty?*

No one with any real experience on a ship of any kind, much less the *Defender*, much less a parent or someone who spent any time with children, would ask a question like that. Certainly not aloud. With enough experience, they knew better than to even *think* such a thing. It equaled slapping the universe in the face and issuing a challenge.
~~~~~

Usually that challenge was answered in the most uncomfortable and embarrassing manner possible.

M'kar wished she hadn't been standing within a kilometer of the idiot who had just issued that challenge.

"If anything is going to happen—" she muttered.

"It'll happen to him," Norgon said from behind her. He shrugged and offered a lopsided grin when M'kar turned around to meet his gaze. "Even I know better than to say something stupid like that. He's a new guy, but that's no excuse."

"You'd think after what we went through with Draxonis and then frying the Ankuar," Anya said from a few steps away, "the new crew would have figured it out by now." She raised a hand, beckoning. M'kar turned to see Taggert come around the long display wall. In a few seconds, Anya related what she, M'kar and Norgon had overheard, and gestured at the knot of crew, who were signing up for some adventure trip. "Think we should step in and try to help?"

Taggert screwed up his chubby, ebony face, nose twitching the entire while he thought. Then his gaze met M'kar's and something delightfully malicious glittered in his big, dark eyes.

"There's the trade-off to consider. We get points with Enlo for trying to rescue the idiots from themselves and whatever bad luck that one just drew down on them."

"Or we get too close and have it rub off on us," M'kar finished for him.

"It could rub off on us for refusing to help." Norgon shrugged, and his slightly dopey smile got wider. He had long been considered a bad luck charm. However, a patient and encouraging commanding officer had turned that bad luck around. He was intensely loyal to the command crew of the *Defender* because they had given him a chance. He was also sympathetic to the newbies and klutzes he encountered.

M'kar privately had a wager going with herself that someday all the help and sympathy and encouragement Norgon offered to others would tip the scales. He would become a golden core of good luck, to the point that everybody would be fighting to have him in their crew. Enlo had to reward such patience and endurance. She had seen the All-Maker's hand at work enough times to know that eventually, everything did balance out.

"Compromise. We warn everyone, we warn the mouth, and then we get as far away as possible," she offered, when the other three looked at her.

Norgon offered himself as sacrificial lamb, to warn the loudmouth and his friends that he had just challenged the universe. M'kar took the duty of going to the compound shared by the command crew currently on shore leave, to warn Genys.

For the sake of control, since where one drac was all the others wanted to be, most of the drac parents were taking shore leave at the same time. Brea and Tahl couldn't take shore leave together because one of them had to be present in Medical at all times. M'kar was just grateful for the chance to be on hand while Decker made more adjustments to the drac treats he was developing. It amazed her, sometimes, how much control he had over Spitfire, when he was clearly the most indulgent drac parent of the six of them.

Decker agreed with Spitfire that until she could consume the various Draxonis plants that would fuel her fire-breathing abilities, she still needed to live up to her name. So how could he enable her to spit fire? The answer came to him in a candy Tress Lore had offered to Spitfire and Barroo once, with mixed results. The candy fizzed and popped loudly when wet. Enough candy in the mouth had painful results. Spitfire liked the experience more than Barroo did, which M'kar was grateful for. Decker played with the formula, inserting a diluted phosphorous compound.

The formula wasn't quite what Decker wanted, but the dracs all loved being his test subjects. Spitfire passed out samples every time he came up with a new recipe. The courtyard of the compound certainly provided enough room for the dracs to test out the treats. There was plenty of that fresh air Treinna kept chuckling about, to waft away the stink from failed recipes.

When M'kar reached the compound, she found Tress and her gaggle of friends playing some game that involved blindfolds and balls with chimes inside them. All the young dracs were playing too, and some of the adult teacher dracs. All were having great fun, according to their chirps and squeals. Treinna was relaxing in the corner farthest from Decker's worktable. If "relaxing" could apply to untangling more of the Castitaran language, matching audible words with written, and finding the parallels with the Draxonis plates. M'kar supposed being a linguist, untangling languages was fun for Treinna. M'kar settled in a lounging chair near her table, knowing that would ensure her hours of quiet.

Some of the children's parents were at other tables in the courtyard, or the doors to their huts stood open, meaning they were relaxing indoors while monitoring their children. M'kar reflected that Tress had the good sense to pick clever, good-natured, relatively obedient and adventuresome friends. More important, they all had intelligent parents with a strong dose of common sense. Meaning none of them spent more than ten seconds reacting to M'kar, the first time they got close enough to see her facial tattoos and realized she was Nisandrian. By the third time she growled or hung the children by their ankles, the children giggling helplessly the entire time, none of the parents turned white or choked on whatever they had been eating.

All in all, this shore leave promised to be a good time, relaxing, spent in the company of people who made her feel comfortable and almost invisible. Being the daughter of Chieftain Ashrock, with a drac perched on her shoulder, M'kar could never be quite as invisible as she wanted.

"Look out!" Jorgan Pace darted across the courtyard, waving his arms. His pet light snake, Sparky, squeaked from inside the tiny environmental chamber the boy wore around his neck.

Chapter Five

M'kar jerked out of her doze, rolled out of her lounging chair and flung her arms up in the air to shield herself. Then she saw the two dracs directly over her head, hot pink and brown, spinning in a complicated dance.

Jorgan was ten Standard years old and if Jasper Lore had anything to say about it, would be married to Tress before either of them left the ship to go to the Academy. The boy was an intuitive engineering genius. If anything happened to his parents, Jasper would probably adopt him.

"What are they doing?" M'kar crouched on the painted tiles and narrowed her eyes. Barroo certainly seemed excited about something, rather than angry with Spitfire.

"Chief Decker got the formula right," the boy said with a grin, and dropped down in a crouch that mimicked hers. "Spitfire won't share. They're playing keep-away."

"When you say right ..." M'kar kept an eye on the circling dracs as she got to her feet. It made her eyes hurt, but she managed to also watch Decker at his worktable in the far corner.

Sure enough, the Security chief, clad in his idea of casual wear -- saggy, baggy, stained, rip-proof and fire-proof -- stood at his table with the rest of the ship's complement of dracs circling in the air above him. They knew better than to land on the table. Not that Decker would scold or offer them anything from the assortment of bowls and beakers and boxes scattered across the table in front of him. Spitfire had them all well-trained so they only took samples from her, no one else.

"Don't be a Pinky-dink," M'kar said.

Spitfire let out a squawk and stopped circling with Barroo. She dropped down and darted over to M'kar, to look her in the eye. Her expression was offended for a moment or two, before shifting to contrite. Not that M'kar would ever maintain a mental link with anyone else's drac outside of emergency situations, but she and Spitfire had come to an understanding, of sorts. The little pink drac didn't boss her around, and she didn't call her Pinky or any variation of nickname with Pink in it. Use of it did serve to be a rap on the knuckles and get Spitfire to be nicer. Or in this case, share.

Barroo dropped down to M'kar's shoulder. He held out his forepaws and bobbed his head three times, meaning "please." Spitfire hovered in front of M'kar, looking her in the eyes for a few seconds. Then her mouth dropped open and her tongue lolled out. She let out a few chirps of drac laughter, and held out one paw holding four sparkly, red-tinted globs the size of large seeds. Barroo cheeped the drac equivalent of "thank you" and took one. Spitfire popped one of the remaining three into her mouth. Both dracs squeaked and a small flash of lightning erupted from between their closed lips. They leaped up in the sky and opened their mouths. Flames erupted in a flash. A glob of something hit the colored tiles, flared, then disintegrated in a shower of sparks. Interestingly, no residue remained on the tiles.

"Wow." M'kar took a tentative, testing sniff. Definitely phosphine stink, but not as bad as she had feared. Some overtones of sulfur, and something sweet.

Barroo wobbled a little as he glided over to rejoin her. His mouth fell open in his usual doggy grin and his eyes spun a few times. M'kar swore they spun in opposing directions. She watched Spitfire as she darted ahead and flew back to Decker. The little pink drac wobbled in her flight, too.

"Congratulations, I think you created catnip for dracs. Or worse," she said, when she reached Decker's worktable.

"Back to the drawing board." He shrugged but didn't seem worried. In fact, she thought he looked pleased.

"What else were you trying to do, besides let Spitfire live up to her name?"

"How fast did the fires go out, once they hit?" he asked instead.

"Hmm, maybe five seconds."

"The bigger the dose, the longer it should last, probably." He nodded and made a notation on the tablet lying on the worktable.

M'kar thought about reminding him such technology wasn't allowed, but she considered how close the compound was to the administration building. They were probably just within the boundaries of permitted technology.

"You're thinking of having our dracs as backup for security?"

"If people know they're too young to flame, or they think the kiddies don't have access to the right plants to support flames …" He shrugged, a slow, malicious grin stretching his lips for a few seconds. "Might make them careless."

"I am so glad you're on our side."

He gave her a shallow bow and held out a bowl of more red globs to Spitfire. She gathered up a double pawful and leaped into the air. Barroo followed her as she trilled and the other dracs gave up circling Decker and came to her.

"What gave you the breakthrough?"

"That variant of the firebreath vine we took off Forbidden Island. Brea confirmed it lacks all the elements the kiddies are allergic to. Spitfire loves it, says it smells yummy."

M'kar choked. Decker constantly surprised her with the things he claimed Spitfire said. Somehow, she never would have expected him to say "yummy."

"Wait a second. After that run-in with the Ankuar on Maqaffree, I thought all those plants were destroyed."

"Hmm, maybe I confiscated them, in the interest of ship's security." He gave her the closest he could come to an innocent expression. "One nice little side effect is that the new vine has a calming effect. It'd take a lot to build up in the blood enough to put the kids to sleep. According to Brea, anyway," Decker added with a shrug. "I figure, if things are bad enough we need them to spit fire, don't want them to get over-excited. You know?"

Later, M'kar wondered why she hadn't worried more when the young dracs ate enough of fire-jewel-candy to make them all sleepy. Or that the teacher dracs refused to eat it. Decker frowned and remarked that Spitfire hadn't eaten enough of the vine all by itself to put her to sleep, when they were on the ship. Then he shrugged and declared he would have to adjust the formula. All M'kar cared about right then was the delight of the young dracs at being able to spit fire at each other.

~~~~~

The dracs were still napping when M'kar and Treinna gave in to the pleading from Tress and her friends to take them to the marketplace next to the administration center. It was clearly a tourist trap, full of treats and useless bits of pretty stuff people would never need, but wanted because it would "remind us of this shore leave."
~~~~~

M'kar enjoyed the first twenty or thirty minutes of shopping, especially the children chattering about the trinkets and toys and fake weapons. About the time Jorgan and Dafna brought up the idea of having a training mission out in the jungle, a niggling sense of something wrong began to itch at the base of her scalp. She thought at first it was an instinctive sense of doom, at the idea of taking children camping in territory she hadn't studied first.

"I know why," Treinna said, when M'kar finally told her something felt wrong. She gestured around the shopping area, all the bright, useless, tempting junk. "What does this place remind you of?"

M'kar looked around and thought. It looked like any other public market around a dozen spaceports she had seen on just as many worlds. The kind of places that offered the flavor of that world without having to cross the boundary line, stepping off Alliance-held territory. She couldn't seem to push her brain into the right direction to get the answer. Finally, she shrugged.

"It's the prize shop at Castle Zooks." Her friend managed not to laugh or even grin, but amusement was bright in her eyes.

"Well, as long as no Ankuar walk in, we're fine." M'kar tipped her head to her empty shoulder. "And our dracs stay napping."

"You've just doomed us, you know."

"Sorry." She shrugged again, and Treinna shared a long sigh with her. They turned back to keeping the children from becoming too enamored of something they couldn't or shouldn't buy. Something either too expensive or too big for the limited living space on the ship.

M'kar gnawed on that comparison while she managed to give coherent responses to more questions and ideas thrown at her by all six children. All the tempting junk, the noise of the surroundings, the numbers of strangers walking around didn't add up to enough reason to be uneasy. None of them were in uniform, to attract attention from someone with a general grudge against all military. There were enough people with strange face paint, she doubted her facial tattoos were attracting attention. Still, she had always trusted gut instinct over facts.

Someone is watching us, she signaled Treinna in the abbreviated sign language they had created just for their crew.

We have the only children in sight, her friend offered.

M'kar grinned, acknowledging she was right, and laughed at herself for not thinking of that little variable to attract attention.

Still, it might be wise to get out, Treinna added.

The children only gave token protests when M'kar announced it was time to head back to their quarters. They were likely tired, maybe overwhelmed with the smells and sights and sounds, but not too tired to be obedient.

M'kar led the way. Two girls hung on her arms, still trying to talk her into taking them camping. The two boys were walking backwards, in front of her, adding to the begging. Tress and Dafna walked with Treinna, who brought up the rear. M'kar repressed a sigh of relief when they reached the archway to exit the marketplace, down a cobblestone path between tall ferns.

A man called Treinna's name and stepped out of a shadowed doorway to the right of the archway. She froze and went pale, eyes widening. Then she gestured for the girls to go to M'kar, and hurried to meet the man.

Silver hair, deep blue eyes, square chin and cheekbones.

M'kar shuddered at the clashing colors that draped the man from head to toe. Nisandrians never claimed to be knowledgeable about fashions, but this man looked like a gaggle of color-blind three-year-olds had dressed him, in multiple layers of cloaks and scarves and beads. He had to be sweltering in the near-tropical climate of Mendax. She would have labeled him a Maniterr, but he didn't have the characteristic too-lean build.

"Who could that be?" she muttered, not really expecting an answer.

"That's Uncle Fin," Tress said. "Why is he dressed that way? He looks silly." She frowned, watching as Treinna and the man looked around and stepped back into the shadows of the doorway, clearly trying to stay out of sight.

Treinna was an only child, so Fin had to be one of Jasper's foster-sibs. M'kar ran through the names and what she knew of the careers of the group of derelict ship children. Fin Seeway was a mixture of many different genotypes, like all the other children. Someone had once remarked that they looked like all the ethnicities from all the Human worlds had been mixed in a centrifuge.

"Oh, great," she muttered as she led the children at slightly doubled pace toward their compound. The details she recalled made Seeway's appearance a harbinger of doom.

The impending bad luck from that loudmouth in the plaza a few days ago was about to fall on them. She just knew it.

Seeway was prisoner of a contract he had been tricked into making as a cultural liaison—meaning troubleshooter and path smoother—for Vitiarre and his team. If Seeway was here on Mendax, that meant the former ambassador was close by. No wonder he was dressed like that.

"No, no, no, no," M'kar muttered as she hurried the children down the tree-lined, cobblestone path to their compound. She tried to block out the horrid idea dawning in her mind. Thinking it could make it reality.

Ten teacher dracs teleported into the air, shrieking worry, above M'kar's head. The combined sound wasn't that particular chord that could liquify dymcrait/Hiver brains and make people want to peel off their own skin, but it was close.

"Go!" she snarled to the children and gestured down the path to their compound. M'kar went to her knees and pressed her fists over her ears. She concentrated on breaking through the cacophony of ten increasingly frantic drac minds, all talking at the same time.

Those six children knew how to obey when it mattered. She thanked Enlo and watched them vanish around a bend in the path. Then she focused on her heartbeats and sharpening her force of will into a battering ram to get the dracs to shut up, audibly and psionically.

The two teacher dracs assigned to her and Barroo quieted first and landed on the cobblestones in front of her. Whimpering just enough to be audible, they put their forepaws on her thigh and looked up at her with such sad, beseeching expressions, she needed to cry. M'kar held onto her strength of will and asked, as kindly as she could, despite the ache in her battered ears, what was wrong.

An image of five young dracs curled up in one pile, asleep … felt wrong. That was the strongest impression.

She remembered the soporific effect of the fire-spitting treats Decker had created for them.

The need to let out a long, loud stream of Nisandrian curses died under the sudden onslaught of rich, spicy, musky aromas. The tangle of clashing scents was thick enough in the air to taste. With a second breath, the texture of the air changed on her tongue and against her bare skin. With the third breath she thought maybe she didn't want to breathe anymore.

The dracs let out yips of disgust and whirled up into the air. M'kar silently called them cowards and got to her feet before turning around. The breeze was coming from behind her, from a handful of men in eye-watering, clashing shades of rich colors. Every breath of warm breeze across those flowing robes and scarves stirred up more scent.

The dracs hovered overhead, doing the drac equivalent of pacing in mid-air.

"You -- barbarian." The tallest man of the group gestured, at her and then up at the dracs. His sleeves flashed so many colors, M'kar had to guess how many layers there were.

Who's he calling a barbarian, wearing that nuclear alert test pattern and threatening to make my eyes bleed?

"You will make the pale green one and the lavender one come to me."

M'kar laughed, and instantly regretted it. Laughing required she take a deep breath of air. Her sinuses and her gag reflex punished her.

Fury brought massive red splotches to the man's neck where his mask of makeup ended. He tipped his head back, inhaling in a visible threat of a roar. Everyone behind him in the group cowered back. That posture identified him. She hadn't recognized him without his fancy jeweled headdress. Maybe that was taken away with his position as ambassador?

"Vitiarre?"

"Ambassador Vitiarre, you moronic Nisandrian floozy."

So he knew what her tattoos signified. She wasn't in uniform, so maybe he didn't realize she was Ashrock's daughter? Could she use that for advantage over him?

"Here, Uncle," a strained tenor voice warbled, and a young man M'kar didn't recognize hurried down the path, dragging a Mendax security guard with him. How many nephews did Vitiarre have, and discard when they failed him? "He will help us. I told him this barbarian stole our dragons."

Oh, so that's the lie they're telling now? Thanks goodness they don't have the brains to employ quantum physics and rewrite reality with the power of belief ...

M'kar thought of and discarded a dozen responses to the implied accusation. She was encouraged by the disgusted expression the security guard didn't do much to hide, followed by his wink for her. She bared her teeth in a grin that got a few gasps from some of Vitiarre's sycophants. Then she tipped her head back and mentally told the worried dracs to go, she would catch up with them. They popped out of sight.

Vitiarre let out a strangled cry of frustration. "I told you--"

"First lesson in dealing with dracs." M'kar swallowed hard as she willed her senses to go numb before all those heavy perfumes made her heave all over his jewel-encrusted shoes. Or maybe she should? "They're dracs, not dragons. You find dragons on Castitarus. Dracs are from Draxonis." She muffled a chuckle when Vitiarre winced at that name. "You don't *tell* dracs to do anything. And if you know what's good for you, you won't try to tell *me* to do anything, either."

"How dare you?" one of his underlings wailed. The only way M'kar knew that quavering falsetto voice belonged to a man was that the Maniterri were such misogynists, no woman would be permitted the "honor" of serving even a disgraced ambassador, except perhaps to clean the cabin on board his ship.

"I dare because I am the firstborn daughter of Chieftain Ashrock of Ba'e'do'stra Clan of Nisandros. I'm as royal as you can get without being a deity."

"You?" Vitiarre inhaled sharply and took a step back. So did everyone in his group. "You are his ... spawn? The half-breed?"

A dozen vicious, taunting responses clogged in her throat.

"She's Fleet, " one of them squeaked. "She has to obey you."

"Think again, *no'ca'wimp'fysh'ti*," she spat. "I'm on shore leave. You have no power here. You're not part of the Alliance, so the Fleet doesn't have to obey you either. And you can get a lot farther in life if you ask instead of throwing around orders. Ever think of that?"

From the way the Maniterri blinked rapidly in unison, like a bad caricature of a robot in a cheap drama-vid, none of them had ever considered the idea.

"Where did the creatures go? How did they fly away so fast we didn't see them?" someone else in the group asked.

"They teleport, remember? When your idiot nephew and his bumblers violated twenty different regulations to sneak on board

Anwesta and try to capture them?"

"My brother did no such thing," the nephew squealed. "He was kidnapped. He was framed!"

M'kar snarled out a string of Nisandrian that sounded utterly awful. All she said was that the squealer's brother regularly wet his pants and didn't wash his hands between picking his nose and eating with his fingers.

The Maniterri scowled and gasped and blustered and Vitiarre inhaled for another bellow of fury and orders. She gave them sign language for "we'll talk when you grow up and take a shower," and got out of there as quickly as she could without running. Every step she took, the air got a little cleaner, a little thinner. Her nose had indeed been getting numb. As her senses recovered from the cloud of scents that had hammered them, M'kar thought her stomach might revolt at any moment.

As soon as she put a building between her and the Maniterri, she ran. She found the nearest fountain and put her head directly under the flow of icy, stone-flavored water. She drank until her stomach was heavy, her tongue didn't feel coated with gritty slime, and she washed the scent off her face and out of her hair. She could endure the scent clinging to her clothes until she got back to the compound.

The teacher dracs hadn't been mollified or reassured by her promise to get there as soon as she could. Genys and Tahl came running down an intersecting path toward the compound, urged on by the teacher dracs for Battleaxe and Ha'ess. When they reached the compound courtyard, the communication pack was flashing. That had to be Brea, calling to ask what had Boomer so upset.

"Boomer." M'kar sighed. That would help. Boomer hadn't been among the dracs begging the fire-spitting treats from Decker and Spitfire.

Decker roared her name and came running, cradling Spitfire. She raised a hand to signal him to be quiet while she activated the communication pack. She noticed Genys' hair was wrapped in a towel, her clothes were fastened crooked, and her face and bare arms and legs seemed to be coated in something glossy and smelling of salt and spices. A good guess was she had been indulging in a spa treatment. M'kar only hoped the appearance of dracs trying to drag the captain back to the compound hadn't done any damage to relations with the natives of Mendax. Tahl was in exercise clothes. Probably she had been somewhere quiet, enjoying some solitude without Ha'ess clinging to her.

"What's got the tutors so twanked?" Brea asked, once the link opened. "Boomer can only tell me everybody's asleep and sick."

"Send him down here so I can send something up to the ship. The babies ate it, and I've got the feeling whatever we thought was good ..." M'kar met Genys' and then Tahl's gazes. "Wasn't."

"Right. He's on his way. Well, as soon as I can get him calmed down. He's kind of scared to go down to the planet, like whatever got the others sick will get him."

"Sick? Are you sure Boomer said they were sick?" Tahl asked, stepping up to the communication pack.

"That's the impression I'm getting from him. Half the time I'm glad the kids can't talk to us, because we'd get drowned with 'why?' The other half, I sure wish they'd learn some words, you know?" Brea sounded like she was trying to laugh. "Hold on while I focus."

"What are you thinking?" Genys asked, as they waited for Boomer to calm down enough to understand what Brea wanted from him, and teleport down to the planet.

"There are some species that essentially go into hibernation when they've been badly injured, or they're sick to a certain degree. That's where Neoma and the Le'ankan Masters got the idea of creating healing trances." Tahl frowned thoughtfully at Decker, who looked back and forth between all of them, his expression stony, yet somehow conveying a sense of desperation. He rocked slightly on the balls of his feet, cradling Spitfire.

M'kar had never seen the little pink drac so still and limp. She could almost understand why Decker was beside himself. At least, as beside himself as she had ever seen him.

She absolutely refused to picture Barroo, limp like a rag doll that had lost half its stuffing.

"She's gonna need the formula." Decker hesitated, then held out Spitfire for M'kar to hold.

He stomped over to his worktable and snatched up his tablet, brought it over to the communication pack, and tapped until he got the link. Boomer popped in and fluttered for a few seconds as if he didn't know what to do. Then the lemon-yellow drac settled down on top of the communication pack and chirped once. He sounded so much like someone saying, "Well? What did you want?" that earned a few smiles.

"The formula for what they ate is on its way up to you," Decker said. "I didn't think I'd be poisoning them …"

"They're sensitive enough to know when something is dangerous," Tahl said. "However, this is an alien world, and some native compounds might be different enough, they don't know what's dangerous and what's benign without some exposure to teach them." She took a deep breath, and glanced across the courtyard, at the basket where the other four dracs were sleeping. "Or could make them sick."

"That's the thing," Decker said, a threat of a wail in his voice. "I didn't use anything native here. I used what's native to them. That variant of the vine from Draxonis. Figured that would be safe."

"I have the awful feeling we're going to wish someone had thermo-bombed Forbidden Island, instead of telling the dracs to keep everybody away," Genys muttered.

With the formula Decker sent up and the samples Boomer carried back to the ship, Brea eliminated a number of time-wasting theories and possibilities. The vine was the spicy component and glossy red tint of the fire-spitting treat, and had elicited an allergic reaction. Only the young dracs seemed susceptible. She reported later that the adult female dracs went into fits of sneezing when they got close enough to smell the fumes from the crushed treat.

Brea recommended a simple treatment, to avoid complicating the situation. Everyone was to encourage their dracs to drink lots of water once they woke up, to flush their tissues of the allergen. She would work on a detoxifying tonic and send it down with Boomer once she had it ready.

Decker immediately hurried to clean off his worktable and put all the ingredients into the disposal system.

While they waited, M'kar changed her clothes. Then she had to explain why she came back by herself, why the children had gone to their quarters, and why her hair and clothes were wet. By then, the dracs were awake but still groggy enough to want to just snuggle. They were pliable enough to obey and drink water.

While they were tending the dracs, Treinna returned. She

verified M'kar's theory. Seeway had come looking to warn her and Japser. He hadn't known the *Defender* was on shore leave on Mendax until his friends on the ship had told him. They were all women, charged with ship housekeeping. None of the men watched their conversations around the women, who told Seeway the plans hidden from him. Vitiarre had followed the *Defender* to Mendax, determined to take their dracs, relying on the same tactics that had failed to force Jasper to work for him. Seeway couldn't get to the bridge on his ship, to communicate with Jasper, but the women helped him sneak away and take a provisioning shuttle down to find *Defender* crew and warn them.

Vitiarre needed a drac desperately now, to regain his position as ambassador and solidify Maniterr's claim to Draxonis. He intended to again lay claim to obedience from Jasper, as Seeway's foster-brother, and Treinna, his mate. By Maniterri law, everything that belonged to Treinna belonged to Jasper, and through Seeway's contract with Vitiarre, belonged to Vitiarre and Maniterr. He intended to use Maniterr law to lay claim to everything on the *Defender*. Because the *Defender* had a female captain, Vitiarre declared it leaderless. He had already filed claims with Mendax authorities to seize the ship through space salvage laws.

"You did tell him he could seek sanctuary with us, didn't you?" Genys said, when Treinna finished relating the warning.

"He doesn't dare. All those stupid Maniterri laws make it illegal for an inferior to break a contract. Only superiors can break contracts. The only way he can break free is to be fired." Treinna shuddered. "We need to cancel shore leave and get out of here, before I have to tell Jasper what happened to Fin."

"Captain," Decker began.

"Do you even need to ask?" Genys said, with a threat of snarl in her voice. "Emergency evacuation, effective now." She slapped her palms on the table, startling the sleepy dracs. "Go!"

Chapter Six

Captain's Log
Personal

Thanks be to Enlo. Vitiarre is so deeply in trouble with Maniterr, there were no diplomatic repercussions from our flight from Mendax. He had no one to complain to and no one to file legal claims against my crew or ship or file complaints and claims with Fleet. I've heard from several superiors who thanked me for possibly delaying the need to negotiate membership with Maniterr for a few more years.

Yes, the misfit luck of the Defender strikes again.

On a positive note, the request for a Le'ankan Master to oversee the developing psionic Talents among our ship's children has been granted. Master Thyal, M'kar's classmate and hearth-brother and drac parent of Infrenx, will be joining us when we return to Le'anka.

On a negative note, diplomatic nepotism strikes again. The misfit luck of the Defender is working against us on this one.

The Mirror Monsters will soon invade our ship. I have filed numerous protests and requests to rescind those orders before we reach Le'anka, but the total silence from several layers of superiors does not bode well. Not for me, but for M'kar and Thyal.

The Mirror Monsters is the name M'kar and I came up with for Nyssa and Nyx, children of minor royalty on Qahngress, when they were inflicted on us during Basic at the Academy. What makes them special on their world is how rare twins are, especially twins of mixed genders. They came to Le'anka to study and faced the first disappointments of their pampered lives. First they realized how un-special they were, on a planet full of Talents. Then they weren't welcomed into Master Reydon's special, anomalous Talents class. Their twin-bond does not qualify as a Talent. Then Nyssa decided Thyal was her destined mate. He proved how smart he was when he disagreed. He has evaded every attempt to trick him into the bonding ritual of Qahngress, which she still, as far as I know, believes will open up the bond between their souls.

What's sad is that the twins are gifted healers, but not Talented. Even sadder: someone, somewhere, with the authority to put those two on my ship, is gullible enough to be charmed by Nyssa and do her bidding. Even sadder than that, Nyx doesn't have a brain in his head, and he let his twin convince him he's in love with M'kar.

I suspect Nyssa did that to put a wedge between Thyal and M'kar. She sees M'kar as a rival. I wonder how she'll react if she ever learns about the communication link between the two of them.

I don't dare ask, though. I'm not sure of M'kar's reaction if I propose to her there is a deeper bond between her and Thyal than their hearth-kin vows and near-death battle with the dymcrait. Either she'll laugh until she passes out, or she'll get violently sick, or she'll just get violent, period.

Enlo, please, show us some mercy and keep the Mirror Monsters off my ship.

Captain's Log
Personal
Multiple apologies from superiors many levels up do very little good when complaints and requests and prayers to Enlo are not answered. The Mirror Monsters will be joining us.

Yesterday, we arrived at Anwesta. Thyal was waiting. Nyssa has been hounding him ever since she and Nyx returned to Le'anka. He took refuge on the station. I have done the best I can, assigning him crew quarters as far from the Medical crew quarters as I can. I have also asked Battleaxe to tell the dracs on the ship and the station that Nyssa and Nyx are bad-selfish-toy-stealers-stinky-hearts. But what are our chances those two will be so intimidated by our dracs they will request reassignment?

On a positive note: Granny is still so infuriated with us for leaving again without her, she is giving us the silent treatment. That includes our six young dracs. She keeps the teacher dracs off the ship and flying attendance on her on the station, but she scolds our drac children when they try to join the family.

M'kar insists Granny is up to something, and she's cutting our six out of the loop so they don't slip up and tell us. I must sadly agree.

~~~~~

Fleet Command, Le'anka
Admiral Harrendon
To Captain Genys Arroyan, AFV Defender
Captain Arroyan, you will soon receive official orders to proceed to Tierfallon Station, to transport a team of diplomats for a high-
~~~~~

priority mission.

This advance warning is a courtesy and in recognition of the invaluable service you and your crew have provided the Fleet and the Alliance.

Forget the fancy military protocol, Genys, this is a sincere apology. I have filed every protest I can, to shield you from risking scuttling your career.

The mission is -- brace yourself -- to Nisandros.

I am well aware of all the notations filed everywhere possible, requesting, recommending, and warning that Lt. M'kar must never be sent to Nisandros, with full details of the personal danger she faces, as well as the diplomatic repercussions if any of the competing elements on Nisandros ever get custody of her person. Starting with her ability and willingness to commit mass murder to stay free, and ending with Nisandros having a temper tantrum and declaring war against the Alliance.

However, those in higher authority, with louder voices (I must doubt their intelligence and common sense) believe the mission, to open negotiations with Nisandros to finally join the Alliance, is of high enough priority and sensitivity that sending her as a representative of the Fleet, the Alliance, and the Le'ankan Academy to her homeworld, will do far more good than harm.

I'm sorry, Genys, from the bottom of my heart. Even though you cast doubt on its existence often enough when you were my favorite student. Say a prayer for me. Now I have to notify Ashrock about this whole mess.

I'll be praying for you, and depending heavily on the bizarre, inexplicable luck of the Defender. *If anyone can survive this mission with their sanity, skins and the Alliance intact, you can.*

Enlo's starlight guide you.

~~~~~

Genys read through the particulars of the assignment multiple times on the voyage to Nisandros, looking for every loophole and weak point. Especially wording that could be twisted and re-interpreted to essentially hand M'kar over to her clan, or to the leaders of the various religious factions who wanted to either partially deify her or sacrifice her in a bloody, ancient ritual of racial and genetic purity. Worse than death was the possibility of finding out M'kar had been married by proxy to the heir of whichever clan would make the most profitable alliance with her father's clan.
~~~~~

"I want you to promise me one thing," M'kar said, when Genys revealed the assignment to her command crew. She looked around the conference room at her fellow officers. "If the nosepicker shows up at the welcoming ceremonies and he's wearing my clan colors along with his own, somebody has to kill me."

Many of those in the conference room thought she was joking. Genys didn't laugh. M'kar's closest friends only managed smiles, but not laughter. They knew she was serious.

~~~~~

Captain's Log
Personal

We survived the mission. I'm not sure yet what we survived.

All was quiet here on the ship, once the flamboyant welcoming ceremonies ended and the diplomatic party settled in for negotiations. Thyal kept in constant communication with M'kar, and reported to me on an hourly basis what was going on with her on the planet's surface. I didn't know whether to laugh at him for being so oblivious to his own feelings, or pity him, when he had to suffer with her through what turned out to be an elaborate courtship campaign. Every eligible son of high enough rank came to pay court.

I'm surprised M'kar didn't return to the ship with white hair and swinging from her one remaining nerve.

There was a period of about ten hours when Thyal lost contact with M'kar, and the diplomatic party reported some badly hidden panic over the disappearance of the entire courtship group. When they reappeared, every single suitor dropped his suit. M'kar returned to the ship with some mysterious cargo she won't let anyone see, and requested medical leave for the remainder of our mission.

She has promised me a full report later, once she has had time to digest what happened, and refers to the whole adventure as the "All the Boys I've Loathed Before Incident." I'm not sure I want to know what that means.

Captain's Log
Personal

Six days out from Nisandros.

M'kar thinks she found pieces of a broken Gate!

She brought pieces of a broken Gate onto my ship!

I'm going to kill her. Somehow. When she least expects it. I am going to ambush her and pound her to within a grain of death.
~~~~~

I understand the stress she was under, and there was some massive time and space dilation when she and all those narding indiferps trying to trick her into matrimony were chasing her and fell through that malfunctioning Gate -- malfunctioning with not a single blip showing up on any ship's sensors, which doesn't do much for my nerves, because what's the use of all those sensors taking up half the ship's systems, focused on finding Gates, when we can't even detect a malfunctioning one sitting right underneath us?

I'm so proud of her, and so grateful she got back alive, I just want to throttle her.

Maybe I'll do worse. I'll point out the feelings between her and Thyal that neither of them seem aware of, and let her just melt down from embarrassment. That'll fix her.

~~~~~

"We have a problem," Treinna announced, coming into the ready room for the morning briefing.

The *Defender* was two days out from Le'anka, after a long delay at Science Station Tyers to drop off the pieces of the theorized Gate. Most of that delay had come from needing to put the entire *Defender* and its crew into complete quarantine while everything and everyone went through a thorough examination: physical, mental, emotional, psionic. The results of exposure to the unclassified, unidentified, and as-yet unnamed mineral that made up the heretofore never-before seen core of a Gate had to be studied and analyzed, and everyone classified as physically, emotionally, and mentally unchanged and undamaged. That quarantine had included complete communication shutdown, to avoid any outside emotional or intellectual influences that might skew the intense studies conducted by station personnel.

"We do not have a problem." M'kar stretched out languidly on the couch and gave everyone in the room a sleepy grin. "The Mirror Monsters are so completely *ot'friq'zi* by their first mission with us, they're pulling every possible string to get off the ship. Life is good."

"Yes, we do." Treinna waved her tablet. "The *Dandridge*'s people have been marking all their linguistic and sociological data from Castitarus for our eyes only."

"And nobody protested? Nobody at the Academy cared about being cut out of the loop?" Genys glanced at Veylen. He nodded, his face wrinkling with the same concern she felt on her own face.
~~~~~

"They've been busy with that theoretically abandoned civilization the *Inquest* found, about two luns after the Castitarus Chute opened up. They were glad to leave all the fussy details and tedium to us." Treinna rolled her eyes, and finally sat down next to M'kar. "So much data piled up while we were on the other side of ten jump gates, and then when we were in quarantine ... my team is only about halfway through all the backlog of data." She paused, glancing around the room. "It's starting to repeat itself."

"And nobody knows, because nobody else is looking for or looking at that data, but us," Genys murmured. "How long ago did the repeating start? Real time."

"Three decs and four days."

Genys tapped her desktop to open a link with the communications station. "Sylvy, get me a direct line to Fleet, Commodore Malcom, priority level orange. Tell them I think the *Dandridge* might be in trouble."

Four hours later, after looking through the regular reports sent from the *Dandridge* by message pods, picked up by the survey teams on Draxonis and sent through the Chute every five days by courier ship, a disquieting pattern of repetition emerged.

"Disquieting?" Genys said, when she got the report from Commodore Malcom. "Try frightening. There were three -- only three -- distinct messages reporting the status of the ship and their work studying Castitarus. Each has repeated three times, and no one looked closely enough to realize that. Word-for-word repeats."

"What is Fleet doing?" Taggert said.

The rest of the bridge crew was quiet. Many of Taggert's team were filling in the auxiliary seats on the bridge, waiting for the news. Castitarus and the Chute leading to the planet were of special concern to them. Genys suspected more than a little resentment at having their discovery in the hands of another ship and crew. Especially since that ship and crew now seemed to have either messed up on a galactic scale, or were in trouble.

"Sending an investigatory probe. Following up with one of the Draxonis survey ships, depending on what they find. And before anyone asks, yes, I requested we be assigned the investigation. Draxonis and Castitarus are our discoveries. We have a responsibility to figure out what's wrong. Especially if the *Dandridge* is facing danger we should have faced." She shook her head. "They're purely scientific. They don't have the weapons, the higher-level defenses we carry. They don't have personnel trained to look for threats."

"Why would they?" Maora offered. "Their mission is to just orbit the planet and eavesdrop on the culture for two years, and then serve as a jumping off point for the infiltration team."

Genys knew Maora said that to ease the guilt and frustration she felt. It didn't do much good.

Until the probe got through the Chute to Castitarus and sent back the first report, they were to stay on their course, heading to Le'anka to file reports, divest themselves of Nyssa and Nyx, put their dracs through another checkup at Anwesta, endure another tirade from Granny, and then wait.

Genys thought she understood a little better now why Captain Shryne did some of the things she did, revising orders to suit the situation, or proceeding without orders. Waiting had a suckage factor off any measurable scale.

~~~~~

Returning to Le'anka, the *Defender*'s dracs again grew fidgety, meaning Granny was calling them and demanding a mission report. That was normal.

However, her temper tantrum was short-lived and did not repeat, and she didn't give the drac parents the silent treatment. None of them found it believable that Granny had learned her lesson. M'kar did some investigating, questioning the dracs on Anwesta and their handlers. Granny was clearly up to something.

"Situation red," M'kar told a meeting of the *Defender*'s drac parents. "Granny knows about Castitarus. She knows about the numenjax. The Anwesta dracs refer to them as 'the big ones,' and they think the numenjax are relatives, not another species."

"Let me guess. The old biddy is going to demand we take her to Castitarus to find them?" Decker said.

"No," Genys said, her tone quiet and cold. "There is enough trouble going on there. They don't need a starship suddenly dropping down into possibly a regressed society, with that silver geriatric menace flying around, demanding they turn over their dragons for her to boss around!"

Tahl chuckled, getting stunned looks from the others. "Wouldn't you like to see her try it? Remember those drawings,
~~~~~

giving a scale perspective between the dragons and a drac?"

"With our luck, she'll succeed," Treinna drawled.

Soon, though, the crew of the *Defender* had far more worrisome images to occupy their minds. The first report came back from Castitarus.

The probe sent through the Chute had found the *Dandridge*. All automatic communication requests had been ignored. Moving in closer, the probe discovered a slowly dispersing cloud of data packets with emergency retrieval beacons attached to them. Those beacons had been removed from the *Dandridge*'s life pods, which only deployed when massive damage required evacuation of the ship. The probe gathered up several data packets as it came in closer to the *Dandridge* to do a basic life signs scan and assessment of damage. No hull damage could be discerned. However, ship's power had been reduced to one-quarter normal levels. Many basic functions were dead. The *Dandridge* was essentially blind, deaf and mute, which explained why the automatic communication requests were ignored. The probe did several passes of the ship, determined there were more life signs on board the ship than the mission manifest indicated, then went back through the Chute to deliver its gathered data to the ships waiting at Draxonis.

Of greater concern was the second ship found in a lower orbit around Castitarus. That started a cascade of reactions, because no ship should have been able to get past the ships at Draxonis to go through the Chute. A check of the relay beacons at the mouth of the Chute leading to Draxonis revealed a ship had passed through, after giving the required security all-clears, along with coding that ordered the monitoring system to ignore the passage of the ship.

It was Maniterri in origin.

Disgraced former Ambassador Vitiarre's ship.

The probe did basic life sign scans and equipment scans of the Maniterri ship. Three-quarters of the expected life signs were missing. The ship's systems seemed to be functioning, but there was no response to the probe's communication requests. A closer scan revealed all the Maniterri shuttles were missing. The probe registered several slowly dispersing debris fields. It also noted several satellites orbiting Castitarus were missing, and the debris fields loosely matched the positions of the satellites.

The survey teams at Draxonis met to determine what to do.

Their first action was to open the data packets, which contained a report from Dr. Teodosia, head linguist on the *Dandridge,* acting captain now that Captain Seldun was incapacitated.

The Maniterri ship had come through the Chute broadcasting orders allegedly from the Alliance Congress, ordering the *Dandridge* to turn over all data and to cease operations. Vitiarre's ship and people were there to make contact with the government of Castitarus. Captain Seldun quite logically doubted the orders and set about verifying them. By the time his communications officer confirmed all the official codes and clearances were falsified, Vitiarre's ship was close enough to launch magnetic scramblers that effectively blinded and crippled the *Dandridge*'s systems. They were a science vessel, and weren't equipped for defensive or offensive situations. Their efforts to take back control of their sensors and communication system opened the ship's systems to invasion by programing sent in the communication bursts. Within an hour of receiving the first hail, the *Dandridge* was effectively slaved to the Maniterri ship's control. Vitiarre's crew set up repeating cycles of reports and designated all data to the attention of the *Defender.*

Genys noted in this point of the discussion with her command crew that Vitiarre's people obviously still had illegal information sources in Fleet. They knew the *Defender* was otherwise occupied with the Nisandros mission and wouldn't retrieve that data for decs. Probably the same information source had provided the Maniterri the means to get through the security around the Chutes.

Vitiarre claimed Castitarus as a protectorate of Maniterr, and promised the crew of the *Dandridge* that if they didn't cause trouble, he would obtain pardons for their actions against the best interests of Maniterr, which could be considered an act of war.

The *Dandridge*'s scientists didn't even have to pretend to play along. Vitiarre's people ignored them from that point forward. All their efforts focused on regaining eyes and ears on Castitarus, since they couldn't communicate through the Chute. They observed a regular relay of shuttles leaving Vitiarre's ship and going down to Castitarus.

After five Castitaran days, the shuttle trips grew irregular. After eight days, two shuttles no longer left the planet's surface. On the twelfth day, two shuttles launched and commenced chasing satellites. One knocked three out of orbit, causing enough damage that they shut down functions. The fourth satellite crashed into a fifth and they exploded. The sixth satellite collision resulted in both shuttle and satellite exploding. After destroying four satellites, the second shuttle crash landed back on Castitarus, in the sea.

On the thirteenth day, all the women from the Maniterri ship fled to the *Dandridge*. They reported that the men had gone insane. Their language skills had deteriorated, they were highly emotional, given to fits of rage, and their battles for control of the ship had damaged basic functions. What the women considered more disturbing, the men were neglecting their grooming rituals, didn't care about makeup or clothes, and stopped washing. A team from the *Dandridge* took the Maniterri shuttle back to Vitiarre's ship and boarded with no problem. They subdued half the men on board and weren't able to get through blockades to the remainder. They took their prisoners back to the *Dandridge* to determine what had happened to them, leaving the rest to survive the best they could. Several men reported an odd smell that could not be explained by the growing filthy conditions or the ubiquitous Maniterri perfumes and incense. It was dusty and sweet, sometimes bitter, and seemed natural enough not to be "natural" for the Maniterri. Several *Dandridge* men had sneezing fits, suffered hives, and reported feeling unusually sleepy for a short time after returning to their ship. They were treated for allergies. All efforts by this time were focused on trying to free the *Dandridge* of the Maniterri programming. It appeared to be a self-replicating and constantly modifying worm program.

On the eighteenth day, some *Dandridge* men displayed the same symptoms as their prisoners: deterioration of language skills, emotional outbursts, fits of crying, memory lapses. Unfortunately, all the medical personnel were male, and affected, likely because they were dealing directly with the prisoners. A check of the ship's environmental controls revealed the Maniterri sabotage had shut down the systems that would have warned them about biological contamination. The sensors had detected the entrance of alien organic substances, but no alerts were raised. By the time someone thought to check and activate filters and countermeasures, the entire life support system of the *Dandridge* had been infected.

Dr. Teodosia took command once Seldun showed symptoms of the decline. She had the report put together and dispersed with the beacons, depending on someone eventually realizing something was not right with the *Dandridge* and coming to investigate. She reported that all the women seemed unaffected, and what little medical investigation they could perform indicated some sort of hormonal overload in the men, essentially sending them backwards in their mental and emotional development, or perhaps more accurately, sending them into senility. Teodosia effectively put the *Dandridge* into quarantine and requested that any personnel involved in rescue operations be limited to females.

~~~~~

"Is it just me," Decker said, "or does this strike anyone else as entirely unfair?"

The command crew sat around the conference table. Everyone was silent after going through Dr. Teodosia's report and the follow-up reports from the survey ship that had been chosen to begin rescue and relief operations.

"I mean, don't we have the right to be a *little* happy at those nitzicks digging their own pit, filling it with an entire ship's worth of bio-waste, and then tripping themselves so they fall in head-first with their mouths open?" The security chief looked up and down the table, hands spread, begging them to agree.

"I'm sure we are, at some level, Chief," Veylen said. One corner of his mouth twitched upward. "Unfortunately, we're also conscious of the negative implications, and quite frankly ..." He sighed and turned to Genys, at the head of the table.

"We're all thinking the same thing, people," Genys said, nodding. "This is equivalent to a comet streaking toward a target on the ground, with our name written on them both. Vitiarre did what he did because he's a spoiled brat who didn't get what he wanted. We stood in his way. He's going to pull us into this mess, one way or another. I don't doubt right this moment, some department on Maniterr is putting together complaints and rewriting the details to put all the blame on us."

"You're right," Tahl said. "So I'm going to get to work on what limited data they've sent us so far. I want to be ahead of the game coming up with a defense, if not a cure, before we get sent in." Offering a thin smile to everyone at the table, she got up, and her senior medical officers got up to follow her.

Genys was proven right, and she regretted and resented it,
~~~~~

when a Maniterri shuttle was observed launching from Castitarus two days later. The captain of the survey ship elected not to intercept it, in case there was a weapon on board. There were no life signs, meaning it operated on automatic pilot. The survey ship escorted the shuttle through the Chute. When it reached Draxonis, the shuttle broadcast a message, which repeated for four days straight before falling silent. Then all functions shut down and the shuttle started to drift. The survey ship then towed the ship through the Chute, to take to the nearest Fleet station for examination and extremely careful handling.

Meanwhile, the message had been sent through several channels, to reach Fleet and the Academy as speedily as possible.

Vitiarre did not identify himself, but his voice was distinctive enough to be recognizable, even though he sounded like he was drunk. His words were slurred, he repeated himself, he mispronounced nearly a quarter of the words, and broke into distinctly childish giggles every other sentence.

The message: Matriarch Chercha, head of the Castitaran Senate, sent greetings to the Alliance. The Senate wished to open diplomatic relations, and specifically requested the *AFV Defender* and no other ship to come into orbit. The diplomats were to be led by Ashrock of Nisandros.

The Senate had been informed that the *Defender's* crew were in possession of dracs, the stunted offspring of the numenjax, their revered and long-missing guardians, judges and teachers.

Chapter Seven

At this point in the message, Vitiarre had broken down in fits of giggles, and when a woman said something to him in Castitaran, he grew sulky and kept saying no. At one point it sounded like he was spitting. There was a break in the recording, then the woman came on, and spoke in Castitaran.

Treinna was the most fluent in the Castitaran language on this side of the Chute. She translated, sent the remainder of the message to Fleet and Le'anka, then copied Genys.

The Senate wished to learn the full story of the presence of the dracs. They were certain the entirety of the story had not been told to them. Perhaps many alarming details were shaded by personal vendettas that had no place in such a momentous historical event as two cultures making contact across the stars.

"That's what I call diplomatic language," Veylen said, once Genys had convened the command crew and shared this newest development. "They know how to call the Maniterri bald-faced liars without actually using the words. Maybe they're signaling they trust us to tell them the truth."

"Or it's a trap," Maora said, shaking her head.

"You're thinking what I'm thinking?" Genys said. "The Maniterri have found kindred souls, and this is a great big time-wasting, badly disguised trap?"

"My brain is catching on the detail that it's very clearly a matriarchal society. Why would they let a bunch of overdressed, swaggering men drop down on them from the sky and believe *anything* they say? Especially men who are more prone to lecture them on how wrong they are to be a matriarchal society. Honestly, from some odd things I've sifted from the *Dandridge*'s reports, I'd theorize that something happens to the men's brains when they reach maturity. They're *unable* to function in society, rather than they're not permitted."

"The same thing that affected the Maniterri and the *Dandridge* men is, what, natural to Castitarus? A virus?" She nodded.

"The fact they requested us and specifically said it was because of our dracs … that worries me," M'kar said from her place at the far end of the long table.

In chorus, the ship's six dracs let out chirps and croons that very clearly signaled agreement.

Genys shivered, wondering if the total absence of the twelve teacher dracs was something to worry about, rather than be grateful for. While she trusted Battleaxe and the other five young dracs to protect ship's security, the older teacher dracs were clearly under Granny's thumb. Or the drac equivalent. Why weren't they spying on this meeting? What were they up to?

"Maybe they just want some clue what happened to their dragons," Veylen said. "Maybe they're ready to consider us messengers from Enlo, because we have dracs and our leader is a woman."

"If only it were that simple," Genys muttered.

~~~~~

While waiting for the Alliance leaders to come to a decision and respond to the invitation from the Senate of Castitarus, M'kar studied the dracs on Anwesta. Thyal helped her. Granny and her closest minions were unusually well-behaved. She was polite and cooperative with Dulit and Flinders and M'kar. She didn't order around the *Defender's* six young dracs. The lack of spying and prying while the *Defender* attended to maintenance in anticipation of a new mission was worrisome.

Decker noticed Spitfire being somewhat twitchy, looking at ventilation grills far too many times to be a coincidence. He turned on ship's maintenance sensors and discovered teacher dracs hiding in the ductwork and access tubes throughout the ship whenever there were meetings of command crew. Granny still had spies everywhere, and they had learned to hide.

"She knows we have been requested to represent the Alliance. She knows the Senate wants to learn about dracs," M'kar reported to the meeting of drac parents.

"She's planning on going with us," Genys said, speaking slowly, as if testing each word before she let it off her lips. "The scheming old biddy knows she hurt herself with her temper tantrums and then giving us the cold shoulder, so she's changing her tactics, trying to lure us into relaxing our guard. She probably even knows Jasper is making headway on the drac-proof fence."
~~~~~

"The question is if we let her know that we know," Tahl said just as slowly. "Honestly, there could be some benefits in having such an old drac, the matriarch of the entire race, with us when we make contact. Especially when the people of Castitarus venerate dragons, of some sort. However, her recent behavior makes her less than ideal as a member of a diplomatic party in what could be a tricky situation."

"Translated: can we trust her to behave herself and not make things any worse than the Maniterri already have?" Treinna chuckled sourly.

"I don't want to take the chance," Genys said. "Let's be honest, the Senate requested us because of what Vitiarre told them about us. It could be a trap. The Senate trusts that blowhard and is helping him get what he wants. Our dracs. And," she said, nodding to M'kar, "a chance to hurt Ashrock by dragging him into a situation possibly dangerous to males. The only way to survive this is to go in expecting a no-win situation."

<div align="center">~~~~~</div>

Genys had dinner that evening with the Lores and discussed the problem of making sure Granny stayed on Anwesta. Despite the advances Jasper had made on refining the drac-proof fence, it was nowhere near ready to be deployed throughout the ship. The best he could offer was to create a box enclosed by the field, to keep a drac or two in one place. Getting Granny into the box long enough to turn on the field would be the challenge. Genys felt safe discussing the idea with Jasper and Treinna because Moonrise and Battleaxe weren't there. The images her little black drac had shared with her indicated they were having some kind of celebration. A mated pair on Anwesta had laid three eggs.

"I think we could get something workable put together within a dec, once we finish that asteroid-sized pile of reports on Castitarus." Jasper tapped the screen of his tablet to close it, putting away the diagrams and data relating to the field. Just before dessert, he had given up trying to hide it on his lap and put it on the table between him and Tress.

Genys sighed. It was better than nothing. "Something you want to ask, *baba*?" she asked, seeing how the girl looked back and forth between all three adults at the table.

"Are the dracs in trouble?"

"Which ones?"

"Ours." She gestured at Genys' empty shoulder. "Moonrise is almost never home, and Battleaxe didn't come for dinner, and Aunt Brea said Granny is making Boomer and Ha'ess hide all the time."

"Ah." She raised her eyebrows, adult shorthand for "She's your kid, you handle it," and nodded to Treinna.

"Well ..." Treinna looked to Jasper. He cocked an eyebrow at her. "Basically, Granny wants to come on a mission with us, but she's needed here to keep all the dracs in line who are tending the cocoons. She's bullying our dracs, probably to pester us until we give in and say she can come. Our dracs obey us, but she's Granny, they don't like to say no to her. So they hide."

"You can't keep Granny from coming if she wants to. She can teleport from a whole orbit away." Tress' tone clearly implied that someone was being dense, but she was too polite to point out who.

Genys muffled laughter into a snort. They had managed to leave Granny behind before, but common sense said their luck would run out sooner or later. They had to find another tactic, different from the last time, because the old biddy really was clever. And stubborn.

~~~~~

"Is that ... your father?" Cherise, the mother of Callan, a very determined and bruised boy of eight years, gestured at the door of the auxiliary shuttle bay where M'kar was holding lessons.

M'kar didn't look up right away. It was never a wise move to take her gaze off a student learning to twirl tangle stones.

Cherise took a step just a little too close to her son, as if she needed to get closer to the door to see. She barely flinched when two of the six stones on the twirling strings slapped into her thigh. With the skill and aim she had likely earned through harsh practice, she caught hold of the strings and deftly yanked the weapon from his hand. Danger nullified, M'kar turned around.

Now she realized what her mother had meant when she wrote to say they would be talking soon, and she and Ashrock had something important to share with her.

Ashrock stood about four steps inside the shuttle bay classroom, his clothes unusually sedate. He was dressed all in black and silver; calf-high boots, trousers, a long shirt with full sleeves covered in silver embroidery of clan symbols, and a long vest-jacket
~~~~~

that flowed down past his knees. The cut was that clever style that somehow slimmed while emphasizing just what a big man he was.

He called them his traveling clothes. The ones he wore when he needed to make a good impression. When it was wiser not to use his fun-loving, harmless lunatic persona to ease the fears people felt when they realized the man smiling down at them, with tattoos and scars all over his face, was Nisandrian.

Dr. Jeyn stood next to Ashrock, smiling at M'kar, and also in traveling clothes. Long blousy tunic, loose trousers tucked into knee-high boots, vest-jacket, all in a deep red-purple trimmed in gold that complemented Ashrock's outfit without looking like they were a matching set. Which they were.

Am I too late to warn you? Thyal said. *Father sent me a message that I didn't open until my morning class finished. Congress has decided to comply with the request from Castitarus.*

They know men are susceptible to something down there. How many people have argued not to send my father? Yet here he is. M'kar signaled her students to stop what they were doing, or trying to do. *There's no reason for my parents to come, unless someone is using this against my father. They want the mission to fail.*

Unfortunately, I have to agree.

Her brain stuttered to a stop for a few crucial seconds. She couldn't find adequate words to express the maelstrom of emotions churning in her chest.

We have the mission. Has anybody told Genys yet?

I have to assume your parents have just told her. They brought message packets from my parents. If it's any comfort, Father apologizes. After all the time wasted in debate, now we are tasked with hurrying and making up for the delay.

Typical diplomats and politicians ... Somehow, the ability to find a little humor in all this helped her gain some clarity and calm.

She took a deep breath and gestured across the shuttle bay to her parents. Most of her students had been putting away their practice equipment and hadn't turned to look yet. They turned now, and M'kar could almost laugh at the wide eyes and little mouths dropping open. It was one thing to learn about the clan symbols and the meaning of Nisandrian tattoos. It was another thing to see them on the face of a living Nisandrian who could pass for a small mountain.

Tress muffled a giggle of excitement and waved to Ashrock and Jeyn. Several other children gave her disbelieving looks. M'kar didn't think any of her students were afraid, but they were smart enough to be alert and aware of possible trouble, just because these were strangers to them. Strangers to everyone but Tress.

Praying Ashrock wouldn't do something outrageous and embarrassing, even if amusing, M'kar crossed the deck to her parents.

"If it helps any," Dr. Jeyn said, "I brought a crate of *done'ei* and *mezipa*. We're all going to be doing some therapeutic eating before this ugly little failed trap disintegrates."

"The only thing the Maniterri excel in is being oblivious idiots," Ashrock grumbled.

"I love you both. So much." M'kar embraced her mother, then went up on her toes to kiss her father's heavily tattooed cheek. Behind her, students and their watchful parents whispered. She tucked her arm into Ashrock's as she turned to face the group. "Would you like to meet my students? We've just begun their hand-to-hand lessons." She grinned. "I was thinking I'd fulfill a promise I made a while ago. Actually, more of a threat. I'm going to blindfold them and send them into the zero-g compartment. See how well they navigate and if they can learn to work together without someone *telling* them they need to work together."

"That sounds like a catastrophe waiting to happen." Ashrock squeezed her hand tucked into his elbow. "Sounds like fun."

"I thought we could play Monster in the Maze."

"Can I join in?" Thyal said, as his hoverchair glided through the doorway.

M'kar hesitated. It was one thing for Thyal to get into the zero-g compartment with the children to play with them. She loved seeing him set free from the restraints of his paralysis for a little while. The children weren't as careful as they should be, bouncing around with him, but this group was small enough they couldn't do too much damage. Infrenx was always careful to teleport in and snatch him away from nasty collisions before they happened. However, everything changed when Ashrock got into the zero-g compartment, simply because he took up so much room. He always used too much force, deliberately, so he ricocheted off walls, laughing with every awkward impact.

"Let him be the monster," Ashrock said with a thoroughly evil grin. "I'll be the space barge for the children to launch off me."

By the time lessons ended, all the children had fallen in love with Ashrock. Thyal acquitted himself quite impressively, creating snarls and growls and howls that made the children scream in believable terror. They turned off the lights in the zero-g compartment, instead of blindfolding the participants. Infrenx and Barroo were worn to a frazzle, trying to defend Thyal from bumps and bruises and collisions. They slept through a large portion of the formal dinner to introduce newly appointed Ambassador Ashrock and Ambassador Jeyn to the command crew.

The *Defender* left orbit around Anwesta and Le'anka late in the night shift and headed for the Chute to Draxonis, and then to Castitarus.

~~~~~

"We've got a problem," Genys said two mornings later, as soon as M'kar responded to the hail that woke her from another uneasy sleep full of strange dreams.

It was far too early for problems. Her eyes were crusty and her mouth tasted awful. She hadn't indulged in a gorge, so she didn't have a carb-and-fat hangover. Some dreams were just too realistic.

"As in?" She winced at the creak of her voice. Shreds of dreams wafted up from the back of her mind and she held still, hoping they would go away.

"I got a panicked communique from Anwesta. Dulit and Flinders were both away, checking on the *Corona*'s children in their boarding schools. They got back and discovered Granny had vanished. Nobody believed them, and it's taken them this long to verify. Everybody else is more than willing to leave discipline up to them, and wringing some understanding from those devious little ... Turns out the little monsters have been playing a scam game."

"They've been covering for her." M'kar closed her eyes and rolled onto her back, fighting not to bury her head under her pillow. Part of her wanted to let go with the loudest psionic yell she could muster, to reach to the farthest nooks and crannies of the *Defender*, and mentally drag Granny to face her. Problem: she didn't have much to muster.

Now she had a logical explanation for her weird dreams, and
~~~~~

how she felt. Granny had stowed away and came out at night to trespass on M'kar's dreams and learn about the numenjax. If the dream shreds were accurate, the scheming little drac thought she had authority over the numenjax and they would do her bidding. M'kar sent up a quick prayer that Enlo would dispense full justice on Granny, and she would encounter a species who would either ignore her or laugh at her. Or even better, had the psionic power to make her knuckle under.

"I'll ask Axe and Moonrise and maybe ask Thyal to help track down Granny," Genys said after M'kar voiced her theory. "She's a stowaway. Nobody was saying no to her. She wants to see the numenjax, even though we made it clear to her they were all gone."

"She knows what she knows, and facts don't get in her way."

"What do you suggest we do?"

"Let Granny keep playing her games. Don't give her the satisfaction of looking for her. She can't try to order us around as long as she's hiding, and that will eventually frustrate her so much she'll come out on her own."

M'kar sent out a stern warning to all the ship's dracs. The game was over, and they had forgotten an important rule: on the *Defender*, Granny was not the boss. Genys was the head of the tribe, and they endangered the safety of the ship by keeping secrets.

"We have a problem," she announced two hours later, walking into the morning meeting of what some called Dragon Planet Lessons. Breaking some crew of saying "dragon," when the proper name was numenjax, was frustrating.

Maora and her teams of sociologists and anthropologists had sorted the information provided by the *Dandridge* into lessons, creating a foundation to prepare all those who had a chance of going dirtside. Which teams went down would depend on how the first meetings with the leadership of Castitarus went.

"As in?" Genys' eyes widened. "She's not on board?"

"Told you," Decker muttered. He flinched when everyone else at the long conference table turned to look at him. "Spitfire came to me, all upset because M'kar just about called her a liar."

"Did not," M'kar said. "I just asked her twice." Barroo chirped at her, his tone a little sharp. "Okay, maybe it was three times."

"Our dracs don't lie," Brea said slowly.

"That we know of," Genys said. "I asked Battleaxe after we

talked, and she insists she hasn't seen Granny since Anwesta. Maybe Granny had the sense not to show her face to Axe, knowing she'd report her … so where is she?"

"That's not exactly the problem I was thinking. Yes, our dracs all say they haven't seen her. Almost all our dracs." M'kar turned to Treinna, who sat up straighter in her chair. "The teacher dracs refuse to answer. That tells me they're hiding something. I also can't get a response from Moonrise."

Treinna closed her eyes and pressed her mouth flat with the effort of concentration. She sighed. "Moonrise won't answer."

"Well, there goes our plan not to let Granny know we know she's on board." Genys shrugged. "Let's focus on the mission prep for now. She can't go anywhere until we get to the planet. Hopefully by then, Jasper will have the smaller version of the containment field working."

"If you don't mind my saying," Decker said, partially raising his hand. "We're going to a place that has been listening to all the lunacy Vitiarre has been telling them for more than a lun now. Yeah, they were polite, but who knows what crazy demands they'll make once we get there? If our dracs came from their dragons, they could argue that makes the dracs theirs. Is it really a good idea to create something that would let outsiders not just get their hands on our dracs, but keep them?"

"You might be right, Chief," she said after a long moment of silence. All the drac parents present held their breaths. "That's something to think about and deal with. Later. The mission prep comes first."

M'kar settled down at the table, next to her father. For once, Barroo stayed utterly still on his perch on the back of her chair. He never begged any treats from Ashrock, and her father didn't offer.

Twenty minutes after the meeting ended, Treinna sent word that not only couldn't she find Moonrise in all the usual spots, but Tress was missing as well. She had contacted E'bett and Maenta, asking if they had seen her daughter. The next step was to track down Tress' gang, to see if they were involved in some complicated game or adventure. M'kar contacted Thyal and asked him to join in the search. Since he focused on the children showing signs of awakening psionic Talent, he knew the "scent" of their minds and might be able to trace the girl's presence.

Within an hour, he contacted her. M'kar was in Medical, conferring with Genys and Tahl on the progress in unraveling the hormonal overload that affected the men on Castitarus. With her father thrown into the mixture, M'kar had more visions of possible ways for the mission to go wrong every day.

You need to meet me and a certain young lady in storeroom seventeen. Thyal shared with her an image of a very subdued Tress sitting on a shipping crate, with Infrenx sitting next to her and Granny curled up on the little girl's lap. Moonrise hovered over Tress' shoulder, looking somewhat droopy and greener than usual.

Bring Treinna or Jasper to deal with her?

Let's ease her into it gradually. Granny is really the guilty party. She took advantage of Tress' training to be obedient to her elders.

"Granny isn't her elder," M'kar blurted.

"Found her?" Genys said. "Where?"

"Thyal found her. Let me deal with those guilty of aiding and abetting stowaways, then you can join in."

"Oh … boy." She shook her head.

~~~~~

"I am very disappointed," M'kar said, stepping into the storeroom exactly twelve minutes later, "to learn the daughter of the Chief Engineer and Chief Linguist is most certainly not obedient to her elders."

She had considered scowling and snarling when she entered. The problem was that all the children knew she was teasing when she played fierce. They knew she was serious when she was calm and her voice was just a little quieter than normal. M'kar kept her hands clasped behind her back, stepped up to Tress with a good meter of space between them, and waited.

The little girl visibly shrank down into herself. Her big silver eyes got even bigger. On her lap, Granny tipped her head back and let out a few defiant chirps.

"Keep it up," M'kar said, bending down to meet the little silver matriarch's gaze. "Her father is working on a field that will keep your kind penned in one place. And I've got a hankering for a new silver hide belt."

She normally would have said "boots," but Granny didn't have enough hide for a pair of slippers, much less traditional Nisandrian battle boots, with loops and hiding places for knives and darts and
~~~~~

poisoned needles.

"You wouldn't. Would you?" Tress' voice cracked a little.

"Try me." Her voice went even softer.

Granny whimpered and clutched at the front of Tress' jumpsuit. The girl wrapped her arms around her, nearly hiding the little drac from sight.

Thyal ruined it all by snorting.

Granny let out a chirp and turned to glare at M'kar.

"Try me," she repeated.

The drac sighed and the colors of her eyes shifted to her more normal, good-humored, slightly scheming disposition. Arrogance might be a better description, M'kar decided. Confidence, cubed. Granny needed it, to control her band of rogues and tricksters and make sure newborn dracs didn't brain-drain every adult who came near them. Maybe they should be grateful Granny was so determined and scheming and able to figure things out and manipulate everyone to accomplish her goals. The fate of the entire drac race had essentially rested in her paws.

The story was simple, and M'kar had figured out most of it on her way down to the storeroom. Granny had finagled and coerced her followers into a routine that let them cover for her and convince the authorities she remained on Anwesta. Then she took advantage of Dulit and Flinders leaving the station. Dulit had neglected to give Granny specific orders that she was not allowed to leave the medical base while he was gone. That had been the loophole she had slipped through. After all, she had agreed to put herself under Dulit's command.

Granny had the intelligence to go to the one person on board the *Defender* who would be sympathetic and want to help her, with the know-how and the freedom of the ship to provide her with a hiding place. The teacher dracs had cooperated to keep Granny's presence hidden from the *Defender*'s drac children — all except Moonrise. Granny had intimidated her into keeping silent, and helping Tress feed her without raising alarms.

"It seems that children are such a normal part of this ship, they have slipped into the background," Thyal observed.

M'kar muffled a few snorts of laughter, imagining Treinna and Jasper's reactions when they got the details, and realized they hadn't noticed their daughter's unusual behavior. The times she took extra food from the processing unit in their quarters' kitchen nook. The slightly spicy scent of drac hide had probably been building up in Tress' room, because Granny hid much of the time there. But the Lores hadn't noticed. Granted, Moonrise also lived in the Lore family quarters, but she had her cushioned basket and toys in Treinna and Jasper's bedroom.

M'kar decided to leave it to Treinna to interrogate her own drac and find out just what Moonrise had done as a partner in the conspiracy.

"All right, time to take this to the captain." She sighed and didn't watch Tress as she added, "And your parents."

M'kar contacted Treinna to ask if she and Thyal could come meet her, and learned Genys was already in conference with the Lores in their quarters. Thyal suggested, in the interest of saving time, he send the recording of Tress' interrogation ahead of them, so her parents would know everything by the time she got there. Moonrise let out a feeble little squawk and teleported out. M'kar could guess she had finally responded to Treinna's call. Infrenx and Barroo were subdued, flying escort as M'kar guided Tress down the corridors, Granny cradled in her arms, and Thyal bringing up the rear in his hoverchair. All six were silent. M'kar had to wonder what expression she wore, because the crew they passed in the corridors gave her questioning looks but never said a word.

Chapter Eight

Finally, the march of doom was over. The door to the Lores' quarters slid aside as soon as Tress stepped within sensor range. She hesitated. M'kar gave her a little nudge between her skinny shoulder blades. The girl gave her a grudging glance, and she had a hard time not snorting laughter. She could only hope she kept her face straight. Treinna and Jasper stood in front of the couch, with Genys to one side and Battleaxe on her shoulder. All that could be seen of Moonrise was the tip of her snout, poking out from the decorative pillows on the couch.

"Thank you," Jasper said, when Tress responded to his silent summons, pointing at a spot on the floor in front of him. "If you don't mind, I think this is something we need to settle as family, first, before we deal with shipboard discipline."

"I'll leave it up to you to handle her punishment." Genys stepped over to the door where Thyal and M'kar had stopped.

Battleaxe let out a trumpeting sort of cry. Granny flinched, then hunched her shoulders, and sat up to face Treinna and Jasper. Moonrise poked her head out from the pillows and made a crooning sound.

"Granny ..." Genys waited until Granny turned her head and looked at her. "You are supposed to be a leader, a good example. There's no excuse for what you did. The other dracs are depending on you. The healers at Anwesta are depending on you. The people in those cocoons are depending on you."

A creaky croon escaped Granny.

"You've gotten Tress into enough trouble. Come with us."

M'kar braced herself for an argument. Granny submitting to someone else's authority would be admitting she was in the wrong. The most likely response would be to pretend not to understand what Genys said.

Infrenx made a coughing sort of sound. Granny turned enough to look at her, sitting on Thyal's lap now. Head hanging slightly, she spread her wings. Tress let go. She flapped and leaped up toward the ceiling. She hovered a few seconds, then swooped to the doorway, and out. Genys sighed and set off down the corridor. She moved slowly so no one could guess she was actually chasing the elderly drac.

~~~~~

Boarding teams in isolation suits took over the Maniterri ship and had taken custody of the infantile remnants of the crew. The ship's systems and records were so badly mangled by the multiple battles to take control that much data had been lost. Identifying the crew who were in custody and determining who was missing, either marooned on Castitarus or killed in the shuttles, was delayed by the refusal of the sick men to cooperate. They either had constant temper tantrums, or they sulked, or they treated everything like a game. Jasper's foster-brother, Fin Seeway, was one of the first identified as missing. Vitiarre was the only one definitely known to be on Castitarus, either a guest or prisoner of the Senate.

The *Dandridge* had been freed from the programming enslavement of the Maniterri ship and had resumed its mission. Now that Castitarus was aware of the visitors from beyond the Chute, some communication had been established. It was audible only, because Castitaran technology was unable to handle the multiple communication streams used by the Alliance. Learning the Castitaran language was proceeding with tripled speed now, and Treinna admitted she was both excited by the advances and discoveries being sent to her every day, and frustrated, because she wasn't there yet, hands-on involved. The Senate was open to using translation devices, and their academics were eager to gain access to computers. For the first face-to-face contact with the Senate, Treinna would act as translator, as a matter of honor and respect for the matriarchs of the Senate, and to raise Genys' prestige.

They all agreed that even though Ashrock's presence had been requested, he would not come down to the planet until Tahl had a better understanding of the threat to the men, and some method of protecting them. She didn't like playing games with the endocrine system and artificially controlling hormonal balances. That always led to trouble further on in a patient's life.

By the time the *Defender* had passed through the Chute to Draxonis, an assessment of the damage resulting from the destruction of the satellites had been completed. Basically, there was no harm to the planetary communication system, reinforcing
~~~~~

earlier conclusions. Several locations that had been exchanging signals with the satellites had been either damaged or destroyed, however, these stations were on a smaller continent showing signs of volcanic activity. Loss of the stations seemed to have no impact, and there was no sign of Human habitation on that continent. Analyzing their function would have to wait, but Genys added offers of making repairs and improvements to the list of items to be discussed when she finally met with the Senate.

~~~~~

The *Defender* made audio contact two hours after it came through the Chute and entered orbit around Castitarus. All the dracs insisted on being on the bridge for it, even after M'kar made them understand they wouldn't see numenjax. Granny insisted "the big ones" were indeed on the planet. She clearly communicated that M'kar and Genys were being lazy or selfish, refusing to locate them immediately.

M'kar finally got irritated enough to challenge Granny to go find the numenjax herself, and then come back and show the rest of them how to get to "the big ones." Granny gave a loud sniff that clearly meant "suit yourself," and vanished.

Her snit was forgotten when a thin alto voice responded to the hail from the *Defender*, far faster than anyone on the bridge expected.

"Greetings in the name of the Senate of Castitarus," the computer translated on the forward viewscreen and audibly, in a hushed tone that didn't interfere with conversation.

Treinna went through the planned introductory phrasing, declaring she was on the *Defender* and Captain Genys Arroyan and her crew had come as requested by the Senate. M'kar was relieved to discover she could generally follow what both sides said. There was a vast difference between practicing conversation in a language they had only heard in recordings, and actually conversing with a native speaker.

"We are relieved and grateful to speak with you," a new, richer female voice said, once the greetings had been exchanged. "I am Matriarch Chercha. In the days since in our own defense we imprisoned these rude children who descended on us, much ridiculous talk has spilled from their mouths. We chose the higher path and have waited until you could come and speak reason and
~~~~~

we could learn facts and truth from you."

"Please accept our apologies for the unpleasantness. These men are representatives of one of many worlds, and they broke protocol and regulations to contact you." Treinna glanced at Genys, questions in her eyes. Genys nodded and spread her hands, palms up, giving her full freedom to speak. "Our tradition is to observe a new world from a distance, learning about your ways and beliefs, learning your language and your history, so that when we initiate contact we may do so politely and respectfully, avoiding generating fear or disruption in your culture."

"Yes, so we had hoped, so we had inferred from some of the slanderous things the childish ones declared about you."

"We would gladly remove the burden of their presence as soon as you wish. Our authorities hope you will allow us to pass judgment on them and dispense punishment based on our laws. At the same time, we will give full respect and consideration to your laws and traditions."

"Take them, and gladly." Matriarch Chercha chuckled quietly. "However, you should be aware that these rebellious children have become infected with the bescere. We did not realize at first that they had not been infected because their behavior was so rude and immature. Not until their behavior descended still further, did we dare think ..." She sighed loudly, sounding like someone trying not to weep. "We dared to hope the people of your worlds do not suffer the bescere. We took hope, despite the fact you came from the star well that has brought so much trouble to our people in the past."

"The bescere?" Treinna glanced up from her tablet, where Genys sent her notes to guide the conversation. "Is this the mental deterioration that has affected those left on the invaders' ship?"

"Yes, the mental descent that afflicts all males once they have reached maturity. Perhaps you know it by another name, in another form, perhaps to a lesser degree?"

"I would need to consult our ship's medical team, but I am not aware of any disease that specifically focuses on just males."

"Thank Praestantaes, other worlds are not touched with our affliction. You indeed bring us hope. We feared at first they had come from the sister world, returning to trouble our clans and guilds. When we determined they came from beyond the sister world, we welcomed them and then regretted it."

Genys tapped quickly into her tablet. Treinna glanced at her and nodded.

"Matriarch, my captain wishes to speak. She is still learning your language, and she requests your patience and forgiveness if there is misunderstanding or insult. All are unintended."

"Gladly, and I am honored. Welcome and greetings from the Senate, Captain Genys Arroyan."

"You honor me with your patience," Genys said slowly, studying her tablet screen.

A translation prompt program spilled words across multiple columns of the screen as she spoke. From where she was standing a few steps away, M'kar could see the tablet telling her what she was saying in both Castitaran and Standard. The third column wasn't showing any suggestions for better word choices. So far.

"In the name of the Alliance, I am authorized to offer help to the full extent of our ability and knowledge, regarding difficulties and diseases. Our principles forbid us to disrupt the culture of any new world we encounter. This bescere, this mental disease, do you know its origins? How long has it been part of your culture? Most important, are you qualified to speak for all of your world, all your clans, to request our aid?"

"The bescere has stolen the minds, the maturity, the sanity of our males for four generations now. Since the numenjax vanished and the star well closed and the air turned cool. I dare to speak for all the matriarchs, all the clans, all the guild mothers, when I ask for your help. You have proven the words of the invaders to be lies, and we are grateful. Even though we had hoped you could bring back our numenjax, we gladly relinquish that hope to regain our males and restore them to their wives and children and mothers."

~~~~~

While Treinna and Genys worked out an agreement for the first face-to-face meeting, which tradition demanded be turned into a grand festival and tournament, an all-female Security team headed down to Castitarus. Female crew who had experience dealing with angry, injured, and sick wild animals came along as backup. Most of the men from the Maniterri ship had been contained in one place. That qualifier, "most," worried Genys. She asked for clarification. Then she learned a rebel faction had broken into the holding facility, kidnapped some of the Maniterri men, and
~~~~~

stole one of the stranded shuttles. Vitiarre was among them. Genys added the issue of rebel factions to her growing list of likely sensitive topics. It was enough to know the missing men were being searched for, to be rescued and returned.

The prisoners had been provided food, water, and blankets, but the Castitarans had avoided any further contact. M'kar could understand that. She knew exactly the kind of arrogance and condescension Vitiarre had likely dumped on the female leaders of Castitarus from the moment his party landed.

M'kar theorized there were more than a few rebel factions on Castitarus who disagreed with the Senate's handling of the whole situation. Some people obviously believed the invaders were from the sister world Chercha had mentioned, which backed up the theory about a war between Draxonis and Castitarus the last time the Chute between the worlds had opened. On the short walk from the landing field where the last Maniterri shuttle sat, she saw women in leather and metal armor, armed with spears, swords, and shields, keeping people pushed back out of sight behind buildings and stone and wood fences. The sounds of angry voices and arguments weren't so easily hidden.

Maora had speculated that the appearance of the invaders from the stars could have caused major social upheavals already. Some people might want to cut off all contact with other worlds. Others might be taking advantage of the upheaval to change things they didn't like about their world.

Then the retrieval team came to the place where the Maniterri had been corralled for several decs. M'kar put away her considerations and worries for later. The team stood for a good ten minutes, looking down into the small, bare stone canyon of the Maniterri prison.

"Please, please, please tell me we can keep pictures for our private 'don't be caught dead like this' collection?" Sh'hari said.

M'kar shuddered, imagining the contingencies that had prompted the very visible adjustments to the canyon, smoothing the walls into slabs more than four meters tall, angling inward and upward, and impossible to climb to escape. Had the changes been made just for the Maniterri? Or was this pit used on a regular basis, to deal with other men who suffered the bescere?

The floor of the pit was flat, packed dirt, with grooves maybe half a meter wide and a meter deep, crossing one semi-sheltered end. There were dark splotches on the edges of the grooves, and the stink clearly identified them as makeshift latrines. The forty-some men in the pit looked generally bruised and ragged and dirty. The few visible blankets were torn and dirty. Maybe the men had fought over them.

"Can't say they don't deserve it," Sh'hari said.

Decker had assigned women to this team who had experience with Maniterri misogynistic rudeness. He couldn't say it aloud, or even hint, but it was understood that he wouldn't take seriously any claims that his personnel were "rude" to the prisoners.

M'kar reflected that sometimes she really hated having to take the high road and attempt to be morally, spiritually, and ethically superior to idiots who certainly deserved their current misfortune.

"We need to be careful. You know the minute we start gloating, something will turn around and give us twice as much grief," Sh'hari added.

"The good old *Defender* misfit luck." M'kar nodded and looked back over her shoulder. Standing as high as they were, they could see the waiting Maniterri shuttle. "Sure hope Hanni can drive one of those. I do not want to cram all of that stink into one shuttle."

"I say we get a bucket brigade going, and give them a bath before loading," another woman offered.

"You know what we need?" Sh'hari said after a few more seconds of contemplating their unpleasant cargo. "A really strong telekinetic. I would really love to knock them unconscious until we dump them in their holding pens on their own ship."

"I don't suppose there's anybody in the team you've got a score to settle with, that we can put in charge of restraining the stinky boys?" M'kar said.

The Maniterri were so relieved to recognize Fleet uniforms, they didn't notice the people freeing them from the pit and herding them to the shuttle were women. Several of them cried out in tearful gratitude when they were instructed to stand with legs spread, hold their arms out at their sides, and close their eyes and mouths, before getting three buckets of water poured on each of them. Then they were given two blankets each, to wrap around themselves for warmth and decent coverage. Long sample bags replaced their missing shoes. They squelched and slipped and tottered into the shuttles.

Hanni proved her intelligence and foresight and came prepared, with ration bars doctored with liquid tranquilizer taken from the Maniterri ship. The men devoured the bars. They were all starving, and all asleep before Hanni untangled the badly conceived sabotage someone had done to freeze the shuttle's controls, and got it off the ground.

M'kar and her team were more than relieved to get the Maniterri back onto their ship and turned over to the medical personnel who would be treating them and trying to find the cause and a cure for bescere. All female, wearing isolation suits to prevent taking the disease back to the *Defender*. She felt sorry for the *Dandridge*'s male crew, who had been transferred to the Maniterri ship to keep all the patients in one place.

The invading organic element had been identified as numerous plant substances, but none of them registered as toxic or viral in nature. The medics' preliminary theory was that some reaction to a combination of several of those Castitaran organic substances had triggered the hormonal imbalance. They would need further study to determine if the change went down to the genetic level, if it could be reversed, if it could even be considered damage. Not enough was known to guess if bescere was an adaptive virus. There was a chance it came from a parasite too different from anything medical science understood to be identified as a living organism. Bescere could be as "simple" as an allergic reaction to some substance secreted by the parasite. The Maniterri women and the *Dandridge* female crew would have to serve as a control group, to determine the difference between their bodies' reactions to the invasion of the bescere and the male reactions. Why weren't they suffering the hormonal overload and imbalance?

~~~~~

During the preparations for the first official face-to-face meeting with the Senate, Genys brought up the question of why Ashrock was requested, if the people of Castitarus knew the bescere was a danger to men. She wasn't at all surprised to learn Vitiarre had told the Senate Ashrock was a woman, the most powerful ambassador in the Alliance. Chercha apologized profusely, assuring her Ashrock would not be expected to come down to the planet until there was some assurance he wouldn't fall victim to
~~~~~

bescere. She also shared more details about the many lies Vitiarre had told. The Alliance was a society of dictators. Castitarus needed to protect its freedom by forming an alliance with Maniterr and Ankuar. He also insisted the *Defender* was responsible for the enslavement and abuse of the Castitarans' beloved dragons. He refused to say numenjax. Essentially, everything Vitiarre said about the people of the Alliance, the matriarchs chose to interpret as the exact opposite.

The formal meeting of Castitarus and the Alliance was to take place on Congregation Island, set in an inland sea in the center of the continent. It contained all the government buildings and the headquarters for all the guilds. All the clan and guild leaders would be there to meet the *Defender*'s diplomats. A guesthouse was being prepared for the women to stay on Congregation until they could be sure they wouldn't take bescere back up to the ship with them. A field had been set aside, with a tall fence, where the shuttle could land and be secure. When the shuttle landed, a ceremonial walkway would be assembled, to lead them to the arena for the welcoming ceremonies, followed by a tournament of all the best warriors and athletes. If the *Defender* wished to send some of their warriors to participate, they would be most welcome.

Genys, Maora, Treinna, Tahl, and M'kar went down to the planet. Half the Security detail would accompany them and stay in the guesthouse, the other half would stay on the shuttle, practicing isolation and decontamination, so they could travel between the ship and planet with samples and equipment.

Granny accompanied them. Genys hated how the little drac preened as soon as she knew she got her way. However, making her an official part of the team increased chances of her behaving herself and obeying Genys, as opposed to her just teleporting down and sticking her muzzle in wherever she chose. She had developed a habit of vanishing for half a day at a time, with none of the dracs able to find her. That worried Genys, despite all the trouble Granny caused. Better to soothe her pride, to keep her out of trouble. Granny would ride on Maora's shoulder. Everyone else's dracs would wait in the shuttle until called for. At least they could be depended on to obey.

The team arrived in dress uniform. A low-level, adjustable security field in their belts, and body suits to shield against low-impact blows, small things like darts and knives, provided some protection, without being visible or possibly offending their hosts.

"That's not an island," M'kar commented from the co-pilot's seat, as the shuttle settled low enough in the atmosphere to see Congregation with the naked eye. "That's a small continent."

Besides being the center of the government, Congregation hosted major trading activities, spring and fall ceremonies and celebrations, and athletic tournaments. The sociologists and anthropologists theorized the tournaments served as a pressure release valve for the population, helping to resolve disputes and avoid wars through mock battle.

Maora refreshed them on details of the expected tournament, after M'kar described the arena they had passed over. Thick clumps of people were milling around. Tents surrounded the amphitheater, with flags in the colors of the ten clans visible everywhere.

As the shuttle slowed to land, Genys rehearsed her greeting speech, which was all she would need to speak in Castitaran before turning on the translators. Treinna nodded slowly as she listened to Genys practice. Her lips and the corners of her eyes didn't twitch, usually signs of something mis-pronounced.

With a final bump-jolt, the shuttle landed. Tahl turned on the master control to synch all their bio-monitors, disguised as decorative bands on their necks and wrists. The light energy level repelled and analyzed most forms of biological invasion. Hopefully, data to help in understanding and defeating bescere could be gathered today.

"Here they come," Sh'hari announced from the pilot's seat.

Everyone held still, listening to the soft thuds and hints of scraping, as the greeting party trudged across the fenced-in field where they had landed. Sh'hari turned on the outside audio pickups, to hear the discussions, the sounds of wood being moved, supports being pounded into the ground, the ripple-snap of cloth being spread out and caught in the breeze. Treinna closed her eyes and listened. Every few sentences, she translated the orders for the assembly of the ceremonial walkway.

Sh'hari studied the multiple security monitors, watching the women work. "These ladies outside may look like something out of the days of bows and arrows and catapults, but they know their engineering. They studied the outside of the shuttle for a while and I saw them doing calculations, adjusting for the hatch. Think they've all gone downhill, lost their technology, thanks to the disease?"

"That just raises more questions," Maora said. "Maybe the bescere is an invader from off-planet, traveling on an asteroid from another system. The alternative is something they did to themselves, but that implies more advanced science than what is visible. Could they have forgotten all that and regressed in just a few generations?"

"Implying a massive coverup," M'kar said. "Refusing to accept blame. When disasters like that happen, the first response is to point fingers. Usually at the person you were trying to sabotage when everything hinked and you ended up biting yourself."

"Or it was something that was building up, adapting, for many generations," Genys suggested, "before something went wrong and triggered the change. You have to figure even if the women seem immune to the mental deterioration the men suffer, maybe they only *seem* immune. Maybe the deterioration is slower for them. Which is why they're reduced to bows and arrows, while they're using a pretty sophisticated planetary communication system."

"My vote is that they did it to themselves. Like the Q'endrissi," Tahl offered. "Their search for immortality ended up shortening their lifespans, giving them brittle bones and hemophilia."

"Trumpets up," Sh'hari announced, turning from the screen where she was watching the activities outside the shuttle.

A silvery peel came from outside through the audio pickups. All gazes turned to M'kar. She took a deep breath, stood, tugged her uniform straight, then sputtered when Barroo leaned around to rub his muzzle against her nose. She lifted him down from her shoulder and cuddled him for a moment before setting him in her seat. Another tug on her uniform and she stepped to the hatch.

Based on the strong warrior element in this culture, Genys opted for prestige points by sending M'kar out first. Even wearing a pristine uniform, with her hair pulled back in tight braids wrapped around the back of her head, her Chief of Talents had the ability to project an image of a barbarian barely tamed. It wasn't just her facial tattoos. The long ceremonial knives hanging from her belt added to the image. M'kar had exchanged her everyday, regulation-permitted knife for three long blades in sheaths heavily embroidered with gold and silver threads in her clan symbols, the handles of carved and stained bone embedded with precious stones. Maybe most of that implied threat came from the cold stare M'kar had once been clocked at holding for twelve minutes and fourteen seconds. Some of their crewmates joked that she could stare holes through reinforced quad-alloy. Genys hoped they never faced a situation where she had to prove that was true.

The hatch opened. M'kar stepped out and down. Maora got up and followed her, with Granny perched on her right shoulder, sitting on a silver and amethyst-beaded starburst of knotwork, made especially for the situation. Granny had preened to the point of irritation, when M'kar made her understand she could pick the colors of beads and Maora would make it just for her.

Genys waited until M'kar moved out of view and Maora stepped down after her. She took a deep breath, got up, exchanged glances with Treinna, then looked around the passenger compartment at their four waiting dracs.

"You behave, you hear me? Granny is here for show, to impress the natives. You are here as crew, and I want you to make us all proud."

Battleaxe touched the side of her face with her right paw. Genys muffled a chuckle. She could only guess where Battleaxe had learned to salute, because nobody did it on the *Defender*. Maybe from all those hours spent in the classroom with the ship's children. Probably something they had seen in video historical records. Before she turned toward the hatch, Genys caught a glimpse of the other dracs trying to mimic Battleaxe. That heavy weight in her gut vanished. She stepped up to the hatch, with Treinna and Tahl right behind her, and five members of the Security team, in dress uniform, prepared to follow at a discrete distance.

Enlo, guard us. Guide us. Give me wisdom.

Chapter Nine

Then the air of the planet touched Genys for the first time, no longer blocked by the air pressure vents in the hatch blowing outward. She held her breath for a second, an involuntary reaction. She silently scolded herself and took a deep breath as she put her boots on this alien world. Not on soil yet. A thick carpet that barely gave under her steps ran under the canopy that rippled softly in the breeze, held up with long poles every three meters.

There was no trace of that faint, musky, dusty smell that had been described in the air of the infected ships. That had to be good. Genys took another breath. Now she and her team were committed. They had been exposed to whatever made this planet a danger for males. Checking their blood chemistry and the estrogen side of the equation every few hours might reveal something that would help cure the men.

M'kar walked slowly, her usual long, ground-eating stride reined in. Maora walked four steps behind her, and Genys four behind her. Semi-sheer curtains hung down the sides of the walkway, muting the brilliant sunlight, rippling softly in the breeze. Silhouetted figures stood between every other support pole, facing outward, wearing long tunics, trousers and calf-high boots, with a spear in each hand, braced on the ground, arms outstretched before them. No one said a word.

Two people waited at the far end of the walkway. Genys studied them, straining for details as she strode forward. They looked to be about her age, in long-sleeved robes in some dark shade, black or midnight blue, with high collars that rose up to frame their heads. They stood with their hands tucked in their full sleeves, no weapons visible.

Both women flinched and their gazes followed M'kar as she stepped out of the shadows of the walkway and faced them. Yes, facial tattoos and that killer glare worked better than a full array of weapons pointed at a possible enemy. M'kar crossed her arms over her chest and bowed, then held out her hands, palms down as she straightened. One of the women held out her hands, palms up, and they exchanged greetings, host and guest. M'kar stepped out of sight to the left.

Both pairs of eyes widened, and the mouth of the woman on the right dropped open as Maora stepped into the light, with Granny on her shoulder. Voices rose up beyond the curtains, gasps and what Genys hoped were cries of happy astonishment and wonder. Granny rose up on her haunches, spread her wings, and trilled a dozen notes. The crowd, invisible beyond the walkway curtains, went silent. When she finished her song, a wave of sound crashed over them. Maora exchanged greetings with one of the women, then stepped to the right of the opening. Genys again silently asked for Enlo's guidance, stepped into the opening and stopped. She went into parade rest, hands clasped behind her back, and slowly surveyed the scene.

The walkway had taken them through the gates into the arena. In front of her, step-seating that could easily hold several thousand people formed a u-shaped cup in the landscape. The people were dressed in bright colors with so much variety, there was no telling any one shade apart from the others. Flags waved in the fresh breeze that smelled of flowers, freshly cut wood, clean dust, and the distinct hay-and-sweat perfume of horses.

The two women standing at the end of the walkway separated now, one to each side, revealing a group of silver- and white-haired women in long robes, walking with staffs taller than their heads, each staff crested with the emblem of a clan. Genys crossed her arms over her chest as M'kar had done, and bowed, careful not to let her head drop lower than the height of the middle of her chest. She had studied the children's decorum lessons until she thought the words and visuals were painted on her eyelids. As she straightened, Genys held out her arms also, but she stepped forward, past the two guarding women, and approached the leaders of the Senate walking toward her. She kept her arms stretched out, palms facing downward, waiting for her hosts to answer the ritual.

The woman who stepped forward first gave her a narrow-eyed smile. Genys respected caution and a touch of suspicion rather than a veneer of pleasantries that could easily shatter.

As the woman held out her hands, palms up, Genys spoke the carefully rehearsed Castitaran words, announcing her name, her mother's name, grandmother's name, the planet of her birth, her ship, and her years of training. She finished with a translation of her vows when she took command as captain, joining the quest to find the Gatekeepers and reunite the scattered Human race. Treinna had trimmed out some details that would generate too many questions. The general implication of a quest and loyalty to the Alliance were what mattered.

Matriarch Chercha, the first to step forward, recited her name and lineage and her vows to serve the Senate and her own people. Then she stepped back and let each of the other leaders make their greetings and welcome Genys.

From there, Treinna and Tahl stepped forward, and Treinna took over the introductions and greetings. Last, she introduced Granny. Genys wondered which ached more by this time, Treinna's head or her tongue. As planned, Treinna gave a short explanation about Draxonis. She emphasized that the *Defender* had found the dracs on Draxonis. While saying outright that Vitiarre had falsely accused the Alliance of kidnapping numenjax and shrinking them was not wise, some proactive steps needed to be taken to clear up misunderstandings and prevent an interstellar incident.

Finishing, Treinna bowed, then gestured at Granny. The little silver prima donna stood up again on her haunches and spread her wings. Then all twelve of the ship's teacher dracs popped into sight overhead. They swooped and dove and flew circles around each other in an aerial dance, to the delight of the people in the arena.

Granny cast what was clearly a smug glance at Genys.

I am going to strangle her one of these days. Genys sighed and decided better to enjoy the moment than work herself into a headache. This display and one-two punch of inflicting wonder on their hosts might help in the long run. She hoped.

~~~~~

M'kar had read about the physical training and the need for mounted, armed patrols to defend the settlements against the constant encroachment of wildlife. Roaming bands of males who had escaped protective custody and work farms had to be recaptured before they caused damage. They were referred to as "wild bulls," in public service announcement warnings about their migration paths. M'kar tried not to speculate on what was involved in the "wild bull hunting parties" mentioned on some
~~~~~

communication channels.

Because of the planet's sometimes brutal conditions, feats of skill and strength were admired. Aggressive tendencies seemed to be handily dealt with by putting warrior types on the front lines of defense. The tournaments handled any disagreements that might otherwise have turned into war. Maora and her team were of the opinion that wars rarely occurred because of low birth rates and far too much land for the low population to properly handle. Only fools destroyed what resources had been wrestled from the unfriendly wilderness.

Tall, milk-skinned, flame-haired Aniskara presented herself as M'kar's guide when the time came for the tournament. Since Granny had let an entire colony of cats out of the bag with her stunt, the diplomatic team called their dracs to come sit on their shoulders. M'kar had Barroo retrieve her weapons, and clothes to change into. Battleaxe and Ha'ess helped fetch the larger bulky pieces from the ship. The women in the preparation house were fascinated, first by the little dracs popping in and out with their burdens, and then by M'kar's weapons.

Yes, she had to admit, she did have a nice assortment. She also admitted it was fun to "talk shop," as they traded questions about each other's weapons and backgrounds, and especially how they got their scars. Most of the women in the preparation house approved of the Nisandrian tradition of highlighting all scars with tattoos.

Aniskara was a grandmother, looking forward to her first great-grandchild's birth in another moon-cycle. She was indeed as young as she looked, the equivalent of late forties in Standard years. On Castitarus, they married young. The males had such a short time span when they were safe to have in the home, around children, before needing castration to curb the emotional flames that led to brawls and deaths. The trend was for a girl's first mate to be her romantic one, the love of her life, chosen in her teens. As she got older and took other mates, successive choices were made for political and breeding purposes.

Discussing grandchildren and family lines confirmed details that Maora had only speculated on. Castitaran society traced family lines through the females. When a son was given to his mate, he was considered the property of her family, and his mother and sisters essentially wrote him off. When bescere set in, most men forgot their birth families. It was enough of a struggle for a man to remember his mate and their children, if they were lucky enough to have more than one together, after he was removed from the house. M'kar confided in her new friends that her mother hoped to be a grandmother someday, but wasn't putting any pressure on her, and she was grateful. Then, listening to gut instinct, she added that her father would make an incredible grandfather, and spoil any child of hers utterly rotten, each leading the other into trouble constantly.

"On your world, are you in contact with your father?" Aniskara asked. That was definitely longing visible in her gray-blue eyes. "You would trust him with your child?"

"My father … in many ways never had a chance to be a child. His world is a warrior culture, taken to stupid extremes. That's just my opinion. He gladly settled in to be a perpetual child, when he left our homeworld. The children on my ship adore him, and after a few strange looks, the parents trust him implicitly."

"On your ship?" She tipped her head back, as if she could see through the vaulted roof of the preparation house. "You have facilities to restrain your men, so they can voyage with you?"

"I don't think you understand. Our men don't suffer the bescere. There are other forms of mental and emotional deterioration that we still struggle to combat and cure, but that affects both genders. Age does not automatically condemn our males to becoming brutes. Granted, on my father's homeworld, they *choose* to be that way. I'm positive there is some genetic disposition to utter stupidity, and shining examples of testosterone poisoning causing permanent brain damage, but …" M'kar shrugged and tried to smile. She had the awful feeling she had just caused some trouble that Genys and Maora would have to deal with eventually.

Oh, yeah, she had made a great impression.

Aniskara laughed and reached out to hug M'kar. The low-level chatter of the other women stopped with an almost audible click.

"You give us hope." A big, coffee-and-cream-skinned woman stepped out of the shadows where she had been listening. Her head was shaved, except for a topknot sporting a long braid of silver hair. She had a number of scars, crisscrossing lines of white that made

M'kar shudder, imagining the headaches she likely suffered from repeated impacts. "Lexa," she said, and crossed her arms over her chest, giving a short head-bow.

"M'kar." She repeated the salute, bending forward enough that Barroo, who had stayed silent on her shoulder all this time, chirped a protest. Then he mirrored the bow.

That earned laughter from most of the women.

"Hope that your people will find the cause and the cure, and someday we will have lifemates again, as our great-grandmothers had," Aniskara offered, before M'kar could decide how to ask the question. It must have been very clear on her face. "Our leaders give us some information, but they withhold much that has been communicated between your ship and the Senate, to protect us from disappointment."

"I would choose steep slopes of hope, followed by steep slopes of disappointment," another woman said, coming over to the bench facing M'kar's seat. "Rather than living in ignorance, protected by those who don't think I'm woman enough to handle that disappointment. At least we know *something* is being done."

That seemed to open the floodgates, and questions soon came quickly enough M'kar got lost. She asked permission and explained her translator while looping it around her neck, then inserted the earpiece. Soon the questions came so fast, the translator linked together three different questions into one, causing more confusion and much laughter. The program increased its vocabulary and M'kar increased her own understanding of the language, catching nuances through body language and expressions.

Before they were summoned to step out into the arena for the ceremonies to open the tournament, M'kar had several invitations. To visit estates. Talk to doctors who had been researching the problem of the bescere. Go on hunting or patrol trips. She didn't hesitate to accept an invitation from Aniskara and Lexa, who offered to put together a wild bull hunt, so she could see examples of the most extreme effects of the bescere.

Jasper's foster-brother, Seeway, was still missing. Maybe he had made it out into the wilderness and found shelter, however tenuous, among the men who had escaped to freedom.

~~~~~

Matriarch Chercha and her peers in the Senate kept Genys to
~~~~~

themselves, separating her and her Security shadow from Treinna, Tahl and Maora, and their shadows. After getting a few updates and listening in on their meeting with lower ranks of the planetary leadership, Genys was grateful. The upper echelon of the Senate clung to decorum, so they didn't speak over each other, and gave her time to think before responding. They were fascinated by the translator equipment. The constant babble of questions surrounding Treinna, Tahl and Maora made her ears ache. Chercha and her peers asked their questions one at a time. Whenever Genys caught the pattern of what the matriarchs were building up to, she tried to anticipate the questions and offer information so they wouldn't have to ask. That visibly earned her additional respect from her hosts.

The formalities, clarifying what was expected from both sides in the diplomatic negotiations and arranging for access to Healers Guild members and historical records, for the sake of finding a cure for bescere, proceeded smoothly. Genys and the matriarchs had time for a pleasant lunch. Battleaxe preened and posed and did her part for good relations with Castitarus. She allowed the ladies to stroke her head and examine her wings. They asked questions about her age and teleportation ability and how soon she would be able to breathe fire. To break the ice, Genys related the incident with the fire-breathing treats Decker had concocted that put the dracs to sleep. Her hostesses laughed, then she could almost hear the questions forming in their brains.

"Yes," she said, when the laughter faded. "My Security chief is a male. He is somewhat truculent and ready for a good brawl, but that's Decker's personality, not illness. He's fully mature and fully self-controlled. If his drac doesn't send him into an early grave with her antics, I expect him to be in service to the Fleet for another forty or fifty years. He's not the type to take his savings and retire to settle on a colony world."

"Could we meet this Decker?" Matriarch Phileda asked, some hesitation in her voice. "I find the concept of an older man who is still in possession of his faculties utterly fascinating. We have tales in the old books of older men who were quite charming, clever ..." She sighed. "The sort of man we would like to have with us in our declining years."

"I must wait until the medical team is confident in some sort of protection, before we risk any of our males visiting the planet," Genys said after a moment of deliberate hesitation. She and Tahl and Maora had already anticipated this question, and she had her answer ready. However, she had learned that hesitation always gave the impression of thoughtfulness.

When the tournament began, Genys was ready and grateful for a break. The contestants paraded around the arena, and the chanter announced their names and pedigrees and battles. She muffled a few chuckles at the reactions when M'kar's battle record included the assassination attempt she had faced and defeated when she was only four years old. Genys got her improved humor totally under control by the time the feats of skill started on the field below her. She had to keep a calm expression under the attention of what felt like half the audience, after M'kar sent Barroo off the field to sit with her and Battleaxe.

The first contest was a race, over various types of hurdles, then scaling a wall and crawling through an obstacle course of what looked like massive clay pipes. They finished by racing up an inclined slope of wooden planks that adjusted haphazardly, changing angles, dropping, even tipping sideways. The matriarchs' pavilion sat at the perfect angle and height to see the women underneath the construction, pulling levers and manually moving the planks. They couldn't see who was climbing the slope, who they had just sent sliding downwards or nearly toppled over the edge. Upon reaching the top, the contestants slid down ropes or climbed down ladders, or if they had a good angle, jumped off for the final sprint to the finish line.

The order in which they reached the finish line determined who they would fight in the next phase of the games. As each woman reached the finish line, she had her choice from an assortment of weapons waiting on a long table.

M'kar came in third in the race.

"How do you think she's doing?" Genys asked Barroo.

The little brown drac bobbed his head a few times and let his tongue loll out in his doggy grin. Genys supposed that was a good sign. He wasn't worried, he wasn't picking up any negative impressions from M'kar, and he wasn't sulking that he couldn't play with her.

"I'm at a great angle to catch everything," Treinna reported, in the few minutes of lull between events, as the contestants paired up. Her voice in Genys' ear, with no echo from the translator, was a welcome change.

"How do you think we're doing so far?" she asked, voice soft so the translator wouldn't broadcast her words for her hosts.

"It's interesting. The healers talking shop with Tahl have so many questions, so eager to learn all our medical science. I agree with the theory that this society suffered a major slide backwards in technology. Their terminology and understanding of concepts are far beyond their tools, based in historical texts they keep referring to."

"I'm glad I don't have to deal with the question if we're justified in returning them to their previous level of technology and science. Let the Academy handle that headache."

"A couple have already tried to get Tahl to promise we can fix things before we have enough data to figure out what we're up against." Treinna's pause was so characteristic of her, Genys could almost see her chewing on her bottom lip. "We sure don't want to get them mad at us. And not just because I really like these ladies. Even the itchy twitches are kind of fun."

Genys muffled a snort of laughter. "Do they truly want a cure, or is it all political talk?"

"The healers do. They know what's happening to their men isn't right, even if it's the norm. They know this isn't the way Enlo made us to be – and yeah, we've heard enough for Maora to have a good idea of their spiritual beliefs. The parallels with their Praestantaes are numerous enough. The name might be different, but the general idea of a loving creator who got kicked in the face by the bratty kids, keeps offering a second chance, and stands back to let them face the consequences of their choices, it's all there. Although I'm getting the feeling there's more lip service than actual true devotion and belief. But who am I to judge? I'm guilty more often than I like to admit, getting so busy I forget to take care of my soul's feeding and exercise too many times."

"Yeah, me too," Genys sighed. "Backing up. So they admit other parts of society don't hope for a cure?"

"Some don't want help from us, because they like the current set-up. Some people originally thought the Maniterri came from the sister world, and they were ready to go to war. Some historical grudges there that Maora needs to investigate."

"Any hints of malcontents and rebels who might be upset to the point of violence, to have us here? Should we be grateful we're on this island? The last thing we need is to create an interstellar incident by defending ourselves from an angry mob that thinks we're the monster in the castle."

"Preach it, sister," Treinna murmured.

Genys sighed, smiling, grateful they could both find some humor in a situation that might turn fatally tricky at any moment. "So bottom line, the people you're talking to, the authorities on the subject, still have an active hope for a cure?"

"I'm getting the sense they have hope, but they don't put as much stock into that hope as they'd like to. If that makes any sense."

"Too much sense. Ah — they're getting started. Need to turn the headache back on."

"Never turned it off," Treinna said, ending with a chuckle. A soft background humming from the people surrounding her died away, indicating the link had closed.

The contestants went to quadrants marked in the mossy groundcover that carpeted the center of the arena. Removing the racecourse components had cause the delay that gave the competitors time to rest before the next phase of the games.

M'kar had chosen a long pole, while her opponent had a length of rope with what looked like weights woven into it near one end. Genys had a good view of their weapons because they stood almost directly in front of the pavilion where she sat. She suspected that was on purpose, maybe as a gesture of politeness. M'kar only glanced up once, nodded to Genys, then focused on her opponent. Genys studied the woman, a head taller and maybe thirty kilos heavier, all tanned muscle and dozens of thin metallic bands on her arms. She hoped those bands were decoration rather than some kind of defense. That could imply something about the woman's fighting style.

The *blat* of an alto horn rang across the arena. M'kar's opponent twirled her rope slowly, playing out the weighted end bit by bit. M'kar held the pole in both hands, circling her, face calm, legs bent, shoulders hunched, presenting a smaller target for that rope to hit.

Snap — out went the rope. M'kar slammed the pole into the turf and swung her legs up into the air. She vaulted over her opponent.

The rope swung out like a darting snake, trying to catch her. She caught it with her free hand, keeping a grip on the pole with the other. A good hard yank made the other woman stumble forward. She didn't let go. M'kar spun and danced backwards out of reach. Her opponent gathered up the rope and backed to the other side of their assigned square.

M'kar focused on the pole, sliding her hands farther apart down the length, and seemed to be twisting it. Genys muffled a gasp when it came apart. Then another gasp when M'kar's opponent took advantage of her few seconds of distraction. She lunged, snapping back on the rope instead of twirling it. The weighted end leaped with an audible crack, straight for M'kar's head.

She wasn't there. Genys swore she had just seen her teleport. A dark blur resolved into M'kar somersaulting in a curve, in the opposite direction of that rope lash. One half of her pole arrowed straight at the rope-woman. She ducked, putting her chest right into the path of the second half of the pole. With an audible *ooph*, she went down. Genys saw her chest shuddering as she struggled to regain the breath knocked out of her. M'kar looked up at the pavilion, then turned to the rest of the field. Several of the pairs had either already knocked out one opponent or had paused to watch the match. A little woman scurried down the field, calling something, waving her arms. She reminded Genys of Granny, silver hair and silver clothes and the spry way she moved. Genys braced for trouble. That sinking feeling in her stomach never lied.

Then the little woman laughed.

M'kar walked over to her downed opponent and held out a hand, offering her help. Genys held her breath until the woman reached up. She smiled, still looking a little breathless, and rubbed the spot on her chest that would probably have a huge, dark bruise in the morning. She kept hold of M'kar's hand when she got to her feet, and pulled her arm up high in the air. Cheers erupted from a large portion of the arena.

"Quite impressive," Chercha said, leaning over to Genys. "Thelda has never been so quickly taken down. The intimidation factor usually means we have some amusing displays of acrobatics as her opponents try to stay out of her way and wear her down, until she makes a mistake."

"Is the pole supposed to come apart?" Genys had to ask.

"Yes, but not all the poles offered do. It is the luck of the draw. Your champion is clever, to figure it out."

"She's a survivor."

Thank you, Enlo.

M'kar didn't come off so well in all her matches. Genys hoped those losses were deliberate, to strike the right balance between proving the visitors could hold their own and not insulting their hosts by making them look bad. When M'kar joined Genys in the pavilion, dark splotches visible on her bare arms and face promised colorful bruises. She was sweaty, with smears of moss and dirt on her face and clothes. An impressive collection of delicate, colored chains, designating her ranking in each contest, hung around her neck. She bowed gracefully to each matriarch, despite probably feeling like one massive bruise, and accepted their compliments. Then a guide led M'kar to a bathhouse for the traditional hot bath and herbal oil treatment provided to the contestants. A short time later, Chercha summoned a guide to lead Genys and her Security crew to the guesthouse.

The guesthouse was a long building, two stories tall, large enough to house at least two dozen people. It sat close to the massive administration building on one side, and the feasting pavilion on the other side, where the festivities would take place until nightfall. Treinna, Tahl and Maora were waiting inside. They looked exhausted. And uncomfortable.

Eight boys waited in a neat row of seats on the far side of the main room, facing the three women. What looked like travel sacks sat at the feet of each one. Nervousness widened their eyes and put a sheen of sweat on their faces. After all the questions thrown at her today, Genys guessed the matriarchs had taken the first step in providing study subjects for finding a cure for bescere. The boys looked terrified of what would be done to them.

She prayed they were there to help find the cure, and not a follow-up to some bald hints that she wasn't getting any younger and needed to start thinking about producing some heirs.

Chapter Ten

Genys mumbled a few words she thought were pretty close to Nisandrian oaths of deep mortification. M'kar hadn't translated but explained the crackling words were the equivalent of heart-felt pleas to Enlo to please get her out of this mess or kill her right then and there.

"Please tell me they aren't what I fear they are," Genys said, after remembering to turn off her translator. She gave the eight boys a tight smile and nod, as she crossed the room to the chairs the other three women were sitting in.

"Test subjects," Tahl said, with just a hint of a smirk.

Which meant she knew what had been going through Genys' mind, and she had enjoyed seeing that momentary reaction of why-didn't-I-become-a-doctor-like-my-sister?

"Thank you, Enlo." Genys dropped into the closest chair. Another glance at the eight boys. They were like dolls she had seen in a shop, all the same face, in a stair-step progression of ages. "So what's the problem? We have room on the ship. We can put them in isolation suits to travel from the shuttle bay to the isolation ward in Medical."

"They expect to stay with us, whether we cure them or not." Maora sighed. "They are our property." Granny crooned sympathy and nuzzled the woman's hand that cradled her like a baby.

"You should have seen the tearful farewells with their mothers," Treinna added. "They think they will be cured and join the Alliance and grow up to be heroes like they've heard in stories about their great-great-grandfathers. Before the bescere hit."

"One step at a time," Genys said. "Pray. A lot. More than we already have been. Like E'bett said in chapel the other day, this might be an uncomfortable situation for us, but maybe Enlo put us through the things we've endured to be the right tool and right approach to meet the need."

"I have never accused the All-Maker of being cruel or having a nasty sense of humor," Maora said, "but there have been times lately when I come close." She sighed again. Then that mischievous twinkle came back to her eyes. She raised her head and gestured with a lift of her chin at the eight guests. "Let's not be rude." She reached over the side of the chair and pulled out her translator headgear.

"If they're going to be on the ship with us, they need their own," Genys said, more to herself than to the others, starting a list of things that needed to be done to outfit and deal with their guests. Treinna and Tahl stepped up to get to work with the boys while Maora and Genys worked on a plan and their lists.

When M'kar entered the guesthouse, she took one look at the row of boys and went white. Then she took two steps backwards, like she would run. Genys suspected the reasons, and didn't know whether she should feel horrified, amused, or sympathetic.

"They offered you ..." Genys gestured with a tip of her head at the row. All eight boys were focused on Tahl, giving them their preparatory examination, taking blood samples and recording their bio-statistics to establish a baseline. They all had nearly the same expressions of fascinated interest, mesmerized by the whirring and flashing of the medical sensor wand.

"Four of my new friends offered me a son or brother, all utterly flabbergasted that I hadn't had any children yet. I even had a few ask me if I had seen a healer about my problem. They suggested a new mate might be the solution. I shocked some of them when I told them I hadn't taken a mate yet. With the birth rate so low, they can't comprehend anyone not wanting to have children."

"One of Tahl's new friends," Maora said, coming over to join them and pitching her voice just as softly, "told her about a treatment they've developed that reduces the number of male births. She's asked for samples, because the implication is that it kills off Y-chromosome sperm. They only give the treatment to men from bloodlines that show a distinct tendency for rapid deterioration and violent behavior. The bloodlines where males retain intelligence, alertness and self-control longer are encouraged to procreate. Tahl has already speculated that a side effect is that it also lowers the female birth rate, just not as much."

"That's ..." M'kar raked her fingers through her hair, still wet, loosening some of the braids. "Depressing, I guess." She shrugged. "I was going to say barbaric, genocidal, maybe sexist."

"That's a word I haven't heard since Basic," Genys said.

"Actually, I can understand why limiting male births would be considered a blessing. What mother would want her son to suffer bescere? Better not to have any sons, than watch them deteriorate. Taking a mate from a strong, resistant bloodline only makes sense."

"Yeah, well, as long as I'm not expected to contribute to the gene pool ..." M'kar shuddered and glanced over at the eight boys. "Please tell me you didn't accept on my behalf."

Maora laughed, earning the attention of the natives. Barroo jumped up from M'kar's shoulder and glided over to the smallest boy of the group. He hovered in front of him, chattering until the boy's wide-eyed, frozen look relaxed into smile.

"He's the same age as Jorgan," M'kar offered. "Poor little guy. Why did his mother give him to us?"

Genys explained quickly. M'kar's expression shifted from apprehension to sympathy. Then turned to that thoughtful look that sometimes made Genys hold her breath in anticipation of something either viciously witty, or brilliantly outrageous.

"This could be a big leap in solidifying relations with Castitarus." She walked over to stand facing the boy. He looked up at her with an expression Genys had seen most of the ship's children wear around M'kar the first time they met her — a mixture of wonder and delighted fear.

"I don't follow," Treinna said. This showed she had been paying attention while assisting Tahl.

"Good hospitality and diplomacy would be to introduce their children to our children. These are the safest ages of males to bring on board the ship, if I understand what Aniskara was telling me about the onset of bescere. Maybe it's there, but isn't active yet. Weakened, immature. We'd still be exposing our boys who aren't in the sensitive range. Theoretically," M'kar said slowly, forehead wrinkled in thought, "it could be something like inoculation."

"Bad science, yet somewhat valid," Tahl said. "Especially if the bescere is triggered by something biological, and not a virus. They will certainly be more comfortable with our children than anyone else on the ship. We can keep them in a controlled environment and yes ..." She sighed. "This will provide me massive amounts of data to work with. The wider the spectrum of test subjects, the more variables we can gather and study and monitor. Any changes in the children whose bio-stats are known to me will prove helpful." She bowed her head a moment, submitting to the unspoken possibilities filling the air. "Providing this leads to prevention and cure for all."

"Can you give them advance warning through Thyal?" Genys asked M'kar. "The fewer people who hear and are involved, the happier I'll feel."

"On it." She stepped outside, fingers pressed to her temples as she visibly braced for a long conversation with Thyal.

~~~~~

Half an hour later, the five women escorted the eight boys through the gates to the landing field. Their Security crew had gone ahead to prepare. The teacher dracs swirled out of the shuttle the moment the hatch opened. M'kar had been focusing during the short walk, giving the twelve dracs instructions. They spun around the eight boys, chittering and crooning, until each boy was chosen by a drac. M'kar grinned, choking on imminent tears at the astonishment and glee that touched each determined, stoic, apprehensive face the moment a drac landed on his shoulder. The explanation was likely unnecessary, but she gave it anyway: they had been adopted by a drac for however long they were on board the *Defender*. The drac would be their friend and would bring help when they needed it.

Berry, a mottled blue-purple and reddish-purple female, let out a soft, crackling sort of croon. She was perched on the shoulder of the tallest boy of the group. M'kar estimated him to be fifteen, at the most. Berry spread her wings and shook her head.

Then she sneezed.

"Oh ... fewmets," Genys said. Her mind flashed back to how the female dracs sneezed at Decker's fire-breathing treats.

Sneezing dracs were not good. What if that wasn't an allergic reaction as Brea had theorized, but a sign of something worse? The last thing they needed was for their dracs to get sick, maybe go into hibernation.

All the dracs gave Berry and her boy startled looks.

"None of the other dracs are sneezing," Genys murmured. "Something different about this boy?"

"It can't be this easy," Tahl said. "Maybe it's my Ankuar blood, but I expect easy answers to be detours and distractions."

"You're thinking sneezing points out who is infected?" Maora
~~~~~

said, after the women exchanged measuring looks.

"Well, once we get them up to the ship, we'll start in on every test we can think of and invent more. I have a theory, considering the hormonal fluctuations we have already uncovered. The boy's age, the fact that bescere begins at full maturity … something in the blood chemistry makes the victims susceptible, but something that is common among all males." Tahl's tone was distracted as she brought out the medical scanner. "The difference between mature males and adolescents, perhaps."

"Hormones," Genys offered.

"That's too simple." She paused as the scanner woke up and she pointed it at the boy, who was holding very still, perhaps expecting Berry to do something to him he wouldn't like. "Yet how many times has the simple answer been the best one?"

"How many times has the stupid answer been the right one?" Treinna muttered. "Do we dare send him up to the ship if he's infected?"

"I really wish I wasn't handing this over to Brea," Tahl said. "As much as I trust and respect her. Yes, we have to send him up. And avoid physical contact with adult males."

"Better keep adolescent boys away from him," M'kar offered.

"Captain?" Hanni stepped out from the cockpit where she had been preparing the shuttle to launch.

"We have to be back in our quarters, ready for the feast any time now," Genys said. "There's no time for dithering. Go. Warn the ship, trust your staff to take the right precautions. M'kar, impress on Berry that she has to be careful, and she'll probably be donating blood samples, since she's reacting and just …" She waved her hands at the open hatch. "Go."

~~~~~

The feast was easily the most casual and comfortable social event Genys had ever had to endure, considering that she and her team were the focus of the evening. Food was set out on tables scattered through the extensive Senate gardens, under long pavilions. Everyone helped themselves and migrated between seating groups. Granny flittered from one group to another, finding the oldest and most powerful woman in each group. Then she settled down on the arm of the woman's chair and went into her "poor pretty kitty" routine, as Tress Lore had dubbed it. Everyone
~~~~~

adored her. What amazed M'kar, whenever she caught the conniving old biddy in action, was how she put up with petting and cooing and baby talk and other demeaning treatment she wouldn't endure from anyone at Anwesta. There had to be an agenda, because she repeated the pattern, never staying with any one woman longer than twenty minutes.

The team mixed and mingled and answered questions about the Alliance and did what they could to mitigate the damage Vitiarre had done to relations with Caristartus. The Senate already knew far more about the Alliance and its technology and governmental structure than a first contact level permitted. So much could go wrong in this mission that had already been preemptively sabotaged.

The dracs riding on everyone's shoulders protected them from sabotage through the food and ever-present alcohol, and from rudeness and snide remarks. Other than the women who were being suckered in by Granny playing sweet and adorable, most people approached the dracs with some flickers of wariness and always showed respect.

The preeminent healers of the planet surrounded Tahl, assisted by Treinna, asking questions and comparing knowledge and theories. Many presented her with samples of various plants and other compounds they had tried over the years to treat bescere. Genys and Maora stayed together, limited to the company of the matriarchs. Well, that was their job, after all, building bridges across the galaxies.

M'kar was surrounded by the hunters and warriors and athletes. Aniskara and Lexa put her under their protection and introduced her to everyone they considered useful and just plain fun. They worked on details for the wild bull hunt they had promised her, and the location and arrangements changed as more women found out about it and begged to join in. A few of her new friends asked outright how she had become paired with Barroo, and how they could obtain a drac as a friend. Several women commented how they would love to have a drac to intimidate bureaucrats and troublemakers.

The five Security crew were treated politely and with the same respect as the matriarchs' bodyguards. Genys was impressed to see how no one tried to distract them by offering food or starting conversations. She had witnessed too many disasters where well-meaning hosts at large, crucial diplomatic or cultural engagement events had treated guards as guests and got in the way of them doing their job.

"You know what's really disturbing?" Treinna said, when the party finally began to wind down. She and M'kar waited on the administration building steps, within sight of their guesthouse, for the other three to show up. Their Security crew had gone to the shuttle that had returned a short time ago, to check in.

"Besides the lack of comfort food? These are women in stressful situations. They need something indulgent and bad for them, to help them take the edge off." M'kar flinched when Barroo drooped so his head hung below her shoulder. "Finally found your bedtime, did we?" She slid him off her shoulder and cradled him in her crossed arms. He sighed and gave her his doggy grin and closed his eyes.

"Besides that." Treinna nodded, her grin a mere flicker. "Nobody asked us about the boys. It was like they handed over their sons and washed their hands of them. Everybody has to know we sent them up to the ship. It's kind of hard to hide the shuttle flying out and back in again, since there is no other aircraft on the entire planet."

"That we know of."

"That we know of." She nodded. "I don't know if I should be worried that they trust us so much, or they fear to offend us by asking what we did with the boys, or they don't seem to care."

"I think with what seems a hopeless situation, they've learned to at least present a face of not letting it bother them."

"Hmm. Maybe. I know if a female version of bescere was waiting for Tress when she hit puberty, I'd be worrying myself into headaches and visiting a counselor and the chapel every day."

"No, I think you'd make sure you never conceived until there was a cure."

"True. Which just means we have to pity these women, who have to learn to turn their hearts off, or let the race die out to avoid having sons who will suffer."

"Are you sure you didn't drink tonight? Because you sound really depressed, and you're making me depressed."

Treinna made a half-squeal, half-growl, and turned to try to elbow M'kar. Moonrise chirped sleepily and slid down, visibly demanding the same cradling Barroo enjoyed. The two women grinned and for a few minutes were quiet, waiting for their teammates.

Genys and Maora came from one direction and Tahl came from another, escorted by their Security and a few women who had been their hostesses through the evening. Everyone made polite thanks and responses and said goodnight. The team was silent as they crossed the short distance to the guesthouse.

M'kar smelled something that didn't seem right, when she stepped into the guesthouse. She slid Barroo onto the nearest couch and reached for her knives. Too bad there were no lights to turn on. They had to take the lanterns left by their escorts and go around the guesthouse, lighting lamps. Sh'hari was head of the guesthouse Security team. M'kar stopped her when she made a move to go ahead to take care of the lamps. She took another breath, trying to identify the slightly sweet, slightly musty, slightly dusty smell.

Battleaxe sneezed.

"Whoever you are, you might as well come out, we know you're here," M'kar said, in Standard and then repeated in Nisandrian. It always sounded so much nastier that way. Then the translator blurted the words after her.

"Matriarch Chercha said no men were allowed on the island today," Genys said, raising a lantern. Her translator repeated the statement. Sh'hari and Kara separated, moving out to cover as much of the dark room as they could. A nearly subliminal whine indicated the stunner wands were powered up and ready.

A lumpy shape rose up from behind a couch that had been against the righthand wall when they left the guesthouse, but now sat a meter away from it. The shape was covered by a decorative throw. It slid down to reveal a bearded, tanned face. The rest of the man still cowered down behind the couch.

"Fleet?" he said, in Standard.

"Fin?" Treinna cried. "Thank you, Enlo. We were so worried!"

M'kar repressed a whistle of appreciation. Fin Seeway had to be more than two meters tall. How had he fit behind the couch?

Genys gestured for him to come out. Tahl went to the chest of equipment that had been left partially hidden under another of the ubiquitous throws, this one depicting a seascape. The chest had a fingerprint and retina scan lock, to ensure no one could get into it and cause trouble by misusing the equipment.

Seeway settled his hip on the back of the couch and swung his legs over, then slid down, to sit facing them. His footgear was just flaps of leather, held onto his feet with thongs that caught his big toes and another strap around each ankle. His clothes were rough, a loose weave, likely all natural fibers, with a drawstring at the waist of his pants. He wore a sleeveless vest, and he was generally dirty, his brown coloring equally tan and dust. He hauled a rough pack that looked like it was made of skins, and set it on the floor between his feet.

A look of near weepy gratitude twisted his long, lean face for a moment, when Tahl opened up her medical kit and stepped over to begin scanning him. Seeway held still and waited until Genys asked him to tell his story.

Battleaxe sneezed. Seeway flinched, then again when the medical scanner blipped. "Sorry. My nerves have been shot to the nethers since this craziness they call the bescere got hold of me."

"You seem pretty coherent," Maora offered. She cradled Granny, who kept her face pressed into Maora's collar, and only occasionally opened one eye to glare at Seeway.

"That's part of my story."

"Where are the rest of the Maniterri?" Genys asked.

"A few got rescued with me. I don't know where the others are. There are a lot of nice helpful people here, but it's hard telling them apart from the ones who believe in really drastic treatment for what ails us. The ones who treat us like we committed a crime, and the ones who practice not-so-merciful mercy killings." He shuddered, then shied away from the bleeping and flashing lights of the scanner. "Sorry. I'm late for my dose."

"Dose?" Tahl lowered the scanner and leaned back a little, as if that would help her see him better. "Dose of what?"

"You found a cure? A treatment?" Treinna guessed.

"Not a cure, but it lets a man hold onto more of his brains." He gestured down at his pack. "When I heard about the ship, I had to take the chance. To warn other men, if nothing else."

"Calm down." Genys got up from her couch facing him, to reach across the gap and grip his shoulders and look into his eyes.

Battleaxe sneezed three times in a row and let out an unhappy croon. Genys glanced at M'kar, the request in her gaze clear enough. M'kar mentally called all the dracs to her, opened the door, and showed them the decorative ridge on the roof where they could perch. Barroo wasn't happy about leaving her alone, but she gave him a mental image of teleporting in, straight through the roof, with talons ready to defend her. Then she gave him a mental image of him sneezing hard enough to knock himself out of the air. Barroo gave her a disgusted look, not at all happy with her teasing, and flew up on the ridge with the other dracs.

While she had stepped out, everyone had moved into the guesthouse kitchen. Maora was ladling steaming water into an elaborate infuser pot provided by their hosts. A tank of water on the side of the stove was kept filled, always hot and ready to make tea or infusions. Tahl was running a smaller science scanner over the purplish balls of dried leaves spilled out on the table. Seeway's pack sat on the table, with an open drawstring cloth bag sitting next to it.

Seeway explained as the tea steeped. He and five junior members of Vitiarre's team had been snatched from the containment area. The women who took them insisted they were rescuing them. They said they had a treatment to help the men, and offered it in exchange for transportation to the sister world.

"Definitely Draxonis." Seeway paused to swirl the infuser and sniff the steam. He explained the leaves were called tear sop. "They weren't happy when I told them the civilization there had died. Turns out their ancestors were stranded on Castitarus when a rebel faction botched their plans to destroy Castitaran society. Then bescere hit and no one in the ships was willing to risk coming down to retrieve them. They've been running a holding action the last two hundred years, waiting for their relatives to find a cure and come rescue them. When the Chute opened and no one came for them, their underground organization splintered."

"Splintered how? And how badly?" Genys said.

"The people on Draxonis made contact with Castitarus two Chute openings ago. They wanted to run things, but the numenjax somehow prevented them taking over. They had to get rid of the numenjax. During the interval when the Chute was closed to them, they whipped up some biological warfare." Seeway shuddered once. He sniffed the steam rising from the pot. His hands shook.

"Draxonis got biological samples of the numenjax and did some nasty bio-engineering, hoping to shrink them and reduce their intelligence and their psionic powers. Legends say the numanjax got into people's brains. They could talk with people from half the planet away."

"I think we should all agree that our dracs don't need to learn this," Tahl said. "Granny is hard enough to put up with, but tell her she's a downgraded version of the big ones? No thanks. I may be Ankuar, but I'm not that suicidal." She winked at Seeway when he flinched at hearing that confession.

"So … during the last Chute opening, they succeeded?" Genys said.

"Partially. More things went wrong. Besides rebels sabotaging equipment. The first wave of biological warfare was aimed at the numenjax, affecting some plants that promoted their regular cycle of hibernation. It mutated, and the plants are the cause of the bescere. Some substance it releases knocks the whole biological system out of balance."

"Can we say testosterone poisoning?" Treinna muttered.

"There was a huge argument when I told the women who took us there was no one on Draxonis to rescue them. Nowhere to go," Seeway said. "Some didn't believe us, and others got furious enough, they're planning to kidnap some of your people to force you to take them to Draxonis."

"Thanks for the warning," Genys said. "Is that why they took Vitiarre?"

"If the exiles who took me took him, we were kept in different camps." He picked up the pot to pour a cup, then took small sips every few sentences as he continued his story.

Seeway had been trying to persuade his captors to help get him to one of the shuttles. He planned to get up to the ship and turn off the program slaving the *Dandridge*'s systems, and then eventually get through the Chute and send for help. He had taken advantage of the uproar over news of the arrival of the *Defender*, and escaped. He came to Congregation as the most logical place for meetings between the Senate and the Alliance, hoping to contact whoever came down to the planet.

"So explain this," Treinna said, gesturing at the hazy purple liquid in his cup.

Seeway looked into his cup, visibly braced himself, and took a large gulp. His hands no longer shook when he put the cup down.

Some of the underground group's members had earned their way into the Archivists Guild. They gained access to knowledge recorded in encrypted files and systems that had fallen out of use when the collective intelligence of the planet took a sudden, drastic drop in the space of a few years. A generation ago, they had found a recipe for a tea they drank in large quantities, that reduced the worst effects of the bescere.

"Do you know what's in this?" One corner of Tahl's mouth crooked up as she studied the readings from her scanner wand. "How did they come up with this combination? Were they using it for women's problems, before they used it for men?"

"Women's problems?" Genys said.

Treinna snorted. M'kar really hated it when her friend caught onto something before she did.

"Yes, as a matter of fact." Seeway scrubbed at his face with his palms and seemed to collapse a little in his seat.

Genys squeezed his shoulder. "What did they use this for before they turned it to help men with bescere?"

"It was used for women who were showing masculine characteristics after menopause hit. Tempers, fits of violence, shrinking of breasts, body hair."

"High concentrations of estrogen, among other compounds that I need to analyze," Tahl said, "but on a hunch I'd say they balance the hormones. Someone was smart enough to guess what was affecting the men, and did what they could with limited science and data."

"Wonder if it'd treat the dracs' allergy problem," M'kar mused.

Chapter Eleven

Seeway laughed. "Makes sense. If it helps at all, Doctor, I've suffered a severe hormonal imbalance since being tricked into living among the Maniterri. The environment, the food they eat, it started a cascade effect that cut back on my male hormones. I was kind of foggy at the first onset of bescere -- until my implant ran out. Then I regained some sharpness and self-control."

"Once you get a good strong dose of this, we're going to send you and the tear sop up to the *Defender*, and my chief medic will put you through a physical exam that will probably make you regret turning yourself in." Tahl patted his shoulder. "You'll be considered a hero eventually."

Seeway finished his cup, and they waited another half hour, to let it take effect, while he told them everything he could remember from his time with the Draxonan exiles. Then M'kar called the dracs in. Battleaxe itched a little, but didn't sneeze when she got close to Seeway. Granny fussed and didn't want to get within a meter of him, but her glare didn't seem quite so fierce. Moonrise and Ha'ess wrinkled up their noses, but after another half an hour, they let him pet them and didn't scratch afterwards.

"Did you notice Barroo didn't show any reactions? Maybe only the female dracs have the allergy to bescere. We need to run more tests," Tahl said.

"On the ship," Genys said. "And I don't dare send him up until morning. It's kind of obvious when the shuttle takes off and lands. Don't want to generate any inconvenient questions."

The shuttle had returned with equipment Jasper had specially modified for their situation. They needed to be able to communicate directly with the ship if anything happened while they were away from the communication packs in the guesthouse or the shuttle. Jasper had made adjustments to the personal communication packs, reducing their size and extending their range so they could be carried under clothing without being too obvious. There was no telling how much their hosts understood and could guess about their equipment, after the odd bits and pieces of information and Castitaran history they had picked up already. Just because they had lost most of their technology around the same time they lost the numenjax and the bescere attacked their men, that didn't mean they had lost the understanding of it.

M'kar went to her room early, to have privacy to update Thyal. He promised to update her parents, and share her impressions of Seeway with Brea, so she could be better prepared to deal with him when he arrived in the morning.

~~~~~

Barroo woke M'kar, trumpeting an alert and trying to pull her out of bed, shortly after dawn the next morning. People were approaching the guesthouse in a bad mood. The image he passed to her was of exaggerated, scowling features, huge heads and mouths filled with jagged teeth.

"Someday, Troublemaker, you are going to learn to talk and then it'll be a little easier having you standing guard." She rubbed the scratch on her arm where his talons had scraped.

Tugging on the clothes she had laid out to go to morning exercises with Aniskara and Lexa, she hurried, barefoot, through the open common area to the door. Barroo popped out, popped back in, and let her know the angry-snarling-mean-old-females were going to knock the door down. M'kar muffled a snort and asked the other dracs to wake their parents. Then she hurried to the door and pulled it open.

The woman just putting her foot on the bottom step to approach the door was unforgettable. She had loitered at the fringes last night, with a sour expression of disapproval on a wrinkled face under a fuzzy mop of the most glaring shade of hot pink hair that had ever threatened to make M'kar's eyes bleed.

Behind her stood an even dozen other women with a wide range of determined, cautious, irritated and sleepy expressions. M'kar made a wager with herself that the leader of this band of rudely early visitors had hauled the rest of them out of bed. On second thought, their clothes were too fancy for a morning social call. Maybe they hadn't gone to bed yet.

"Enlo's blessings on you," she said, in Standard, though she knew the right Castitaran greeting phrases.

Let these sourpusses assume she didn't know much of their language. They might slip up and say something useful in front of
~~~~~

her. Besides, her mother had warned her that some languages were deliberately tricky, especially in a high-pressure situation such as first contact. Two phrases that sounded alike, with a single intonation changed, could be the difference between asking if someone needed help and promising to do everything in her power to help them.

Barroo popped in, hovering in the air in front of her for a moment, before settling on her shoulder. All the women took a step back, eyes wide with wonder, some of them wide with greed. The pink-haired sourpuss didn't step back. Barroo showed M'kar that everyone in the guesthouse was hurrying to get dressed, and Genys was talking with Seeway. Best if he kept out of sight.

Treinna came to the door, Moonrise on her shoulder, and M'kar moved over to make room for her. The doorway was wide enough for three people to go through, but Ashrock had taught her how to fill a doorway and brace herself so nobody could drag her out. It was necessary when dealing with some of her homicidal cousins. Treinna greeted the visitors politely. Judging from the tightening expression on Pink-head's face, she wasn't mollified. Where were the Senate's guards? What were the chances Pink-head and her cronies were trying to avoid being seen on whatever errand had brought them here?

Pink-head and Treinna went back and forth several times before Treinna gave her a shallow bow, turned, and discretely tugged on the tail of M'kar's shirt as she retreated into the house. She sagged against the wall as soon as M'kar shut the door.

"What do they want at this unblessed hour?" Genys asked. On the other side of the long common room, she and Maora and Tahl were just emerging from their rooms in their dress uniforms.

"Well, the short version is essentially daring us to put our money where our mouths are." Treinna reached up to stroke Moonrise's head. The drac crooned unhappily.

"That sounds ominous," Maora said. "Regarding what, exactly?"

"Finding a cure for bescere."

"We're just starting. I will be spending days just gathering information and samples, and meeting with all the healers who have been trying to deal with the problem," Tahl said.

"You look a little green," M'kar observed. "Barroo's getting some unhappy reverb from Moonrise. What do they want?"

"She tried to trick me into *promising* a cure. Don't worry, I kept emphasizing we could only *try*, that success lay in Enlo's hands. But that really wasn't the issue." Treinna pushed off from the wall and moved over to the nearest couch, to sit and cuddle Moonrise. "They want us to prove we're sincere about finding a cure for their men by bringing *our* men down to expose them." She took a deep breath. "The men who belong to us personally."

"We don't ..." Genys settled onto the edge of the table by her and crossed her arms. "The three of us don't have any men who belong to us, but you two do."

"And we opened our big mouths and told them about my father and Jasper, how controlled and mature they are, and safe and ..." M'kar dropped down onto the couch next to Treinna and hid her face in her hands.

"We can protect Jasper by insisting he's essential to ship efficiency," Maora said. "But M'kar's father came on this mission to help with diplomatic functions, and they know that."

"Knowing Ashrock," Genys said, "he'll be on the first shuttle down. He'll get dirty and sweaty and eat the native food and drink unfiltered water and just dare bescere to come attack him."

M'kar choked, and wished she could laugh, because her captain was right. Ashrock would put himself in front of the gun and taunt the shooter to pull the trigger.

She hurried to change into her uniform, since the workout would have to be canceled. Treinna and Maora conferred over the implications of inviting the visitors into the guesthouse, versus leaving them to stand outside in the morning chill. Welcoming them could create a commitment of hospitality extending to the entire ship. M'kar wondered if her ancestors had decided that being barbarians and treating everybody like a potential enemy was a much simpler and far more honest way to live.

They decided to compromise by taking advantage of the cultural implications of sharing salt and bread, which was universal in every culture the Alliance had encountered. So far. They would take breakfast provisions outside to share with the visitors, and sit on the stone benches in the sculpture garden between the guesthouse and the administration building. That could very likely be the entire purpose of the garden, to provide a neutral place to talk and avoid inviting potential troublemakers over the threshold.

Plus, there was the danger of someone getting nosy, walking into the wrong room, and finding Seeway in hiding.

Pink-head's sour mouth twisted down even farther when Treinna made the invitation, but the rest of her party welcomed it. Perhaps they were relieved? Pink-head couldn't decline, since M'kar and Maora were already in the doorway, holding trays of food. The dracs were soon dipping and soaring and swirling overhead, guiding them to the garden by the power of their excitement alone.

First things first: learn everyone's real name. M'kar knew if she kept thinking of Pink-head *as* Pink-head, she would eventually refer to her by that name at the wrong time, to the wrong person. Pink-head was a matriarch, Lopesi. M'kar pitied Genys, who had spent the previous evening exposed to that eye-bleeding color of hair and her sour face.

Introductions over, they distributed the cups of morning brew before taking the next step. While it smelled invigoratingly spicy, an oil slick collected on top as it cooled. Lopesi opened her mouth to speak, and the communication pack sitting on the paving stones at Genys' feet flashed and blipped. They had brought the pack out to intimidate and impress, and let them keep their personal, mobile communication packs secret. None of them expected the pack to go off. Veylen was too considerate to interrupt their morning routine of exercise, breakfast, and contemplation. Unless there was an emergency.

"Excuse me." Genys managed to get the inflection right in the native words. She bent to press her finger to the flashing plate. "Arroyen here."

"Good morning, Captain," Veylen said. "The new sensors in the communication pack seem to be working with far higher sensitivity than Jasper anticipated. I can register the rising heart rate of six non-*Defender* personnel sitting around you. Is your situation serious?"

Veylen had a wonderful future as a dramatist. His cheerful tone was enough to deceive anyone who didn't speak Standard. M'kar thanked Enlo they hadn't turned on their personal translators yet.

"Serious and social. We're navigating our way through a challenge to, as Treinna puts it, put our money where our mouths are." Genys managed to sound almost as pleasant, and smiled at several of the women in the delegation.

"Meaning?"

"They want us to prove we're serious about curing the bescere by sending down some of our men to risk exposure."

"Ah." A world of communication could spill through a single word. "Should I start putting together a list of the personnel most likely to resist infection, based on our limited data? Brea stayed up all night extrapolating on the hormonal implications of the tea from the data Tahl sent her. She has already synthesized several equivalents, to use as defensive measures."

"Not yet. We're just opening negotiations."

"I will leave you to it, then."

"Say a few prayers for us."

"Yes, Ma'am. *Defender* out."

The lights flashed once, then dimmed. Genys offered another smile, tugged her tunic straight, and sat down slowly. She picked up her cup and make the mistake of looking at the surface. M'kar felt sorry for her. She hoped someday they would be able to look back on this morning and laugh. Her admiration for her captain rose a few more notches when Genys closed her eyes, raised the cup to her lips, and took a long sip, managing to suck down most of the oil slick. That solved the problem of it collecting and thickening into something hard to swallow.

That little bit of intestinal fortitude seemed to mildly impress Lopesi and her cohorts. They readily agreed to having the translators turned on. Maybe because they couldn't understand the conversation that had just taken place in front of them.

They wanted to know about the man Genys had spoken to. Lopesi requested Veylen join them on Castitarus, since as Genys' subordinate that made him her property. That led into an explanation of officers and duties and ranks and reinforcing the equality of genders in the Alliance in principle, if not always in practice. Genys finished by stating that per Fleet regulations, if she wasn't on the ship, her Exo had to stay on board.

M'kar nearly laughed aloud. Genys often complained that Captain Shryne violated that particular regulation nearly every time the crew of the *Inquest* accomplished something amazing and disaster-defying. Generally, Shryne was either accompanied by her second-in-command, his backup, the back-up's backup, and several other senior officers down the chain of command when she went into complicated, only-saved-by-Enlo's-grace situations. Or those officers had to dive in and risk their own lives to pull her and her landing party out of trouble. The general understanding was that officers who had earned command of starships like *Inquest* and *Defender* didn't go on first contact missions unless the situation demanded their presence. Such as here on Castitarus. Their experience and training and knowledge were too valuable to risk losing them to accidents. Too often, new contact civilizations saw the visitors as envoys of evil. They reacted defensively, often overwhelming the first-level defensive shields. Just because Shryne ignored that bit of common sense constantly didn't mean Genys should, or actually did, except when situations demanded. Like now. As M'kar had told her on several occasions, the universe did not need two Captain Shrynes.

Genys wisely didn't use the same tactic to refuse to bring Jasper, as Treinna's mate, down to the planet. She merely stated that his duties ensuring the stability of the ship after their long voyage had higher priority, but if circumstances permitted, he would join them at a later time. M'kar watched Treinna during the discussion and admired her lack of reaction, other than a few drops of sweat at her hairline.

Lopesi and her associates seemed mollified when Maora suggested Tahl bring down some male medics, to do double duty of monitoring everyone's health, including their own. Putting healers at risk of the bescere seemed to impress them, both in terms of sacrifice and bravery. Genys earned more points by agreeing to bring down Decker, when they understood what an important role he filled as Chief of Security. Plus, he had a drac.

That left Chieftain Ashrock of Nisandros and Le'anka. M'kar felt absolutely sick from the pressure of wanting to leap across the garden, grab Lopesi by her elaborate collar and shake her until her eyeballs rattled. Until she got the message: absolutely no, she did not want her father risking getting infected.

She should have known this would happen. Besides, as Ashrock pointed out to her later that morning, when he and Dr.

Jeyn joined them, this was specifically why he had come on the mission to Castitarus.

"Let us be honest, *mi'sho'ki*," he said, when they were all safely inside the guesthouse, with white noise generators purring, to give them a little privacy. "You and I both use our heritage as barbarians as weapons and shields. You enjoy waving the threat of what horrific things you can do when provoked, to stop people from provoking you."

He chuckled when M'kar glared at him and tightened her arms across her chest. He winked at Genys, standing on the far side of the common room with Treinna and Maora. Tahl was busy conferring with Decker, JM, and the volunteer medics. M'kar didn't know whether to be furious with her father for having this confrontation in front of her crewmates, or ... well, she doubted she could love him more. He was her hero and the greatest fear in her life. She wouldn't be who she was without the parents she had, although sometimes she resented all the weight of history they had put on her shoulders by deciding to conceive her.

"And you?" she retorted, after catching her breath and repressing the interior war between laughing and shrieking.

"I?" He pressed his massive hand flat on his chest and looked around the room, eyes wide in pretend innocence. "I merely allow everyone to make ridiculous assumptions—"

"And then you give them a hard push so they trip over themselves multiple times," Dr. Jeyn said. "To the entertainment of many. What still amazes me after all these years is that often, the people you embarrass, in the most public way, end up being your closest friends and admirers."

"That's because he somehow manages to entirely reprogram their brains," M'kar half-snarled.

"Don't waste your breath lecturing him. I've already put in at least an hour threatening him with all sorts of dire punishments if he gets infected."

Decker, JM and the other men settled into their rooms, and joined the group in the common room to finalize the plan. It required a simple buddy system. The men would keep watch on each other, with a woman monitoring them, to catch the slightest change in personality. Bio-monitors would record every reaction to the new environment. Brea and Tahl had worked overtime analyzing the tear sop samples, and added regular doses of the tea to the men's protective regimen.

All of them knew better than to think the cure could be so easy, and so visibly at hand. The question of whether the general population of Castitarus knew of tear sop, and if not, why not, could be dealt with later. What they needed, especially with these hostages to fate, was to find and destroy the cause, and discover a cure for the victims.

They spent time discussing the progress on examining and treating the Maniterri and how to deal with the boys sent up yesterday. Ideally, the dracs assigned to the boys would be the first warning sign of bescere starting to manifest. However, since the females seemed more sensitive, M'kar called all the females to her and asked them to oversee all the boys. Granny didn't respond after multiple calls, to the point of giving herself a headache.

"My impression?" Brea said, when M'kar contacted her to ask if Granny was just sulking. "I've asked Boomer and he says Granny is far away, in a dark, cold place, and she's looking for something. Maybe she's far enough away she can't hear. For all we know, we've found a natural substance, some mineral on this planet, that blocks psionic communication."

"Maybe we can use it in the drac-proof fence," Genys commented, when M'kar reported to her.

Brixley, ship's counselor, had placed the boys in families with children. They had uniformly reacted with astonishment and some envy, when they met children near their ages and learned they shared quarters with their fathers. None of the boys had their biological fathers living in the same house with them. By the time Castitaran boys were old enough to need interaction with a male role model, their own fathers had to be removed from contact with children. When their mothers took new mates, usually the boys competed with the new men in the household. Putting these eight boys with families and showing them how fathers interacted with their genetic children would be a fascinating psychological and sociological study. Brixley's report stated he was proud of the fathers who had agreed to risk catching bescere, to help these young sacrifices to fate.

You're going to be spending a lot of time with them, aren't you? M'kar asked Thyal. *It's a waste of time trying to talk you out of it, or lecture you to be careful, isn't it?*

Are you afraid for me? Thyal managed to keep most of the amusement out of his mental tone.

Of course. We have no idea yet what makes a man susceptible. No concrete idea yet, although Seeway's hormonal problems and the tear sop treatment do give us a big boost forward.

I don't suppose you see me as at least a little heroic?

Why in the name of the Forefathers would that matter to you?

Hmm, I don't know. Thyal's gentle chuckle rippled through the mental atmosphere. *Maybe I was getting a little worried, with all those women pressuring you to exchange some of those prize necklaces for a breeding partner.*

If you tell anyone about that part ... M'kar looked around the common room, terrified for a moment someone would see her reaction on her face.

Don't worry. May I say how proud I was of you yesterday, how diplomatically you turned down the prizes offered you, without insulting your hostesses? You should be flattered. Some were offering you their sons or grandsons.

I was too panic-stricken to be flattered. My mother would be fascinated with the whole sociological thing, and my father would just turn it into a joke, pestering me from now on to make him a grandfather.

He will make an incredible grandfather.

Clay, of the most squishy, sloppy variety in that little brat's hands.

You would make an incredible mother. The children here adore you.

I adore them. She looked around the room, shifting some attention away from Thyal. Good, they were still talking about the boys, the theories for what kind of treatments and examinations and tests to put them through, and the children who had taken the visitors under their wings.

Could I offer a suggestion, to protect you from further matchmaking attempts? he asked.

Such as? M'kar stiffened, hearing something odd in Thyal's mental tone. Not laughter. Nervousness? She couldn't imagine him being nervous about anything between them. The last three years of mental contact had taken down what few walls had remained, after growing up together and then facing death together. His thoughtful tone made her think what he was about to say, he had considered many times.

Next time someone approaches you, explain that you have a long-

standing commitment to me. We each have first claim on each other, and would have to release each other from that commitment before you could consider taking a mate.

With our luck, they would offer to host our marriage ceremony, or whatever formality they use when a woman takes a mate here.

Let them take one look at me, and they'll immediately feel sorry for you, and admire you for showing such honor and loyalty to me.

"You're an absolute idiot," M'kar snapped, trying not to laugh.

She had spoken aloud. Every face turned to her. Something in her mother's expression made her panic, so she scrambled for an explanation.

"I was going over some details with Thyal, about overseeing the boys," she said, and tried to look relaxed. "He was teasing me about a situation I faced yesterday. In fact, I should warn all of you..." M'kar took a deep breath and settled her thoughts. "Because of the low population, all that wilderness that's a constant threat, the need to expand holdings ... there's a strong emphasis on having children, as many as possible." She shrugged. "All of us could be offered diplomatic gifts of good breeding stock from good bloodlines that have proven resistant to bescere."

She caught a smirk Decker wasn't working very hard to control.

"I wouldn't be surprised if we get a lot of offers for our men. Despite being so old." She nodded to Decker, who flushed a little. "Or maybe *because* they're so old, compared to the men who can safely move through society. The possibility they'll hang on a lot longer than most men, self-controlled and intelligent, could make them very attractive."

"And just how did that lead to you arguing with Thyal?" Dr. Jeyn said, not even trying to hide her smile.

"He offered himself as my defense, claiming we have an arrangement." She shrugged.

"If I comment on how happy we would be if M'kar did marry him," Ashrock said, making his voice a rasp, as if he were speaking privately to Jeyn, "I fear she would be quite irritated with me."

"She would be justified in breaking something," Dr. Jeyn said, voice and expression calm, almost bored.

"If I irritate you, *ne'le'shu'na*, would you be tempted to trade me in for a younger model?" He chuckled and caught up Dr. Jeyn's hand to press a kiss on each knuckle.

M'kar's face burned and a happy little ache shot through her. Despite all the time and trouble they had faced, her parents were still silly in love. She wanted that for herself, sometimes so badly she felt sick.

"Are you asking me to?" Dr. Jeyn returned.

I stand corrected, Thyal said.

Hah! M'kar relaxed as the others around them laughed at the teasing between her parents. And grateful for the privacy of their mental bond.

You know what I mean. I am corrected in my thinking. You get your warped humor from your mother, not your father.

Chapter Twelve

Brea called down with her first extensive study of the tear sop and its effects on Seeway. The tea did, as theorized, influence estrogen production and balance out testosterone. There were some small changes in Seeway's blood chemistry within an hour after a dose. Brea theorized that over the long term, the effects of the tea would build up and provide relief from symptoms, even if it didn't cure bescere. The exiles' descendants had been drinking the tea for two generations and were closer to normal relationships between genders than the general population, with equal sharing in carrying responsibilities. Three doses so far hadn't made any changes in the Maniterri and *Dandridge* men. That supported Brea's theory of long-term build-up to do any good. She needed Genys to obtain a steady supply of tear sop, to continue the treatment. M'kar volunteered to ask Aniskara or Lexa, who she felt were more likely to help without asking problematic questions.

The dracs showed great interest in the tear sop tea. Berry stopped sneezing when she had physical contact with her chosen boy. That seemed to make both of them happy. Jasper reported that the boy had found his way down to the low-security level of engineering. Jasper had called Jorgan Pace to act as his guide. The two boys were getting along very well. The Castitaran boy was content to sit on a bench in the corner, watching and listening with a translator hung around his neck and a huge grin on his face. Whether that came from Berry sitting on his shoulder now, or being around men who weren't yelling or fighting or curled up in a corner, weeping or sucking their thumbs, no one was sure. Jasper reported the boy had already asked several intelligent questions. He was also irritated to report that when offered a tablet with a book on engineering principles, translated by the computer, the boy revealed he didn't know how to read. Apparently, it was considered a waste of time teaching boys to read. Jasper had asked E'bett to start teaching the Castitaran boys to read.

"If that man wasn't already taken..." Maora winked at Treinna.

"He certainly is, and don't you forget it." Treinna smiled, with a misty look in her eyes.

The entire ship seems to be rallying to look after the boys, Thyal commented, when M'kar checked with him later. *They've essentially been given up by their mothers. Maybe given up, or at least resigned to their fate, at birth.*

Their attitudes could change if we can offer them hope.

True. How many people's attitudes have changed for the worst, when the reasons for noble sacrifices and noble attitudes have been taken away or cured?

True. She sighed and tried not to be too loud.

Ashrock heard from the other side of the room. He asked her later what Thyal had done now to upset her. M'kar went up on her toes to kiss his cheek. If she had to dig down to the center of this awful, twisted world to fix whatever was attacking all the men, she would. Just to protect her father.

~~~~~

After lunch, the men had their formal introduction to Castitarus. Aniskara and Lexa came to escort the delegation to the Senate chamber.

When Ashrock stepped outside and M'kar introduced him to her new friends, she had a hard time not laughing aloud. Aniskara's eyes widened and she tipped her head back to get a better view of Ashrock. Lexa took a step back and started to reach for the long wooden rod hanging from her belt, the wood dyed in multiple colors. M'kar knew from painful experience in the arena, skilled hands could deal a painful blow with that rod. Lexa caught herself in time. She swallowed hard and glanced at M'kar and gave her a tiny shrug that was clearly an apology.

They controlled their reactions better when Decker stepped outside and was introduced as head of security. Clearly, the idea of a man in charge of keeping the peace and ensuring the captain's safety astounded them. Plus, Decker was a physically fit specimen. He was quite impressive, the tallest man in the group, after Ashrock. The presence of a delicate, hot pink drac sitting on his shoulder, resting her paw on the curve of his ear, detracted nothing from his image of alertness and capability. That nearly constant threat of a snarl curving up the left side of his mouth supported that impression.
~~~~~

"Are all your men so tall and fit?" Aniskara asked, once they had gotten past the gauntlet on their way to the administration building. Gawking, giggling, sneering, skeptical and clearly outraged women lined the path paved with blue-painted gravel.

"Hmm, not all of them," M'kar said, after glancing back at her father, who walked directly behind her.

She was grateful the walk to the first meeting was only a hundred meters or so. The guards who lined the four-meter-wide pathway on both sides had all met her in the arena the day before. A few nodded to her in respect. The others were intent on their duty, which seemed to be to intimidate the women watching the procession and keep them from breaking through. Not all those women were angry or afraid of these mature men suddenly running free and wreaking havoc. Several held out the octagonal disks used for money.

Finally, they were indoors, following a hallway that inclined upward to the Senate chamber. After the formal welcome, they would be handed over to their hosts for the day. Tahl and the medics would go to the Healers Guild hall, with Treinna to help where the translator gear couldn't span the gap. Genys and Decker were to meet with the matriarchs and begin an exchange of planetary and Alliance history. Maora and JM would be leaving the island, with a small troop of guards, to visit places such as markets, schools, hospitals and worship houses, to sample Castitaran society. M'kar and her parents would be visiting with the Warriors Guild. The women warriors were the explorers, the hunters, the peacekeepers, protecting settlements when wildlife and roaming bands of men became a threat.

"If we could grow our men taller, do you know how rich we'd be?" Lexa muttered to Aniskara.

Ashrock laughed, just a few chuckles. Soft, for him, but they broke the somber hush created by the thick draperies on the walls and thicker carpets.

"Warning. My father is an extremely skilled linguist. He learned your language much faster than I did," M'kar said. Ashrock winked at Lexa. Her friend blushed, then grinned.

"In all fairness, Matriarch," she said, giving a head bow to Dr. Jeyn, "I should warn you that before the end of the day, you will have several offers to buy your mate."

"Interesting concept." Dr. Jeyn's lips twitched just once as amusement made her eyes sparkle. "How much should I ask for your father, *Kari-la?*"

"I'm not getting involved in this, Mother. You have to live with him, not me. Set too high a price and his pride will swell so big he'll be a danger to us all."

Lexa snorted. Aniskara's shoulders shook.

"You have very good taste in friends. I approve," Ashrock whispered, in Nisandrian. His translator was turned off, and M'kar was grateful. "Do ask an impossibly high price for me, dearest?"

"Oh, I shall," Dr. Jeyn said, also in Nisandrian. "If only to ensure we don't have an interstellar incident, with our new allies accusing me of bait-and-switch."

He snorted and caught hold of her hand, to raise to his lips and press kisses on her knuckles again. Ashrock nearly didn't finish in time before they came to the door of the chamber. The time for foolery and making friends had ended. The time for diplomacy had begun.

~~~~~

By the end of the day, Dr. Jeyn had received six offers to trade new breeding stock for Ashrock. Genys had received four for Decker, Tahl had received a total of nine for the medics working with her, and Maora received five for JM.

Their party had a tour of the island on their way to the guild halls. They stopped for more than half an hour at the docks for the ferry. The last remaining combustion engine on the planet used to run the ferry, but it had died decades ago. Some people firmly believed the engine was a trick, a puzzle someone had created to be nasty, and it had never worked. For now, the ferries on the four cardinal points of the island were propelled by massive square sails. When the wind wasn't cooperative, teams of men on the mainland pushed huge wheels that operated a simple chain-driven system to haul each ferry back and forth.

Treinna asked to stop and record images, knowing Jasper would be fascinated by the engineering at work here. She was right. He responded immediately when she sent the picture files up to the ship. He found the huge loops of the chain and the gears and cogs more fascinating than the engine. The woman in charge of the vessel nearly wept in gratitude when Treinna told her Jasper had
~~~~~

several ideas and would try to find some way of fixing the engine. She received six offers for him, sight-unseen.

Aniskara and Lexa took M'kar and her parents to the Warriors Guild hall and central training complex. It included living quarters for the teachers, the general support and housekeeping staff, the trainees, and the headquarters for two divisions of warriors. One division handled civil security work, while the other hired out their services to suit the needs of the clans and settlements.

Ashrock was extremely popular, once people got used to his scars and tattoos and massive size. Aniskara had confided in M'kar that men who grew to be so large were either the most animalistic when bescere took them, or the most childlike and docile, and good beasts of burden. She passed that information to her mother, who took notes and made suggestions for a new course of study. The children of the teachers and staff, as well as the students, took to Ashrock quickly. M'kar noted he was especially soft-voiced and kind with the boys, who hung back. What few boys there were. The effort to reduce male births, to spare suffering, was quite evident here. Out of maybe thirty-some children they encountered, only seven were boys.

When they saw the shuttle returning to Congregation late in the afternoon, that signaled the end of their first visit with the Warriors Guild. Bacreen, the headmaster of the Warriors Guild training school, came with them. Tonight, the *Defender*'s delegates would entertain the heads of the guilds at the guesthouse, introducing them to Alliance food. The shuttle contained the ingredients for their dinner, several auxiliary cooking units, decorations, and tablets loaded with translated documents full of history and a first-level schooling introduction to Alliance history.

Sh'hari came to meet M'kar, her parents and their guests when they were still halfway between the guild hall and the guesthouse.

Decker was missing.

Matriarch Chercha was giving Genys a tour of the Archivists Guild house and discussing the process of how the *Defender*'s scholars would search the public archives. Decker had gone to use the sanitary in the guesthouse. There were none for men anywhere else on the entire island. When he didn't return in a reasonable time, a guard was sent for him. Island security had been searching for the last hour now, with no sign of him or Spitfire. Hiding a hot pink drac wasn't all that easy, because her hide stood out against the general background of greens and browns and blues. Battleaxe was searching, but hadn't reported back yet.

M'kar called for Spitfire with all the mental volume she could muster. Ashrock led her by the hand, so she didn't have to watch where she was going as their group hurried to the guesthouse. The rest of their party had gathered in the gardens. All those concerned faces that turned to her ignited a flare of resentment. And frustration.

"I can't reach her. If she was asleep, I'd be able to wake her." She hated the calmly grim expression that took over Genys' face.

"Where's Granny?" Genys said.

"You don't think she'd take him, do you?" M'kar wished she could laugh at the idea, but Granny had been pretty much absent since landing on Castitarus, and when she showed up she ate heavily, slept even more heavily, and refused to say where she had been. Had the little silver drac finally gone over the edge?

"More like if he was in danger, she'd protect him. She has a soft spot for him, but ..." she shook her head. "Any danger Decker couldn't handle would wipe him out fast. By the time enough dracs to carry him responded to her call and got organized, it would be too late to teleport him to safety. How far away could they go that none of them could hear you?"

Battleaxe popped in, chattering and spitting in fury. M'kar held out her hands and broadcasted as much calming as she could muster, in her growing concern for Decker. The little black drac hit her with some force, clear evidence of her concern. The physical contact helped open the mind link and calm her. An image of Spitfire sprawled in a shadowy spot filled her mind.

"Where?" M'kar snapped. *Barroo, go with her, show me.*

The two dracs popped out, followed seconds later by Ha'ess and Moonrise. M'kar explained what she had seen. Barroo gave her a bigger picture, along with smells and sounds, enough to guide her to him. She ran, Aniskara and Genys followed, and within ten minutes they were down at a cove, sliding through a gap that had been forced through the underbrush. From the smell of fresh sap and crushed leaves, the gap had been created a short time ago. The ground turned soft and wet, revealing multiple footprints, just before the searchers emerged through the bushes and short trees and tangled vines. They stepped out onto a pebbly shingle. Spitfire lay in a sprawled heap, one wing extended, halfway in a puddle created by the incoming tide. Battleaxe and Barroo stood sentinel on either side of her, crooning, wings spread protectively.

"Please tell me she's not—" Genys pressed her lips together and held out her hand. Battleaxe jumped up into her embrace and she cuddled her. That took the drac out of the way so M'kar could go down on one knee and examine Spitfire.

"No, she's still alive." M'kar sneezed. For a second, she thought of the dracs' reaction to men touched with the first signs of bescere. Another, more careful sniff. "It's chalky." She tipped her head back and took a deeper breath of the salty breeze coming straight off the water.

"Sleeping powder," Aniskara said, after taking a tentative sniff. She wrinkled her nose. "We use it for dealing with the wild bulls. Sometimes the herds get too close to settlements, moving too fast to handle a few at a time."

"Sleeping powder. Like, you just throw it in the air?" Genys said.

"Makes sense. Someone bombed Decker and it got Spitfire fast enough she couldn't even send out a squawk for help from our dracs," M'kar said.

"Who would do something like that?"

"Many women. Your men are older, stronger, and free of bescere," Aniskara said. "Adding your people's bloodline to ours could grant resistance, maybe immunity."

M'kar silently apologized to Decker for the teasing and the threat of blackmail she had held over his head in the past. He had been kidnapped once before, by a group of women who enjoyed humiliating a strong man. They had drugged him and dressed him up as a toy. This had to be ten times more humiliating and uncomfortable for him. Despite his growling and his passion for finding the worst possible curses, to shock and stun more effectively than any weapon, he was a good man. The fact the children on the ship adored him proved that. There were many men who would be flattered that women wanted them to father their children, but Decker wasn't one of them. He had zero tolerance for men and women under his command who were careless with their reproduction, and even less respect for men who took no responsibility for the children they sired.

The gashes in the mud from the keels of two small boats told the story. Decker had been bombed with sleeping powder and loaded onto a boat. Spitfire had probably teleported out, then popped back in, trying to follow Decker. She had collapsed after the kidnappers had started across the water. That was the only explanation for why they hadn't taken the little drac. They didn't know where she had fallen.

Decker had to already be on the mainland. Aniskara couldn't tell from the smell alone just how strong the sleeping powder was, but she gave an estimate of at least an hour before he woke. He would be dizzy and disoriented, and possibly sick to his stomach for a few hours after that, depending on the strength of the powder used on him. How long it would be until he could call Spitfire and show her where he was, so rescue could come, was anyone's guess. Spitfire had to wake up, first.

The only sensible plan was to send the little drac to Brea on the ship, to examine her and ensure there were no bad side effects from the powder. M'kar sent Battleaxe and Barroo ahead to the ship, with swabs taken from her hide. Hopefully some of the sleeping powder remained, giving Brea a chance to find something to help Spitfire recover.

Aniskara sent out a team to start hunting, and Matriarch Chercha sent for the Senate's guards to help. She admitted there were several likely suspects, rebel groups who would kidnap men for breeding, or to damage the fledgling relationship with the Alliance.

Everyone agreed not to discuss Decker's kidnapping during the evening with the guild leaders and matriarchs. They followed their planned schedule of topics, with plenty of time for answering questions. The mood lightened considerably as the women were introduced to the tablets full of more information than a hundred of their books and scrolls could hold. They were fascinated and sometimes unable to believe the abilities of the tablets, and that the power source built into them would last longer than many of their lives. Lopesi even laughed a few times at the mistakes she made, learning to use the functions to capture images and sounds.

Naturally, the discussion turned to the possibility of finding a cure for bescere. No one balked or took any offense when Tahl and the medics swabbed samples from the hair and skin and clothes of all the guests, to add to the growing data on Castitarus and compare with what had been learned from the boys.

Members of Treinna's linguistics team joined them, one assigned to each of their guests, to provide more refined and intuitive translating. Maora had brought Breska, the woman in charge of the ferries, as one of her guests for the evening. When Genys demonstrated the communication pack, to talk directly to the ship, Breska asked to talk with Jasper, to discuss the combustion engine. That turned into an hour-long exchange. Jasper impressed her with all his questions, his understanding and insight, and the suggestions he had already come up with for fixing the engine and making the towing system more efficient.

The call had come while Jasper and Tress were eating dinner, so the little girl wanted to talk with her mother. She impressed Breska with her growing Castitaran vocabulary, and impressed her more by her intelligent questions about the children her age. Aniskara moved closer to listen, visibly fascinated with the communication system. By the time the conversation ended, Jasper was invited to come examine the engine, and Tress was invited to come to the Warriors Guild to train with girls her age for an upcoming tournament.

Before their guests left that evening, the invitation had been extended to Tress' classmates, and anyone in Jasper's engineering team who wanted to examine the ancient engine. Matriarch Chercha cautioned that some discussion was necessary with the Senate, because of security considerations. Also, there were small groups who didn't want the visitors there at all. They refused to believe the Alliance people weren't really from the sister world. Stories were still told of the problems the visitors had caused, the last time the star well, the Chute, had opened.

Genys cautiously agreed to the proposal for the additions to the diplomatic effort, on the condition that Tahl and Brea and the medics involved in studying bescere thought they could keep Jasper safe. Only female engineers would come down with him, and the parents of the girls who participated would have to agree to the risk, and to having their daughters stay on the planet until they were sure no contagion would be carried up to the ship. After their guests left, Tahl took the shuttle to the ship to supervise the new phase of the investigation, while Brea came down to take her place and follow some theories regarding native medicines. She was the expert in natural remedies, and would be far more useful on the planet from this point on.

~~~~~

When M'kar woke the next morning and checked communications from the ship, she wasn't surprised to find a dozen messages waiting for her. Tress' friends were all eager to participate. Their parents wanted to know more about the invitation Genys had forwarded to them. M'kar was relieved the parents focused on the experience and how it would look on their daughters' records when they went to the Academy, rather than the risks. They trusted Genys not to send their daughters into danger, and trusted M'kar to keep them out of trouble. Everyone understood that until Brea and Tahl made more progress on defense against bescere, if not identifying the source, there would be no field trip down to Castitarus.

Thyal contacted M'kar during breakfast to report that Infrenx was being especially protective of him when he spent time with the Castitaran boys. Infrenx didn't sneeze at any of the boys, but she insisted on sitting on Thyal's lap instead of the arm of his chair, when the boys were around.

Tahl tried an experiment, having the boys, and Seeway, wash in tear sop rather than just drink regular doses. She kept separate the liquid left over from each one's washing and analyzed it. Despite the decontamination field everyone walked through when they entered the ship, and the regular washing with antibacterial and antiviral solution morning and evening, she found a spore finer than dust in the tear sop that had come off the skin of all nine subjects. There was a difference in the size and maturity of the spore, depending on the age of the test subject. She would require much more testing, and more washing to build up enough data for even a tentative conclusion. What she hoped for, though, was that just like the tear sop had a miniscule effect on hormones when ingested, it somehow affected the cohesion factor with human skin. If that was so, then perhaps the hormone levels in each subject directly affected the growth, the viability, and the strength of the spore itself. Perhaps bescere didn't hit males until maturity because it depended on those hormones to develop a stronger foothold in
~~~~~

its victims.

Perhaps the spore was the source of the bescere.

If so, where did the spore come from? What plant?

Thyal might be an integral part of the investigation. He would act as a control, in some levels. Because of his paralysis and the still not-quite-understood aspects of the dymcrait venom, Thyal had regular full-spectrum monitoring every three days. Even a microscopic change in his blood chemistry or hormonal balance would be noted, because of the steady stream of data on his body. Any change in the pattern would be visible and could provide valuable progress in the research. He would also drink tear sop and wash in it, to discourage the spore trying to take root in his skin.

M'kar didn't like the idea of Thyal being exposed to bescere and wished she hadn't encouraged him to join the *Defender*. She wished she had fought not to have the boys sent up to the ship. She should have argued to have them quartered with the Maniterri. Even knowing the medical team needed to be hands-on with the boys, and it would be inconvenient to travel to the ship of victims or conduct research over communication channels didn't ease her sense of guilt. Over the next few days as they waited for some news, a change, an advance in the research, she got a momentary cold flip of dread in her belly every time she thought about the possibility. Thyal going into bescere was even more frightening than it happening to her father. Hadn't he suffered enough?

Thyal laughed when she scolded him to be careful. An impression of a hand gripping her shoulder and shaking her came through their link. *Don't worry, lupi. You won't get rid of me that easily.*

Get rid of you? Why would I want that? You're my captive audience.

Infrenx isn't sneezing, so I'm not infected. Trust her, if you don't trust Tahl or Enlo.

Sometimes, I think she's got more common sense than you or my father put together. He's taking a positively fiendish delight in risking exposure everywhere. Eating the food, getting sweaty and dirty sparring with the warriors, playing with the children, having them climb all over him. I don't know how my mother can stay so calm!

Thyal just laughed and promised again he would be careful.

Then she didn't have time for more fretting. Tress and Dafna and six other girls came down to Castitarus, along with Jasper and his engineers. The girls were M'kar's special responsibility. Their eagerness to explore and meet the Castitaran girls choked her with the need to both laugh and snarl.

Aniskara came to greet the eight girls and formally welcome them, and talk to them about the history and traditions of the Warriors Guild. Then they went on a walking tour of the island. Their first lesson was to see the security checkpoints that kept Congregation safe.

Tress made M'kar laugh. She was more excited about getting to the ferry docks to see the combustion engine her father was working on, than she was about getting to do weapons drills with the local girls. She was her father's daughter and she liked to know how everything worked.

When M'kar and Aniskara and the girls reached the dock for the ferry, Jasper and four female engineers were hard at work with the combustion engine. The five already had the engine half-dismantled and were covered in dirty lubricant, chattering away with the ferry team, using hand signals more than the translators, and seemed to be having a good time. M'kar shook her head. She would never understand engineers. Nothing made them happier than a recalcitrant piece of equipment to fight with and finesse into obedience.

A group of women in the tough, protective clothing of wilderness patrols arrived at the docks, to report to the matriarchs. Aniskara signaled for M'kar to wait and hurried over to talk to them. She shook her head when she rejoined M'kar and the girls, and said nothing until their party had moved down the path following the shore, heading for the guild hall.

Chapter Thirteen

"They have been out hunting for your crewman," Aniskara said, voice pitched low, her gaze on the girls, clearly trying not to let them hear. "All the known spots for the troublemakers to congregate." A little shrug. "The women known for stealing men of good bloodlines, when they don't have the standing or influence or money to get one the proper way."

"It's not right to buy people," Dafna said, looking up at Aniskara with big, troubled eyes.

"Yes, I agree." She gave the child an encouraging if somewhat sad smile. "But that is how it is done here, to protect the men who are unable to think fast enough or high enough to protect themselves. If there is documentation that a man has been given to a woman, then the woman who took him has to give him back, and he is protected by our laws."

"Chief Decker didn't get sold."

"No, he did not. You must say many prayers to give power to the hunters who want to help him. We will find him, I promise you." She patted the little girl on her shoulder. Her kind smile faded as soon as Dafna looked away.

M'kar didn't need any more proof that Aniskara thought Decker's situation was far more grim than she had admitted.

Lexa was waiting at the gates of the guild hall with a group of girls fairly close to the *Defender* girls' ages. The mixture of eagerness and nervousness the two groups displayed as they approached each other assured M'kar friendships would be blooming soon enough. She wasn't worried for Tress and Dafna and their friends. They would have a good time, and useful experience notations on their records. Another benefit of growing up on board a starship.

The Castitaran girls took the *Defender* girls to the barracks to change their clothes. M'kar settled on the bottom row of the seating overlooking the practice arena, to wait, and silently discussed with Thyal the boys left behind on the *Defender*. She made note of the boys who really listened and thought about the explanation why they couldn't go down to the planet with the girls. The ones who weren't pouting and didn't complain that the girls were going to "have fun." Those boys would progress faster than their agemates when they went to the Academy.

That first day at the guild house, the girls did her proud. M'kar wondered how parents managed, because the first few times one of her girls went down in the packed dirt of the arena, she had to grab the bench to keep from leaping to her feet and dashing out to check on her. She didn't have this concern when she was training the children on the ship. Because medical help was only a shout away, and the floor was covered with tumbling mats? Or was there more to it? She trusted Aniskara and Lexa, but she didn't know the other women overseeing the training.

M'kar suspected she would have stress-induced pains by the time the girls moved on to the tournament. Then she grinned and muffled a chuckle, when it occurred to her that she would be a wreck if she ever became a mother, and watched her own child tumble and duck and leap onto an opponent's back.

No, you wouldn't, Thyal said.

Eavesdropping again?

You would be so certain of your child's skill, you'd spend more time worrying about her opponent. Or his.

Hmm, you might be right, she conceded.

I know I am.

How is Infrenx? How are you? Any change in the boys?

Before he could answer, Clytie, daughter of two linguists, released her tangle stones crooked. They wrapped around the knees of another girl, not the target. She went down with a yelp. Before Clytie could react, two of the downed girl's friends bore her down to the packed dirt, pulling her hair. Tress and Dafna leaped in, followed by several native girls, and two instructors.

M'kar had several awful seconds as she ran to intervene. She didn't know what to do. If she touched any of the locals, that might exacerbate the situation. Regan, Aniskara's cousin, picked up a girl, turned, saw M'kar, and tossed the struggling girl to her. That settled that question. M'kar and the second instructor stayed back, taking the girls Regan pulled out of the tangle. They set the girls on their feet and ordered them to sit on the benches. The girls complied with a speed that made M'kar think they were a little frightened.

In less than a minute, the knot of girls untangled. Dafna

emerged, pulling the downed girl out of the bottom of the pile, and trying to free her legs. Tress lay across Clytie, protecting her from a girl who kicked at them both. Regan picked up the kicker and swung her up and out, so her feet were higher than her head for a few seconds. She landed with a thump, with Regan between her and her targets. Regan's shout was enough to make nearly every face in the arena go pale. M'kar didn't need the translator to understand the lecture Regan spilled on the furious, sweaty, dusty girl. At one point, she pointed at the girl who had been tangled with the stones. Dafna had her up on her feet and the two were limping out of the center of the arena. M'kar gave her a nod and a wink, which put a big grin on Dafna's sweaty face.

Then M'kar attended to Tress and Clytie. Both were bruised, smeared with sweat and dust. Tress was going to have a black eye. It was swollen already. Clytie had taken far less damage. The moment she looked at Tress, she burst into tears.

"You did nothing wrong. Mistakes aren't crimes," M'kar gently scolded, and shook her once. "As for you …" She scowled at Tress, which earned a lopsided grin. "You're making so much trouble for your parents. Chief Decker is going to hound them to have you go into Security and not Sciences."

"That was very brave, and very honorable," Sheboli, the other instructor said, coming over to join them. "And a little stupid. Ah, well, you girls were put together to try to forge ties between your people and ours. Today's bruises will certainly start it well." She waited until the translator finished, then held out her hands to Clytie and Tress. "Let's get you cleaned up and put on some cold cloths. You may not like what comes next, but it has worked well for us."

"What comes next" turned out to be an uncomfortable two hours, when Tress and Clytie, the tangled girl, and the kicker went into a smaller arena. They were tied together, right hand lashed to the belt of the girl on her right, and put through a series of timed challenges. At first, the girls either flinched away from each other or glared or tripped one another, trying to shield a friend from the one glaring at her. Then after the second exercise failed, when time ran out, something changed. Their anger focused on the massive time dial hanging over the small arena.

"That's the objective, isn't it?" M'kar guessed, speaking softly.

Not that the girls were listening or able to hear. They were talking now and grunting with effort as they carried long planks through an obstacle course. "Give them a common enemy."

"We find conflict often arises between those who have many similarities. They struggle for strength and dominance, when they need to learn to work together." Sheboli nodded, her flat, satisfied smile widening a little, and leaned back against the tiered seating behind them. The two of them were the only witnesses, besides the women who kept track of the time and adjusted the obstacle course and set up the next test.

By the end of the two hours, bruises had darkened and swelling had reached its maximum on faces and hands and legs. All four girls cheered and gave each other encouragement, laughing as they shaved a few more seconds off their time with the final challenge.

~~~~~

Treinna was seething when M'kar and the girls met up with her and Jasper at the docks at sunset. M'kar cringed and wondered how Treinna had heard about what had happened. Then she saw the struggle for control on Jasper's usually placid face. M'kar could have sworn he was trying not to laugh. He glanced at Treinna and cringed a little. Then a few seconds later, something brought a sparkle to his eyes. Then he looked at her again, and guilt returned. Or was that awe? M'kar wondered if she should point out to Treinna what had happened to Tress, to stop her talking to herself. When a linguist talked to herself, it could get messy.

"Mom, I got in a big fight today," Tress announced, taking the decision out of her hands. Then she stepped into the brightest part of the puddle of light from the torches that had just been lit.

Jasper swore. At least, M'kar thought it was a stream of engineering cussing. He jumped off the platform holding the dead engine and dropped to one knee in front of Tress. His hands shook as he gripped her shoulders and turned her from side to side, studying her black eye and the other marks that had fully bloomed on her face. Treinna nearly knocked him sideways as she snatched at Tress. M'kar braced for the explosion. Tress grinned.

"Ely's black eye is worse than mine, and her whole mouth is swollen up so she had to have mashed fruit and soup for lunch," she announced, pride thickening her voice.
~~~~~

"Who is Ely?" Treinna demanded, after visibly getting control of her voice.

"The best friend of the girl Clytie knocked down by accident, who jumped on Clytie, whom Tress shielded with her whole body." M'kar shrugged. "Girl stuff. Nothing to worry about. Nothing a little makeup won't cover."

Treinna shrieked, eyes wide, and raised a hand like she might wallop M'kar. Then Jasper burst out laughing. Treinna turned to him and they clung to each other and laughed. Tress and the other girls exchanged the "grownups are insane" look that children learned when they were around four years old. M'kar herded her charges down the path, reasoning that Treinna and Jasper still needed to work out whatever was wrong, and could do it best without an audience. She asked Thyal if he had heard anything to explain Treinna and Jasper's moods.

He didn't know. No report had been made to the ship because Genys and Maora hadn't made the end-of-the-planetary day report yet. Brea, Dr. Jeyn and Ashrock joined M'kar and the girls a few moments later, coming from an intersecting path. They had spent the day at the Healers Guild, studying their archives. Jasper and Treinna caught up with them a dozen steps later. M'kar couldn't tell if they had resolved the tension between them.

Dr. Jeyn was excited about a large number of references she had found, confirming bescere, the mental decline of men, and the resulting change in the structure of society, were all relatively new developments in the planet's history. The timeline of when the numenjax vanished and where it coincided with the decline of men might give more clues to the source of the bescere.

The conversation changed to focus on what the girls had done at the guild house all day. They were certainly entertaining, describing their mock battles, glorying in their bruises, and laughing at their mistakes. Everyone laughed when Ashrock sighed and wrapped a massive arm around M'kar and begged Enlo's forgiveness for his daughter, who was teaching her students to be barbarians. The girls' expressions were either confused, or insulted, which just earned more laughter from the adults.

When they reached the guesthouse, Genys and Maora were sitting outside in the garden. M'kar reported no success for the women hunting for Decker and his kidnappers. Genys reported the matriarchs' security team was attacking the problem by seeking out all the leaders of the rebel factions. No results yet.

Then the girls' bruised and excited state had to be reported on. They received well-deserved praise for their actions as semi-official cadets. Dr. Jeyn stated she wanted to go through some ideas with Maora before reporting what she and Ashrock had found. The four medics and JM were waiting in the guesthouse, doing their day's end exams. Brea had to go over everything they had found. M'kar held Treinna back when everyone got up to troop into the guesthouse, to start preparing dinner.

"So, what did Jasper do?" she asked.

"He didn't do anything but just be himself." Treinna scowled and watched the door until it closed, leaving them and their dracs the only ones outside. "I got treated to one of the entertainment venues on the shore opposite the north dock. Music and fashion shows, lots of drinking, and games of skill that seem to be there just to prove how little skill they have once they've had enough stinky drinks to make them dizzy. And gambling. Which they tried to get me to do. Several times."

"You didn't, because I know you wouldn't."

"Darn straight!" She rubbed her temples. "I said I wasn't good at such games. Then I told them I had nothing as a stake."

"Ah." M'kar caught on now.

"Exactly. Oh, they were glad to offer to loan me something to get started, and they were sure I would win enough to pay them back. And they kept trying to get me to drink, so they could persuade me."

"All you had to do was put up Jasper as collateral? And then they would make sure you played games against people who would ensure you couldn't possibly win."

"Who else could I vent to but him? The big ego-bladder thought it was hilarious. He was flattered." Treinna crossed her arms, visibly trying to be furious, but too tired to maintain the steam anymore.

"He should be. Jasper is a wonderful father, and he's smart enough to pull his head out of his engines often enough to treat you like you deserve. Honestly, I don't know how you put up with his love affair with his engines. But you two are happy and Tress is the best of both of you put together, so he isn't a total testosterone-poisoned *bah'creesha'koo."*

"What you said!" She covered her mouth with her hand, eyes wide, laughter lines crinkling around them.

"You have no idea what I said."

"True. Thanks." Treinna spread her arms.

"That's what friends are for." They hugged and laughed a little and headed for the door.

"I overheard some of them plotting to bribe Jasper to ask for asylum. You have to help me block that move."

"Bribe him how?"

"There are caches of old technology all over the place. They think they can get him so fascinated with restoring what they've lost, they can get him to stay." Treinna sighed. "And improve the gene pool."

"Hmm, they might just know him better than we thought." She ducked aside when Treinna made as if to elbow her. They paused at the top of the steps, in front of the door. "First, we tell Genys, send Jasper topside, and have her offer to send down all our *female* engineers to decipher their lost technology. And if they keep playing such tricks ..." She opened the door and gestured for Treinna to go ahead of her. "Maybe we need to pull a Shryne and rewrite the mission instructions to protect our men."

"No," Genys said, raising her head from the tablet she was studying. She watched M'kar and Treinna step into the common room. All the adults were at work on something. A few giggles came from the kitchen area, showing where the girls were clustered. "What happened now?"

"You tell them," Treinna said. "I'm going to sit next to the stud and make sure his ego doesn't blow up enough to send him through the roof."

~~~~~

The next day, when M'kar returned to the training compound with the girls, Ashrock came with them. He suggested that showing what a barbarian with self-control could do in the practice arena might frighten some women into better manners. Especially those trying to steal a woman's husband.

On the walk to the guild house, Tress walked with Aniskara. M'kar tried not to listen in to the very earnest conversation the girl had with their hostess. She was amused that Tress was proving to
~~~~~

be just as gifted a linguist as her mother, chattering away without help of the translator gear. Several times, Aniskara looked over to M'kar, one eyebrow raised in question, or perhaps concern. When they reached the compound, she went down on one knee, held onto Tress' hand, and said something that made the child's face glow. She scampered off to join her friends and the native girls waiting for them. Ely and Marga, the girl Clytie had knocked down, were at the head of the group. They grinned and greeted Tress and Clytie before leading them at a run to the barracks.

"Do I want to know what that's about?" M'kar asked, as she and Aniskara followed at a much slower pace.

"She asked me to make sure nobody tried to steal her father from her mother. She was very concerned that you would defend her parents and get into trouble and maybe ruin the mission."

"Hmm ..." She waited until Aniskara cocked her head to look at her. "I think Treinna can handle those tricksters, so no tribunal in the galaxy could find any fault in her."

"That sounds encouraging." Wistfulness tempered her smile. "It must be very nice, for a girl to be free to love her father so much. You have been given examples of our literature, yes?"

"Some of them. Treinna translated a few of each type. Why?"

"Stories of doomed love are quite popular. I think it is so because we learn to put walls around our hearts when it comes to our sons and mates. We must learn to let them go, to enjoy the moment and not long for what we cannot have. Otherwise we would be crippled and make choices that would doom us."

That morning, M'kar was invited to participate in a wild bull hunt. Aniskara and Lexa both assured her that the men were captured and incapacitated with as much care as possible. However, M'kar had to wonder about some of the women she saw preparing for the hunt, and the glee in their eyes, the excitement in their voices, as they packed nets and spears and throwing stones. Most of the capturing would be done with slingshots hurtling packets of sleeping powder into the midst of the men. She understood that they had to be prepared for the men who were resistant to the powder and fought to defend themselves. But did those women have to look so eager to face that danger?

She had packed a scanner rod to do some short-range scanning of the terrain and what lay underneath it, and get more detailed data, such as mineral content and soil density. The ship's long-range scans from orbit had found signs of what looked like tunnels under the plains, but the thermal footprint of the thick plant life and wildlife in the general area blurred all the signals, so interpretation was difficult. Everything was a guess or theory until more up-close sensor work could be done. Gaining entrance to one of the theorized tunnels might give some clue or insight into the geological and biological features of Castitarus that had spawned the legends of the numenjax.

Legends of other worlds agreed that dragons loved hot conditions. The most logical place to search for signs of numenjax habitation was the small volcanic continent, appropriately called Fire Rock. She had asked, but Fire Rock was considered sacred territory. Lexa told her a handful of stories of monsters in the fog and disembodied voices that frightened the sentries stationed on its shores. M'kar suspected some kind of hallucinogenic gases seeping up through volcanic vents

Ashrock and both sets of girls accompanied the hunters on the ferry to the mainland. Today's training would be an exercise in following an animal trail through the forest and back to the mainland guild house.

When M'kar rode out with the hunters, her last look back showed Ashrock sitting in the courtyard, hands waving and face alight as he told stories to a crowd of girls. Tress and Dafna were acting out some part of the story under his direction, their faces bright with glee. She relaxed in the saddle and turned her attention to the hunt and the chance to explore and gather data She could depend on her father to look out for the girls from the *Defender*.

~~~~~

Barroo rose up from M'kar's shoulder with enough force to startle her. An image leaped from his mind to hers. Granny hovered in darkness, shrieking in fury, her eyes shooting red sparks. An impression of deep darkness and cold washed over M'kar. Before she could catch her breath and ask her drac what was going on, Granny popped into the air above her head.

"Where you have you been?" M'kar demanded, the words startled out of her by the fury that made Granny shudder in mid-air. The little silver drac looked emaciated, like she hadn't been eating properly.
~~~~~

A very clear impression shot into M'kar's mind with a knife's edge of force. Granny wanted her to wake up someone. She wanted her to warm someone. It was too cold, so they were sleeping. They didn't listen. They had to listen to her. Granny wanted M'kar to bring a shuttle and point its exhaust jets at a huge hole in the ground and set it on fire, and wake them up.

"Wake up who?" she snapped.

Shrieking, Granny dove and dug her claws into M'kar's sleeve, and pulled. M'kar's horse reared. The other horses in the hunting party reared and snorted, startled by the little silver fury. Granny's claws slipped. She lost her grip and tumbled backwards through the air, stunned into silence.

M'kar fell. She twisted and kicked, trying to shove herself out and away from the horse. She hit the thick overgrowth of half-rotted vines that carpeted the open ground.

Half the vines disintegrated into thick, choking, sweet-sour dust. The others snapped under her. She kept falling. Sliding. More dust rose up in the air, filling her mouth and nose, and then she jolted to a stop against more vines. Rotting vine dust, everywhere. Slippery and sweet-sour and musky.

"Don't breathe!" Aniskara shouted through the thickness clogging her ears. "Stay still."

M'kar thought of a dozen vicious and funny responses, but that would mean opening her mouth and taking a breath. A gush of water hit the left side of her head, sluicing powdery dust off her face. Gasping, she sputtered and took a cautious breath. Aniskara shouted warning. She shut her mouth and braced, and another splash of lukewarm water. The water had to come from the large waterskins every woman carried on their saddles. Maybe this dust hazard was why they carried it?

"Did you swallow any? How much did you inhale?" Aniskara asked, after a third dousing. She extended her spear down into the pit, nearly two meters deep, to help M'kar climb out.

"Not sure. Is this stuff poisonous?"

"It's the basis for the sleeping powder. It has to be refined, and there are plenty of noxious uses for it when it's been concentrated enough. You'd have to swallow enough in its raw form to fill your stomach, or inhale enough to smother you, for it to put you to sleep, but always wiser to be cautious."

M'kar was right, the waterskins were brought specifically to wash down anyone who fell into the vine pits. Several women fell on every hunt. The vines covered the ground so thickly, there was no way to detect the pits until a horse stumbled, or a hunter on foot fell in. She thought about asking why they didn't warn her to bring a change of clothes, but refrained. The guild house was just on the other side of that ridge to the west, maybe fifteen minutes of riding. The day was warm. It wasn't like she would catch a chill. If she picked up some Castitaran virus or germ, Brea would benefit from it, learning more about the biology of this world.

Barroo resumed his perch on her shoulder as soon as he could, crooning and rubbing her cheek with his head, his worry for her heavy to the point of irritation. When she asked where Granny had gone, he didn't know. M'kar didn't push the point, because she wasn't in the mood to face the old drac again. Not if she was going to resume her inexplicable demands.

As they rode, she learned about the many tactics the warriors used to just keep the vines from taking over more ground. Eradicating it altogether was impossible. Constant fires could only prevent it from gaining ground on the farthest outlying settlements. Any time of the year, clouds of smoke from the burning hung on the horizon somewhere, and the fine, choking dust that resulted was always drifting on the wind. Keeping the fires going was usually the job of men, until they could no longer focus enough to carry out that task safely. When the winds came from the wrong direction, bucket brigades of boys hauled water to rinse people and homes and prevent them being smothered by ash and dust.

M'kar didn't offer Alliance help in combatting the vines. That wasn't her place. But she mentally worked out her approach to Genys, and how to present the proposal to the Senate. This could go a long way toward convincing sour-heads like Lopesi that friendship with the Alliance would be good for them, while they waited for a breakthrough in curing bescere. Jasper would probably enjoy the challenge of incinerating the vines and containing the resulting dust so it didn't choke the surrounding countryside. She would have to talk to some of the botanists on the ship to see if any genetic engineering could be done to slow the growth of the vine, which had no natural enemies that Aniskara knew of. There had to be a better alternative than employing some pan-spectrum herbicide that might set off a cascade effect of damage through the whole ecosystem. Not a good thing to do with people they wanted as friends.

Arriving at the guild house, the hunting party dismounted outside the gates. Then M'kar discovered the many bruises from her fall. She hadn't felt so stiff since that assassination attempt when she was eight. A cousin had greased a flight of stairs and pushed her. She took him down with her and landed on him, but she still had dozens of bruises.

"Go find Granny and tell her she owes me, will you?" she told Barroo.

He cocked his head and blinked a few times, then lifted off from her shoulder with a lazy spreading of his wings. Something didn't seem right about his reaction. Too slow. Maybe sleepy?

She turned around to watch him as he rose a few more meters up in the air, then popped out. Shrieks rose up behind her and she continued turning. A blur of little bodies confused her for two seconds, long enough for the eight *Defender* girls and their training friends to leap and grab hold of her limbs and hit hard enough to send her tumbling to the ground. A louder, bass roar shook the gates of the guild house as Ashrock leaped out of hiding. He grabbed her under her armpits and swung her up in the air. Laughing, ignoring the new bruises making their presence known, M'kar twisted and flung her legs out, knocking him off balance.

That was just what Ashrock wanted. This was the first wrestling move he had taught her, when she was maybe five years old. They went down, Ashrock on the bottom, M'kar sprawled across him, and the girls shrieking with glee and piling on top of them both.

Now M'kar was glad her clothes were still wet. Serve them all right if they got muddy along with dusty and sweaty.

Chapter Fourteen

"The good news?" M'kar handed the scanner rod over to Genys, who had been waiting for her and Ashrock and the girls at the docks when they returned from the mainland. "Lots of data. I wonder if it's possible to use up the storage capacity?"

The two of them turned to watch the girls scamper from the docks to the pebbly shingle of the shore. They laughed and brushed at each other, scattering golden dust as they hopped one-legged and tugged off their footwear. All the girls had exchanged their semi-uniforms for Castitaran costume. Genys assumed the clothes were gifts from the Warriors Guild house.

"I think you'd have to be out in the field and gathering data long enough to wear out the power cell before you'd run out of storage space," Genys said. "What's the bad news?"

A sigh escaped her as the girls splashed each other with kicks and scooped up handfuls of water to fling at each other. She considered sneaking down to the water's edge after nightfall, and indulging in some splashing and silliness, just to break the increasing tension of the mission. Ashrock laughed at them and settled down on a bench at the foot of the docks to examine a spear. Genys guessed that was another gift. A good sign.

"Boring. Lots of scrub land, lots of ravines, lots of sudden drops where you think it's thick groundcover, but you find it's a net of tangled vines covering everything, including holes and crevices. I've got samples of the vines, in different stages of life and death. They smell like and have the same oily glands at the base of the leaves, and give off pollen like those vines we found on Forbidden Island. Which strikes me as suspicious. Seeway's captors said there was genetic engineering of plants, right? Maybe they sabotaged plants on Draxonis and planted them here, or they took plants from here to change on Draxonis, and those growths mutated or ..." M'kar shook her head. "I deal with critters, not plants. Let the botanists untangle and theorize."

"Good idea. We've been twisting our brains in new shapes, trying to figure out how to apply what Seeway learned, and how to make contact with the spies in the Archivist Guild. I don't want to insult our hosts, and we really can't be sure that the exiles were telling him the truth to begin with." Genys tipped her head back and gazed upward, as if she were looking for their ship. "I'm starting to think that Shryne's tactics in situations where everyone seems to be lying ..." She grinned.

"Don't finish that thought. It'll start you down a very slippery slope." M'kar rubbed at her arms and grimaced at the golden dust that floated around her for a few seconds.

"Problem?"

"The vines, the pollen, the sap, the smell." She shrugged. "There's something downright creepy about how the vines are just everywhere. Smothering everything out in the wilderness. I can see why so much effort is put into burning it back, how it can swallow up a whole settlement in a moon-cycle if they can't keep up. They can be downright dangerous. Dirt builds up on the vines, and other plants take root, and you get the illusion of solid ground. But then Granny shows up and has a hissy and spooks your horse, so you get thrown. But you don't land on solid ground. That thick layer of vines is half-rotted, so it breaks under you and you fall into a hole lined with more rotted vines. The stink, when the dust from the dead vines is thick in the air ..." She grimaced and rubbed her arms again. "It's everywhere. I was nearly drowned, trying to rinse the dust off, but it's still coming off me. It's like the stuff keeps growing, the more water you use."

She gestured at Ashrock, who was rubbing his hands on the sides of his pants, shedding shimmering dust. "He and the girls ambushed me when I got back from the hunt." A snort escaped her, and her face relaxed into a crooked grin. "He's a worse influence on them than me!"

"And? From the look on your face, kind of disgusting stuff down there?"

"There's so much dust, everything is slippery." She paused as Barroo popped in and slowly settled down on her shoulder. "Aniskara told me about finding crevices with the bones of people and small animals. Trapped, and can't get out."

Barroo chirped at her and nuzzled the side of her head. The action raised more shimmering dust from her hair. Both women grinned and Barroo sneezed, shaking his head and blinking at the dust covering his muzzle.

"What?" Genys said, when M'kar frowned at her drac.

"I sent him to check on Granny. She seemed bad off. I'm talking skinnier than usual, like she's either been missing meals or pushing herself too hard. All I'm getting from him is what I got before she had a hissy at me. A dark, cold place. She's trying to wake up someone, and they can't wake up because they're cold, and she wants us to start a huge fire in the center of the planet."

"All right, it's official. She's shattered enough connectors in her brain she's a danger to herself, not just our sanity."

"Any chance of getting her to go up to the Maniterri ship and stay?"

"Don't tempt me." Genys sighed. "We still haven't gotten any word on who took Vitiarre. I know he's disgraced and disavowed, but we still have a responsibility to find him and give him back to his own people."

"Yeah … stinks to the celestials to be a responsible adult."

Battleaxe popped in overhead, caroled a greeting and dropped toward Genys' shoulder. Then she stopped. Genys knew it was aerodynamically impossible for a winged creature to just stop short in midair, not without frantically flapping its wings, but somehow her drac managed it. Battleaxe let out an angry shriek and vaulted upward again. Barroo's eyes sparkled green and yellow, indicating confusion. The brown drac leaped up from M'kar's shoulder and went crooked. The two dracs met in mid-air and Battleaxe flew circles around Barroo, scolding him.

"What's with them?" Genys' head ached from the noise and from the backwash of fury and confusion coming from her drac.

"He did something that's got her riled." M'kar closed her eyes and nearly put her fingers in her ears. She froze, the frown puzzled. "He didn't do something he was supposed to do … about me."

Battleaxe dropped down and shrieked more scolding, getting within half a meter of M'kar.

Then she sneezed. Three times in a row.

It cut off her furious scolding and she retreated to Genys' shoulder and let out a whimpering croon.

"I … stink," M'kar said slowly, as if she had to test the word.

"You made her sneeze."

"You don't happen to have a medical scanner on you, do you?"

Genys thought for a moment, her frown deepening. She opened up the portable communication pack and signaled the main pack in the guesthouse. JM answered. She told him to send Brea and a full-spectrum scanner, the biggest and most powerful equipment they had brought planetside.

"And a change of clothes for me," M'kar said. She waited until JM acknowledged the order and ended the communication, then took a few steps back and spread her arms. "I got drenched, to wash the wretched stuff off me, but I'm still shedding it. What if this isn't dust, decayed vine? What if it's the spore Brea found, embedded in the bescere victims' skin?" She swallowed. "What if water encourages growth, instead of washing it away?"

The girls' chattering and splashing had slowed during the drac argument. Now they trotted up the dozen meters from where they had been playing and gathered around.

M'kar groaned.

"What?" Genys had a hard time keeping her voice at normal volume.

"The girls tackled me. We just saw them shaking off more dust." She choked and her eyes went wide and she turned to look at Ashrock.

Genys felt sick. M'kar had to feel even worse. The girls could have the spores on them that Tahl had tentatively linked with bescere. Ashrock had to be contaminated too.

Maybe infected?

"Everyone. In -- " She stopped, remembering what M'kar had just said. Her first instinct was to tell everyone to wash, to get the spore off, but what if water did encourage growth?

Barroo came winging in for a landing, crooning unevenly. Almost like he had hiccups, or he was drunk. Genys' stomach twisted as he missed M'kar's shoulder, folded his wings around himself, and tumbled to the ground. M'kar choked something that was probably a Nisandrian curse and went to her knees, sprawling forward, scrabbling to keep the little drac from hitting the dock.

"It's the allergic reaction, same as the fire-breathing candy Decker made for the dracs," Brea announced nearly an hour later. She ran her scanner over Barroo, still asleep, for the fifth time.

"How can it be the same thing?" Genys demanded. Battleaxe sat on Genys' shoulder, crooning, occasionally releasing a tiny shudder. The impression she was getting was intense sorrow mixed with guilt. How could she communicate to her drac that she hadn't hurt Barroo when she scolded him?

"Just because it's the same reaction, that doesn't mean it's the same element or chemical combination." Brea shook her head.

"No, it's the proof," M'kar said.

She wore exercise shorts and shirt, her hair wet and exposed skin pink from a quick scrubbing with a massive batch of tear sop tea. The aroma was thick in the guesthouse. The girls were in the kitchen, getting scrubbed under the supervision of Maora and Treinna. Dr. Jeyn had hurried past less than ten minutes ago with the largest pot in the guesthouse kitchen, full of tear sop, to help Ashrock wash.

"Proof the vine Decker picked up on Draxonis is a variant," she continued, "or maybe the mother species, of what I fell into today. Makes sense. Aniskara said the base for the sleeping powder they use to control the wild bulls comes from that vine. Of course, she also said it has to be highly concentrated and processed to be used for sleeping powder, but … maybe that's it!" She held up a hand to stop them when Brea opened her mouth to protest.

"The dust goes everywhere. The fires obviously don't kill it, and water encourages growth. And they're constantly washing everything and everyone, when it's burning season *and the dust goes everywhere*. Anisakara told me there was a riot when Vitiarre first landed. People were terrified it was the sister world come to attack them again. They used the sleeping powder to quell the riot, it got on the Maniterri, and you know how obsessive they are about washing. They took it back to their ship, spread it to the rest of their crew, and then to the *Dandridge*."

"Even if that's the answer for bescere, the vine can't be responsible for both bescere and the dracs' allergic reaction. It would take …" Brea frowned and looked up from her tablet where she had been tapping in information, and her gaze went distant.

"Take genetic engineering of the nastiest or the most careless sort, maybe really dumb, bad luck, to create something that affects across the species barrier?" Genys spoke slowly, guessing from the anger starting to draw lines around the medic's mouth.

"Pretty much," she admitted with a sigh.

"At least we have some idea, and maybe some treatment, with

the tear sop," M'kar said. "We can't just toss what we've learned because it's too good to be true, and too convenient."

"Tell me more about this vine?" Genys flinched, catching movement from the corner of her eye.

The girls gathered closer to listen, dressed in clean clothes, with wet hair and pink, somber faces.

"Seems like we could earn some grace points if we figure out a way to deal with that," Genys mused, after M'kar told her everything her friends had taught her about the ubiquitous nemesis vine. "You're sure they have no natural enemies?"

"If the vine originated on Draxonis, there might not be any."

"So maybe the best tactic is to go to Draxonis, find those natural enemies … no, that'll just exacerbate the problem, unbalance things more." She pressed her knuckles into her temples to stave off the headache she anticipated.

"If the Draxonans tinkered with it, to attack Castitarus, there's a chance the natural enemies on Draxonis might not have any effect on it," Brea pointed out. She didn't look happy to say it, but Genys admitted it had to be said.

Just like the first time the tear sop was used for washing, the remaining liquid from each person being washed was kept separate and studied. The spores washed off M'kar were larger, but still tight, smooth orbs when studied under intense magnification. The girls had the same spores, but smaller. Maybe that was proof that hormones affected the growth of the spores, and women were also affected by bescere, just in different ways, too slight to be noticed.

With Ashrock, however, the spores found in his wash water were three times the size of those taken from M'kar, and they had lost their smooth outer layer. Brea's voice was calm, professional, as she stated her theory. The spore had begun to mature, preparing to set down roots in Ashrock's skin, which provided some element that triggered growth. Such as male hormones. Her eyes spoke apology and sympathy.

Ashrock washed a second time, in a stronger batch of tear sop. Brea knew what to look for now and could refine the analysis process. The parts-per-million had decreased to one-tenth of what she had found in the first batch. Dr. Jeyn decreed a third washing before Brea could suggest it. Ashrock responded that she had lied to him all these years, his tattoos did irritate her, and she had finally found a way to remove them. Dr. Jeyn managed to smile as she led him back to their room and the attached bathing room, for the third treatment.

Brea declared him clean, only one spore in the entire batch of used tear sop. M'kar and the girls washed a second time. The leftover liquid was analyzed and found to be clean.

M'kar maintained a level of calm control and poise that worried Genys. She knew how much her Chief of Talents cared about the children under her care. The girls were probably safe just because they were female, and weren't producing the hormones that might make them susceptible to bescere. However, with Ashrock there was no knowing how short a time the bescere needed to dig in and affect his system. While the regular preventive doses of tear sop had to help, there was no knowing how much or how little until some time had passed and they gained more knowledge of the vines. Genys could guess how much M'kar worried about her father, and was probably blaming herself, even though she hadn't been careless.

When Barroo woke up, M'kar gathered up her drac and stepped outside. Tress followed her, and she came back maybe ten minutes later, very somber, and whispered to her mother that Aunt M'kar was crying.

~~~~~

"Do we need a punch-down, *mi'sho'ki?*" Ashrock leaned around the frame of the door of M'kar's room in the guesthouse the next evening.

He had stayed in the guesthouse while M'kar took the girls to the guild house for training. She had been able to forget the events, the dangers and mistakes of the day before while they were tumbling and swinging weapons and dodging. Returning to the guesthouse and the quiet inside, seeing her parents curled up together on a long couch and studying together as if nothing threatened them, unsettled her more than she had liked to admit. She had gone to her room to have some solitude to think, and try to find some answers in all the data she had collected.

Ashrock chuckled when his intrusion made her flinch. She sat up and glared at her father. It was easier to hold back the need to cry when she was irritated with him. She knew it was ridiculous to feel guilty and sick, because he didn't worry about the exposure she
~~~~~

had inflicted on him.

"Maybe we should. I'm still furious with you for coming at all."

"I think you did get infected, but for you, it makes you sloppy." He snorted and finally came into the room. "You're overloading on female hormones, maybe?"

"Po'pa ..." She caught her breath, a sudden calm pushing away the fury and guilt that made her head ache. "You think so? I hate how I can't seem to focus." She gestured down at the tablet full of all the data she had gathered on the wild bull hunt.

"Your mother will likely slap me for saying so, but women have been using overdosing hormones as an excuse for millennia."

"She should punch you, not slap you," she retorted, and stuck her tongue out at him.

"My little one ..." He sighed and sank down on the bench at the foot of her bed. The only other chair in the room was too narrow for his bulk. "You are my delight and my reward from Enlo that I most certainly did not deserve."

"A punishment you did deserve, maybe?"

Ashrock chuckled and reached to cuff the back of her head. M'kar ducked, grinning a little easier now.

"I want you to stop worrying about me and blaming yourself. You did your duty, you are doing your duty. I am very happy to be right here, seeing you doing your best, with people who are your family more truly than anyone of our bloodline ever could be. I approve of your friends, if that matters at all to you."

"Oh, no, not at all. Maybe I should ask for a transfer and start –" She squeaked, ducking another swing of his hand. "Start all over, with new friends."

"Over my dead body. No." He bared his teeth. "Over yours."

"Just try."

Ashrock tipped his head back to laugh. The sound wasn't nearly as loud as it should have been or shake his body as much as it should have. M'kar supposed he was just showing some discretion, some consideration for the people sharing the guesthouse with them. He leaned forward, bracing his hands on his knees, grinning.

"What are you working on?"

"Another puzzle." She turned her chair around and held out

the tablet so he could see the data. "All this information I picked up yesterday while we were out on that hunt. I was just gathering data, in closer detail, refining the general overview that the ship's sensors caught. Things that looked blurred from up in orbit. I filled in some blanks, cleared up some blurs, and it looks like there are more puzzles. The funny thing is, I think I literally stumbled into an answer. Here." She flipped through several screens to show him computer-generated images in various shades of green and gray and black. "These are tunnels of some kind, maybe underground rivers or crevices or … who knows? The readings from orbit were blurry because we couldn't decipher the substance filling in the places where we weren't getting readings of minerals. These tunnels or gaps in the rock could be filled with all that vine overgrowth." She showed him more screens. The coloring changed while they looked at it, indicating the data she had gathered had changed the original readings and findings from the orbital scans.

"It is everywhere, isn't it? If those vines go underground, it could be impossible to entirely root it up and keep it from coming back. They'd have to go underground to get at everything. There could be a king vine, like with viniculture." He shook his head. He sniffled. "I'm so proud of you."

M'kar held her breath. Were those tears in her father's eyes?

Ashrock didn't cry. He got quiet when he was sad. He rarely got sad. He got angry, but most of the time if something bothered him, worried him, hurt him, he channeled that energy into solving the problem.

"Come. Have you shared this brilliant insight?"

"Not exactly brilliant –"

"Time to stop moping in your room and join the team." He caught hold of her arm and pulled her to her feet.

"Moping." She snorted, but she didn't resist. Her father's eyes were clear and not teary.

~~~~~

Brea and Maora had spent the day at the Healers Guild, researching the vine and the development of the sleeping powder. They researched the methods used to try to control or prevent growth. When they couldn't find answers, but rather ran into more puzzles, they ended up at the Archivists Guild. Nearly everyone they talked with seemed a little confused by the sudden interest in
~~~~~

the pernicious, aggravating plant growth. That made doing research hard, because they had to ask the scholars to retrieve all information for them. Only members of the guild were allowed into the archives.

The vine was known by many names, most of them translating as various epithets. It took most of the day just to come up with an official name, zeduk. Then, some clues appeared, and they unearthed a few pieces of useful information

The most important detail: no mention of zeduk any further back than two centuries ago. It had come from Fire Rock, and was first imported to settled territory because of one key quality. It dug in and turned solid rock into arable soil within two years, transforming land covered with lava flows, or burned with chemicals, into fertile, nutrient-rich soil.

"Here's the truly interesting part. The word for *chemical* isn't part of their vocabulary," Maora said. "Our translation program caught it. Our archivist friends just glossed right over it. The word for chemical comes from the vocabulary we took from the Draxonis plates." She pressed her lips flat and looked around the table where everyone had gathered. "That got me suspicious, after the new theories everyone has been throwing around. Treinna found several dozen words our translators have been using that came from the Draxonis plates, but aren't in the vocabulary here."

"No wonder we've been getting some odd looks from the lower-ranked people. Only the people with higher, more educated vocabularies understand the words we've been using," Genys said.

"More proof to your theory," Dr. Jeyn said. "A war between the two planets. Draxonis tried to cripple Castitarus, but they made mistakes and they ended up destroying themselves."

"Does it matter who did what to whom?" Brea offered a quiet, sad little smile and a shrug when everyone looked up and visibly paused, caught by her words. "The ones who did it, the ones who were attacked, the ones who know what happened, they're all dead and gone and the reasons, the explanations are either lost or buried. Both worlds are victims. We need to help the descendants of both sides."

"Just chemicals, no specifics?" Genys waited while Maora and Treinna did a quick search of the transcripts of the discussion with the lower-ranked archivists. There were no specifics. "All right, let's go the other direction. Lava flows. Any mention of when volcanoes erupted? Where they erupted, other than Fire Rock?"

"We have a good idea, with some of the tunnels and areas we detected underground. Some speculation was that they were lava tubes," M'kar said. "But they're hard to analyze because they're jammed with what we speculate now is the zeduk vine."

"Why isn't that changed by now? We register solid rock, but the vine was specifically brought in to turn solid rock into soil for farming. Why isn't it?"

"Something is resisting it, or something is inaccurate in those records," Ashrock said.

"We need to get out there and do some excavating," M'kar said.

"That's going to be difficult." Maora looked up from the notes she was making. "We essentially agreed to stay here on Congregation. It's for our protection from the rebel elements. Which we had to figure out for ourselves. We don't want to stir up the unrest by going where we aren't permitted, and Fire Rock is sacred ground."

"Why is it?" Genys waited, but no one had an answer. "Find out. That could help us ask for and obtain permission."

"Or we could just take Shryne's tactics and do what we know is right, and afterward find the proof that we were right," M'kar offered.

~~~~~

The next day brought more frustration. The new planetary scans performed by the *Defender*, using the results of M'kar's up-close surveys and the new theories, revealed very little new data.

Still no clues had appeared to the whereabouts of Decker and the identify of his kidnappers. There were accusations and people getting into trouble, trying to investigate where they had no business going. Decker had essentially evaporated from existence.

"Maybe his kidnappers have him hidden away some place where the minerals or energy resonance blocks any psionic communication," Tahl had speculated early on the second day after Decker had vanished. Everyone had been waiting for Spitfire to pop out, following the signal of his mind to join him, and then hopefully return to bring rescuers.

Spitfire moped. The fact that she moped and didn't make any
~~~~~

move to leave the ship meant two options: either Decker was kept drugged and incoherent, so he couldn't focus his mind enough for his drac to find him, or he was dead.

More disturbing, though, the absence of Granny had expanded to include all the male teacher dracs. The first day after Decker had vanished and Spitfire woke up, whimpering and frantic, the adult dracs had gathered around to encourage and comfort her. Then, one by one, they went away and didn't return. The dracs were everywhere on the ship, in and out so often they were nearly invisible. No one noticed the reduced numbers because the females were still on the ship, keeping watch over the Castitaran boys.

Then the second morning after Ashrock was exposed to the spore, Spitfire roused from her nest in Medical, where Ha'ess and Tahl were keeping an eye on her. She flew from one room to another, appearing to be searching for something. Then she popped out. And didn't return.

Tila Pace was the first to notice. Her son, Jorgan, and his friends came into Medical to visit Spitfire and try to get her to play every day since Decker was kidnapped. The boy asked where Spitfire had gone. Tahl asked Ha'ess, and her drac could only tell her that Spitfire wasn't listening. No one was listening.

One question led to another, and all the bits and pieces of anomalous behavior were brought together to form a picture with only one conclusion: Granny was up to something down on Castitarus, and she had most of the dracs assisting her. M'kar searched and called the ship's dracs and questioned the young dracs until she was nauseous and headachy from the effort. The only assurance she could give them was that they were all alive and safe, but refusing to talk, refusing to listen, refusing to come.

"That does it," Genys said. "Jasper is making that drac-proof fence his top priority. Either keep Granny contained at Anwesta or find a way to keep all non-Fleet dracs off our ship."

Chapter Fifteen

After dinner that evening, Genys and Maora were in the common room, getting the four-times-daily report from the ship. Ashrock sat down in the kitchen where M'kar was brewing seoli tea and burst into tears. He got control of himself almost immediately, faster than she recovered from the shock. Before she could say anything, before she could decide whether to get her mother first, or send for Brea, Ashrock excused himself and left. She sent Barroo after him while she took care of the tea. Barroo showed her Ashrock catching hold of Dr. Jeyn's sleeve and nearly lifting her out of her chair, then half-dragging her down the long hallway to the sleeping quarters. M'kar counted down the seconds until the tea finished steeping, lifted the infuser basket out of the pot and inverted the lid to allow the basket to drain. Then she went down the long hallway to her parents' room. Before she could lift her hand to knock on the door, Dr. Jeyn opened it and looked out.

"When will the shuttle be going back up to the ship?" Dr. Jeyn asked.

"Mom?"

"I need to get your father under Dr. Tahl's care immediately."

"I'm sorry," Ashrock said, his voice fractured and thickened by tears. "I'm sorry. You were right." He stepped into sight behind Jeyn. His eyes were swollen, his face wet. "I'm sorry."

~~~~~

"No, that is probably the worst thing you can do," Dr. Jeyn said the next morning, when M'kar called up to the ship to check on Ashrock and asked if she could talk to him. "You do not want to get within your father's sight or hearing. I'm considering abandoning ship."

"What is he doing?" An image of Ashrock going berserk and tearing through the ship, targeting her mother, flashed through M'kar's mind. His modified Nisandrian genetics, which granted rapid healing and stronger senses and made her the first female born in their family line in multiple generations, hadn't protected him from bescere. Would he go overboard with all the negative
~~~~~

male hormones that had been the butt of jokes for centuries? Would he have to be sedated?

"Well, between him wanting to be put down like a wild animal, to protect us, and getting all sloppy about how he won't live to see his grandchildren ..." She sighed.

"What has he done? Please tell me he hasn't tried to contact Nisandros and make peace with the clan and agree to that arranged marriage with --"

"Worse." Dr. Jeyn laughed.

Maybe her mother was suffering the female version of bescere?

"What did he do?" It took all her self-control not to scream the question loudly enough to be heard on the ship without the communication pack.

"Well, I caught him in deep conversation with Thyal, begging him to swear on his rank as a Le'ankan Master, he would put him down like a brain-sick *doo'ag*, if he became a danger to us. I was so grateful for Thyal's common sense. Your father will listen to him. All I have to do is step into the room and he starts blubbering about how he ruined my life and we were ridiculous romantic fools and we were never going to change the universe and ..." Another sigh.

"What did Thyal do?" M'kar had wondered why she hadn't heard from Thyal since her parents went up to the ship last night. Wouldn't he have told her what her father was going through, so she could help?

"He agreed to perform the mercy killing. That so shocked your father, he calmed down and agreed he was being ridiculous. Then he thanked Thyal for being able to think clearly and make him see sense." Another sigh. "Then he had to ruin it by asking Thyal to wake up and show some common sense and start pursuing you in earnest."

"He didn't." M'kar choked back the threat to fly up to the ship without benefit of shuttle and give her father the pounding he had been needing for several years now.

No wonder Thyal had been quiet.

"It's not him, it's that dratted self-regulating biology he's so proud of. I swear, someday I'm going to find someone who truly can go back through time, and I will give your father's ancestors a piece of my mind."

That helped. M'kar was able to laugh a little.

The morning passed quietly and far too slowly, even escorting the girls to the guild house for practice. She knew better than to sit by the communication pack, waiting for word. That would guarantee no headway was made.

Some island security women came to watch as she and Aniskara demonstrated some moves for the girls, and stayed to talk. Several expressed surprise that she was a scientist and not handling security.

"You should join the Archivists Guild," Melpone said. She was a cousin of Lexa, with ebony skin and hair so white it was almost colorless.

"Yes, perfect," another woman said. "It's made for people like you, scholars and athletes and warriors, combined."

"How?" M'kar said. "Would it even be permitted, since we're foreigners?"

"Oh, that won't matter with them. It's said they invited visitors from the sister world to join them, the last time the sky well was open." Melpone grinned. "I'm surprised they haven't been badgering you to join them before now. Adding knowledge to the records is all they care about, and you have knowledge many of the highest ranks would kill to possess."

"The guild leaders are likely waiting a respectable time before inviting any of you," Aniskara said. "There are procedures and they are even more strongly restrained by decorum than any other guild." She grinned. "It will flatter them greatly if your mother and Scholar Maora request membership, and then bring them a large offering of information to add to the archives."

That evening, Tahl's report came while M'kar, Genys and Maora were discussing how to go about asking to join the Archivists Guild. Ashrock had been stabilized, but that wasn't as positive a development as it should have been. His hormones had been knocked out of balance and he had gone through four drastic mood swings in the last ten hours that had manifested physically, emotionally, and mentally. He had been stabilized in the weepy phase. The medical team had decided this was the best option, because efforts to get rid of the extremes of depression or rage or euphoria had only aggravated his condition. So far, every effort to balance his blood chemistry had done the opposite.

"Basically, our ancestors' genetic tweaking set my father up for this," M'kar said, after going through the report and discussing theories with her mother. "His hormonal balance was already knocked out of alignment by the tear sop. Tahl and Mom theorize that Nisandrian rapid healing is partly based on higher concentrations of all hormones. They also found the spore got into his lungs and is sending roots into his bloodstream, aiming for the lymph system. It's created a feedback loop, swirling from one extreme to another."

"I'm sorry," Genys said. "You have to feel awful about infecting him."

"He's being his usual aggravating self, a little weepy, but excited about being on the front lines of the battle." She fought to swallow down the thickness in her throat that was either a sob or a shriek of exasperation. "He's stable. Sloppy but stable." She took a quick, deep breath. "He's scared of the black moods. It makes him furious, which just makes things worse. When he realized what was happening, he asked for a strong sedative. When it didn't come fast enough for him, he ..." She shook her head. "My father doesn't get scared. Of anything. He laughs at trouble. This isn't him."

"No, it isn't." Genys' sympathy was bright in her eyes. M'kar was grateful she left it at that and didn't try to make things better with words. "How is Dr. Jeyn handling this?"

"Tahl thinks both my parents will be better off if she leaves the ship and he knows she isn't there, worrying about him."

"That's a little too convenient," Maora offered.

M'kar almost laughed at that, because she had been thinking it. "Reverse psychology. After all these years, he still expects Mom to baby him. Granted, usually he needs to be flat on his back with five broken bones and internal bleeding before he wants babying. And he's upset if she gives in. Mom just does a lot of sighing and rolling her eyes. Then she indulges in some self-defense training that usually ends up damaging a training 'droid."

"Your parents are quite a couple."

"It's their way," Genys said. "Still, there's a big difference between your mother being on another deck and being down here with us, if she's needed."

"He will obey Tahl like he wouldn't obey Mom. He won't fight her or play games."

Before she went to bed that night, M'kar gave in to temptation,

and sent her mind reaching upward to the *Defender*, to contact Ha'ess, and through the drac's eyes looked in on Ashrock. His color looked slightly off, but with all his tattoos, his normal coloring was hard to decipher. At least he wasn't sucking his thumb like he had been last night. Tahl hadn't given in to his teary insistence that he be restrained. M'kar thanked Ha'ess, then withdrew from the link and managed to smile when Barroo turned somersaults through the air. If he could be in a good mood over her father's condition, maybe she should be too.

~~~~~

Dr. Jeyn's return to Castitarus coincided with a response to the query about joining the Archivists Guild. Despite Aniskara's assurances, the Alliance diplomats were politely but firmly refused. The respondents cited the current and growing social upheaval over the presence of foreigners. Premier Scholar Sophria apologized, and said she hoped the advanced knowledge offered by the Alliance would eventually undo the damage done by the last foreign visitors.

The message was followed by a team of scholars. Sophria sent them to bridge the discord caused by the refusal. To answer the many questions about the numenjax, the zeduk vine, and other elements in Castitaran biology and history, the scholars had come with all the scrolls and bound volumes they could carry.

Brea and M'kar sat on the sidelines and listened while the other four women settled down with the scholars. For the first hour or so, Genys and Jeyn didn't get to ask any questions. The scholars were too fascinated and too full of questions of their own. Treinna talked herself hoarse explaining the recorder wands and tablets. She would use them to capture all the information in the documents the scholars brought, as well as record their discussion and translate it. She later reported she thought the scholars were ready to race back to the Archivists Guild house to demand membership in the Alliance, just for access to technology that would make their jobs easier. Those recordings were invaluable when the team went over their notes and impressions that evening after dinner, to make their first reports.

Maora asked a crucial question and the scholars confirmed: yes, the onset of bescere and the vanishing of the numenjax had occurred close to the same time in their history.
~~~~~

Could they provide more descriptions and images of the numenjax? How did the people of this world co-exist with them? The scrolls full of drawings and the bound volumes of data covered the long dining table.

The numenjax were massive, elegant, and silent, and the drawings of them in the ancient records were sometimes full-color and detailed. The compilation program fascinated the archivists, when it put all the drawings together to create three-dimensional approximations of how the numenjax would have looked and moved when they had roamed Castitarus. According to the tales and historical records, they communicated directly into the minds of the people chosen to act as their liaisons with the Humans above ground. The numenjax lived deep underground. They were approached via tunnels that spiraled down deep into the hot depths of the subterranean passageways. When the numenjax pulled curtains of protective vines across the openings of the tunnels, then Humans did not approach them. They needed to sleep during the cold season.

The questions saved for the next day related to which vines had been used as the protective curtains, and whether they were related to the vines that had been genetically tampered with by Draxonis.

The documents the archivists brought proved Draxonis was the sister world. Dr. Jeyn proposed a theory that the numenjax had gone to the sister world and had been unable to return when the Chute closed. The scholars were adamant that their revered teachers and guides would not have left them, for the simple reason that the people of the sister world were rebels and disrespectful. They had tried repeatedly to persuade the people of Castitarus to rise up in rebellion against the numenjax. They were unable to hear the numanjax speak in their minds, so they insisted the creatures were nothing but animals that threatened Human life and needed to be destroyed.

Haji, a tiny woman with a surprisingly deep voice, stood up to lecture at that point.

"The sister world is or was, since the evils associated with her presence have not returned this time -- the sister world was like the evil half-sister or step-sister of fables. Jealous and greedy. She would hang on the horizon like a new moon that had grown out of the darkness. The ancient teachers and visionaries warned us to beware when the sister world appeared, because then people would come in craft that could sail through the airless void, and they would treat us without honor. They had no respect for the numenjax, these arrogant visitors. Some of our ancient scribes went to visit the sister world, traveling in their strange, enclosed ships. They testified that their senses betrayed them. They tasted colors, and sound filled them with heat and ice."

"Sounds like a Chute transition to me," Treinna commented.

Haji recited the unhappy visit to the sister world the scribes had recorded, the indignities they had suffered. The leaders of the sister world continued to insist that the numenjax were not friendly to Humans and should be destroyed.

The archivists went back to their guild hall for the night, allowing the diplomatic team to relax and discuss what they had learned, and put their reports together. The girls returned from a long day of training at the Warriors Guild house, ate their dinner, and went to their dormitory room to collapse, exhausted. That was convenient for the adults.

They kept replaying portions of the recordings of that day's discussions, and the scans of all the documents, long into the night. They agreed the people from Draxonis had certainly considered themselves superior to the Castitarans. They became upset when their "advice" wasn't followed. That advice became orders, then threats. Then when the Castitarans still didn't obey them, the Draxonans schemed to destroy the numenjax and rewrite the culture of Castitarus. All that had backfired against them.

Maora pointed out that all the recorded images and the written descriptions of the numenjax lacked wings large enough for flight. That was one benefit of the genetic tinkering that resulted in shrinking the numanjax into dracs. If the people of Draxonis had managed to do that.

"So … shrink the numenjax, until their wings work, and shrink their intelligence factor too?" M'kar mused.

That immediately got trills of dismay and what were clearly hurt feelings from Battleaxe, Boomer, Moonrise and Barroo. Everyone muffled laughter and tried to stifle their smiles. They spent a few minutes assuring their dracs they were very smart and their adopted parents loved them just the way they were.

"I'm surprised, with all the questions we've been asked about the dracs, why all those supposed experts on the numenjax didn't pick up that little problem," Dr. Jeyn mused, once they returned to the discussion. "The stories and records don't mention them flying. They also don't mention them ever leaving their tunnels. If they never left their tunnels, how did they leave the planet?"

"Maybe they didn't," Brea mused.

"So where are they?"

"Sleeping," M'kar said without really thinking.

Everyone at the table paused, caught in the sudden stillness in the air, the sense that sometimes hit the crew of the *Defender* when a pivotal moment in their mission had arrived.

"Okay," Genys mused. "Sleeping where? And why? Why so long? Yes, the scholars said the numenjax hibernated during the regular cold cycle. The planet's orbit is such that they have especially cold periods every few decades, that last a few years, and that seems to coincide with the numenjax hibernation period ... Oh ..." She muttered a few gutturals M'kar didn't recognize. A glance at Treinna showed their linguist didn't recognize the words either. "What was Granny upset about, before she vanished again?"

M'kar thumped her forehead with her fists, then slumped back in her chair. "She was upset because they wouldn't wake up, and it was cold!"

"The little menace found the numenjax, and she's trying to wake them up?" Treinna whispered.

"How sure is Jasper that those damaged satellites were affecting the weather?" Genys asked.

Treinna sent Moonrise with a note for Jasper. He contacted them within fifteen minutes, confirming that all studies so far of the wreckage of the satellites destroyed by the Maniterri indicated no link with the planetary communications system. If there was any control over the weather, as Genys theorized, that control had never been in the hands of Castitarus. One of his geniuses, Beedlejo, had theorized a day or two ago that the geo-thermal taps they detected weren't to power the satellites, but were there to lower the temperature of the planet.

"What if they siphoned energy away from the volcanoes?" M'kar asked. "Cold. Hibernation." She didn't know whether to laugh or curse. "Tomorrow, ask for weather records for the last century, maybe extending all the way back to the last visit from Draxonis. I'm positive I heard Aniskara say the weather seemed a little warmer than usual for this time of year. Drier, for one thing. Usually the plains where we were hunting would still be wet. Time for the bumper crop in the vines." She slapped her hand flat on the table, making a few dishes jump.

"Is it possible?" Genys muttered. She shook her head when Jasper asked over the link what she had said. "The Maniterri attacked the satellites. Is it possible someone who knew what the satellites did, how the cooler weather encouraged numenjax hibernation, somehow got control of them? Convinced them to kill the satellites, in hopes of raising the planetary temperature enough to wake the numenjax?"

"They wouldn't have to control the Maniterri at all," Treinna said. "All they needed to do was tell Vitiarre the satellites were responsible for the numenjax hiding, and he would have launched an arsenal to knock them all out of the sky."

"His people probably would have, but the bescere took over and they lost the intelligence to fly the other shuttles, or teach anyone else to pilot them," Brea said.

"Any idea how long it will take for the planet to return to normal temperature and weather cycles, once the interference is removed?" Genys said slowly, her tone thoughtful.

That question was passed up to the ship, to wait for the planetary scientists in the crew when they woke up in the ship's morning.

"I read something, one of the children's lessons, I think," Dr. Jeyn said. "A reference to the numenjax sleeping through the cold season. Maora, Treinna, do you remember or is my brain just short-circuiting? Was there a mention of a time when the numenjax didn't come back when they were expected, but they kept sleeping a few years longer than usual?"

"If the scholars from the sister world learned about that," Maora said slowly, her gaze unfocused, meaning she was thinking aloud, "then that might have been the launching point in their plan. If they couldn't persuade the people of Castitarus to rebel and kill the numenjax, then making them sleep and become vulnerable might have been the next best tactic."

Digging through notes and scans Treinna had made gave a

possible answer. Records from nearly three hundred years before noted increasing concern when the weather gradually changed over several years. The numenjax did not emerge from their underground chambers after the long period of sleep. Several years passed of longer winters and shorter summers that weren't as warm or as dry as they should have been. The concern over the numenjax not returning increased because of health problems and food shortages resulting from the changed weather conditions. Then, the weather shifted back to normal, the numenjax returned, and the resolved problems were forgotten.

Around the time of the closing of the star well and the retreat of the visitors from Draxonis, records noted gradual weather changes as well. There were concerns about the rainfall. Droughts occurred where they hadn't before, and floods struck and wiped out homesteads in areas where there had never been floods before. In other places, the growth cycle was shortened, when snow appeared moon-cycles too soon or lasted far into the summer.

"All tied into tampering with the weather, to keep the numenjax sleeping so the sister world could take over Castitarus." Maora shook her head. "So was the genetic engineering program to create dracs a follow-up, or something that didn't happen as quickly as they wanted, or a failure of some kind?"

A querulous, sleepy cheep from the basket of dracs, on the far side of the room, generated weary grins among the women. It was very late, past planetary midnight. They had been thinking and theorizing and researching until their eyes and throats were dry.

"A failure because the dracs have minds of their own and weren't cooperative," M'kar offered, pitching her voice a little louder and sending her thoughts to the dracs. That earned a few purrs from the sleepy creatures.

"Interesting question, though," Genys said, nodding. "Were the dracs the first attempt at control, or the last gasp effort?"

"More research. More questions. And when do we start sharing what we've figured out with our new friends?" Treinna said.

"On that philosophical note, I declare this session ended. We need sleep." She pushed herself to her feet with a groan.

"Sleep on this question: How soon do the numenjax start waking up?" Dr. Jeyn mused. "How many degrees did the planetary temperature have to go down, to force them into hibernation, and how many degrees does it have to go up, to start them waking?"

"We have got a lot of studying to do," Maora said, a fiendishly delighted expression brightening her bloodshot eyes. That earned some chuckles, as the others got to their feet.

"When do we tell our new friends that their numenjax might just be waking up?" Brea asked.

They were all somber and thoughtful as they made their way to their rooms.

~~~~~

The next morning, M'kar woke to the sound of a drac fight. She rolled out of bed and stayed down on the floor. Enough bad experience had taught that when dracs were divebombing each other, the safest spot was as far from mid-air as possible. She reached her door just as a splotch of pink popped into the air over her bed. Barroo popped in, caught the pink drac in his paws, and popped out, taking her with him.

"Spitfire is back!" M'kar reached up, yanked her door open, tumbled out into the hallway, then got to her feet and ran to the common room.

"What gave you that idea?" Genys groaned, appearing in her doorway.

A yelp came from Brea a moment later.

M'kar finally got both eyes open and made sense of the battle going on near the ceiling of the common room. Boomer popped in with Spitfire in his clutches. She twisted free and popped out again. Moonrise vanished, a yelp erupted from Treinna's room, and a moment later, Moonrise popped in, clutching Spitfire.

"I didn't know they could yank each other through the teleportation or whatever it is they do." Maora leaned against the door into the hallway, looking up at the battling dracs.

All right, stop it right now! M'kar's head reverberated with the force of her psionic call. She was impressed. She didn't know she could be that loud. Especially after staying up so late theorizing and studying.

With a chorus of chirps and whimpers, the dracs settled down on the furniture. Spitfire let out a few scolding rasps and fluttered to M'kar, zigzagging. Barroo went after her, scolding. M'kar stopped him with a look. He chirped penitently and settled on her
~~~~~

shoulder, while Spitfire hovered in mid-air at eyelevel with her, giving her imploring looks.

"Did you find Decker?" she asked. Her face warmed, because she had barely stopped herself in time from asking: Did you find your Daddy?

Spitfire's eyes shifted to blue and green happy sparkles. She turned a somersault and flew to the door. M'kar followed her. The other women were close behind, and the girls trailed after them, the last to be awakened by the ruckus. It was that hazy hour just before dawn when the shadows seemed lighter than the air. She pulled the door open, stepped out, and immediately tripped over something huge and dense. She stumbled aside and reached for the lantern hanging next to the door. These people definitely needed indoor lighting that came on automatically.

Treinna laughed and pointed at the heavy and smelly pile in the doorway. M'kar brought the lantern over and groaned.

"So help me, Decker, only you could get kidnapped and worry the entire ship and take time to go fishing on your way back from rescuing yourself!"

Chapter Sixteen

"You know what they say." A dark shape stood up from the decorative bushes to the right of the doorway, along the path to the garden. It wobbled the taller it grew, until finally Decker stumbled out into the light from the lantern. "A rotten day fishing is better than …" His face twisted and his eyes seemed to cross as he visibly searched for words.

"Get him inside," Genys said, and disappeared back into the guesthouse. "What do you say to a really strong batch of tear sop?"

"Make it a bath." Dr. Jeyn leaned out of the door to study M'kar as she shoved the pile of enormous fish, one nearly a meter long, off the doorstep. "Where have they been keeping you, Chief Decker?"

"Don't know." He wobbled forward and nearly went flat on his face with a dopey grin, then seemed to remember that his feet needed to move along with his shoulders and head. "Don't much care. Great fishing."

Spitfire circled around Decker, growing more agitated with every step he took toward the guesthouse kitchen. Barroo tried to intervene and she shrieked at him, then settled into chatter, sounding so much like Granny for a few seconds, M'kar wouldn't have been surprised to see the hot pink hide turn to silver.

"I'm getting the impression she doesn't want Decker to stay here," Treinna said.

"Well, it would make sense to get him on that shuttle and up to the ship where Tahl can get to work on him," Dr. Jeyn said.

Spitfire let out happy trills and her eye color changed, losing the angry oranges and reds.

"I've got half a mind to send him up and not tell the locals we found him," Genys admitted. She stepped back from the doorway of the kitchen and tried to guide a wobbling, sleepily grinning Decker through. The aroma of tear sop filtered through the doorway.

Spitfire let out a dismayed yowl, enough like a cat that got its tail stepped on that the other three women couldn't help grinning.

The pink drac popped out. A second later, Decker let out a howl, followed by a stream of what M'kar referred to as "security foul." The little girls coming down the hall from their dormitory room stopped short, their eyes getting wider with every syllable.

Dr. Jeyn muffled a grin and she and Treinna herded the girls back to their room while M'kar went to see what had happened.

She found Decker mopping at his clothes. Not the clothes he had been wearing when he vanished. Spitfire perched on the top of a cabinet, peering down at him, crooning, her eyes swirling green and yellow. She came close enough to wringing her paws, M'kar had to look twice.

Brea was on her knees, mopping up spilled tear sop tea. The pot they had used to steep baths of tear sop lay on its side. From the purple-tinged streaks on the table and floor, it certainly looked like Spitfire had knocked the pot over.

"Okay, someone doesn't want him drinking that," Genys muttered. "We don't have time to make another batch. I want him in the shuttle and launching before it's light enough for people to see him. Brea, Plan B. Get him washed up, do a preliminary scan. We'll wake up the shuttle crew."

Spitfire let out a happy trill and dropped down from the cabinet. She caught hold of Decker's raggedy, filthy, native cloth shirt, and pulled, as if she would drag him to the bathroom all by herself. M'kar followed them halfway down the hall, then leaned against the wall. Something in the picture just did not add up.

"Is that smell from the fish, or him?" Genys said. "Just proves how much effect the bescere is having on him, scrambling his brains, because Decker is one of the most --"

"That's it." M'kar held up her hand, stopping her captain, while she sent an order to Barroo.

"What did you just think of? And why do I have the feeling we won't like it?" Maora said.

"Decker stinks, but … okay, Barroo asked Battleaxe, because the females have proven more sensitive to the bescere stink. She says yes, Decker stinks of bescere, but not as bad. There's another smell that's like bescere, but it's nice. That's the impression, anyway."

"So what did Decker get into that Spitfire likes, enough that she doesn't want him using the tear sop to negate it?" Genys mused.

"Whatever it is, it's keeping him loopy," Maora said.

"Send him topside, and have Tahl do some intensive studying, comparing his blood chemistry with the rest of her patients."

M'kar notified the shuttle team to be ready to go while Genys contacted the ship.

I'm glad you're awake, Thyal said a few moments later, when she stepped into the kitchen to start making breakfast. *It sounds like you've been having just as interesting a morning as we have.*

Oh, no … what happened? M'kar got a flash of Ashrock, sitting on the edge of his bed in Medical, grinning and chattering and waving his arms around.

Then she caught a glimpse of silver, curled around his neck, hidden by the collar of his huge, fluffy robe.

When did she show up? A shudder went through her, instinct screaming that the sudden reappearance of Granny and Spitfire and Decker all at once wasn't a happy coincidence. Unfortunately, often her instincts were totally incoherent when they screamed, so she couldn't get any useful clues.

Thyal reported that Infrenx had awakened him about an hour ago, insisting that he come to Medical and be very quiet. She led him to Ashrock's room. He was sitting on the floor, laughing and nodding, eating for the first time in more than a day, while Granny hovered in mid-air in front of him, chattering at nearly sonic pitch. Thyal had the uneasy feeling that whatever she was saying, Ashrock understood.

The interesting part is that Granny is blocking Infrenx. She won't let her in the room. Whatever your father is eating smells good, she wants some, and Granny won't let her have any. We need to get him separated from Granny. Your mother and I can control him, and you can yell some sense into Granny.

You wish. M'kar put down the bread she had been about to slice, rubbed her eyes, and turned to leave to find her mother. *We're on our way.*

Her expression must have revealed something when she passed Genys.

"What happened?" For so early in the morning, her captain looked like she had been through several of "those days" without any sleep.

"Thyal just called."

"Your father? He's not getting any worse, is he?"

"Well, he's eating again. Don't know if that's thanks to Granny. Who has returned and won't let anyone near him. I'm definitely going back in time and pounding a few dozen ancestral heads to knock all those genetic tinkering plans out and some common sense in." M'kar gestured down the hall to the bedrooms. "Mom needs to get up there. If anyone can control him or get through to him or ..." She headed down the hall.

After M'kar talked to her mother, she went into her room to throw her gear into her pack. By that time, Brea finally let Decker out of the bathroom. He was barefoot and wore clothes JM had probably left behind, hanging two sizes too large on him. He grinned at them as he and Brea joined M'kar and Genys in the main room. He looked around, in all directions -- even at the ceiling -- turning around three times before he finally sat down facing them. His fingers twitched and his heels tapped, pumping his knees up and down out of synch with each other.

Decker *grinned* at them. She didn't think the permanent sneer in the corner of his mouth would relax enough to let him grin like that. Kind of dopey and young.

"How are you feeling, Chief?" Genys said, voice soft, as if she wasn't sure she really wanted to ask.

"Great. Never better. Glad to get back and clean. Kinda filthy out there." He chuckled. "Did you see the huge ones I got?" He leaped to his feet again. "Where'd you put them?"

"Sit down, Chief," she snapped.

A childish sneer crossed Decker's face. He laughed and vaulted over the chair, heading for the doorway. M'kar leaped to her feet, bracing herself as she held out her arm. It caught Decker partially on his shoulders, partially across his neck.

That move *shouldn't* have worked. M'kar felt a little sick as Decker went down.

He should have ducked sideways, caught hold of her arm, and twisted her off her feet, with a good chop to the ribs in punishment for using such a basic move. Instead, Decker lay there for a few seconds, blinking. Then that goofy grin returned.

"Now I'm officially worried," Genys murmured.

Dr. Jeyn came out of her room, packed and ready to go. She blinked, shook her head, then gave them a crooked smile that clearly said, "Not even going to ask," as she headed for the door.

Spitfire didn't scold M'kar for knocking Decker flat, and that was another warning sign. She clung to the front of his shirt and crooned the entire time their group hurried through the growing dawn light to the shuttle. Decker paid more attention to her than to where they were going, assuring her everything was all right and he would get everything fixed right away.

Decker reverted to tipsy-giddy once they got into the shuttle and prepared for launch. M'kar wanted to hit him with an emergency sedative, but knew better. Intoxication from alien substances prohibited introducing more substances into the victim's blood chemistry. Even if those substances would add to the comfort of everyone else on the shuttle.

On the flight up to the ship, Brea and Dr. Jeyn managed to get Decker to answer a few questions about his kidnapping, his captivity, and then his escape. He swung back and forth between giddy and grinning and sloppy-drippy with tears and contradicted everything he told them. None of his characteristic fury and wounded pride. That was not a good sign. It was almost a relief for them to let Decker slide back into his cheerful, childish mindset, even though he kept offering to show everyone the "incredible, gigundous" fish he had caught while he was on his own.

"I wouldn't be surprised if he made such a pain of himself, the way he is now, whoever snatched him just dumped him somewhere. He made himself more trouble than he was worth as a hostage," Maora commented, once they were on the ship and Brea and four medics led Decker away to Medical.

Dr. Jeyn followed them, to check on Ashrock. M'kar met with Veylen and Thyal in the ready room to go over the recordings of Ashrock's behavior over the last two hours. She couldn't repress the shudders as she watched recordings of her father, from multiple angles, nodding and grinning and responding to Granny's chattering and squealing as if they were having a conversation.

"What if they are?" Thyal said, when she finally voiced her impression. "The oldest writings relating to Talent awakening always tied it to the surge of hormonal activity at puberty. What if the hormonal imbalances caused by bescere awakened something in your father that isn't there or isn't strong enough to be affected, in other victims?"

"There is all that genetic tinkering our ancestors did," she mused aloud. "I would hate to have that information get back to the clan, and let some of those *boostifaks* have a chance to say 'told you so.' Yet it would explain what he's going through."

"And take some of the blame for your unique abilities off your mother's genetic heritage."

She resisted the urge to stick her tongue out at him. Thyal had probably said that to lighten the moment.

Then Dr. Jeyn called up to the ready room, asking M'kar to come to Medical.

"What's wrong?"

"Nothing is really wrong," Tahl said, taking over the link. "Just ... odd."

"As in?" Veylen asked.

"Well, Decker and your father greeted each other like best buddies. We couldn't keep them apart while we were examining the Chief and getting all the samples we need. They're sitting in Ashrock's room now, hunched together like two bad little boys planning a lot of mischief. The problem is that I swear Granny and Spitfire are doing all the talking."

"On my way."

M'kar took a maintenance access tube to get to Medical faster, which meant Thyal in his hoverchair couldn't take that route with her. She hurtled into Medical and her mother beckoned her over to the open doorway of Ashrock's sickroom. Sure enough, the two men sat on the floor, with Granny on Ashrock's shoulder and Spitfire on Decker's. The ship's twelve teacher dracs had joined them in the last couple of minutes. The two men looked perfectly happy. M'kar shuddered at Tahl's description, of bad boys planning mischief. The grins and excitement in their eyes did indeed strike her as juvenile.

"Any way of telling if this *bescere* is causing permanent brain damage?" she asked Tahl, when she stepped away from the doorway. Mostly because she couldn't stand looking at them any longer. From the corner of her eye she caught movement and looked up to see Dr. Jeyn had moved close enough to have heard that. "Sorry, Mom."

"I'm wondering that myself. I think we need to have a conference with your captain. That drac-proof fence sounds like a better idea the longer I think about it." Dr. Jeyn held out a tablet for Tahl to look at.

"What?" M'kar asked, just as Thyal's hoverchair floated into Medical. Both women wore matching flat-lipped frowns of concern.

"I could swear there is something … interfering with our remote scans of their brainwaves," Tahl said. "But the power to do that, and the drugs to enforce malleability in the brains …" Her eyes narrowed as she turned to look across Medical to the hallway to the patients' rooms. "What if dracs, all merged together in that group mind of theirs, can somehow inflict their will on people?"

"That was one of the crimes the people of Draxonis accused the numenjax of perpetrating," Dr. Jeyn murmured.

"But if they downgraded the numenjax when they engineered the dracs, wouldn't that ability, if it actually existed, be downgraded too?" M'kar turned to Thyal. As a Le'ankan Master, he certainly had more knowledge about such things than she did.

"There are fourteen dracs in that room, focusing on two men who are certainly not in full control of their faculties," Thyal said. "Quantity can create strength." He looked around, eyes narrowed in concentration. "Let me try something …"

A moment later, a scolding shriek that could only come from Granny's throat erupted from the patients' rooms. Infrenx popped in and dropped into Thyal's lap. Her eyes sparkled yellow and green and orange with fear and worry and hurt feelings.

"She was caught eavesdropping and got her knuckles slapped?" M'kar asked, as Thyal cradled his drac close. Barroo hunched down on her shoulder and crooned sympathetically. She didn't have to look at him to see the fear in his eyes. He trembled a little when she reached up and stroked down his neck. *Don't worry, I won't ask you. We'll find some other way of figuring out what they're up to.*

"Get that drac fence from theory to reality," Genys said, when they called down to the planet to report their theories.

~~~~~

Four hours later, Genys felt like her crew had been dropped into a training simulation, titled: "Don't let this happen to you."

After Infrenx tried to eavesdrop on the schemers in Ashrock's room, Decker closed the door and turned on sound screens, so no
~~~~~

one could listen in. No one tried, so that tactic wasn't discovered until later. Discovering all the ship's systems Decker had overridden, using his top-level access as Chief of Security, came later.

That was their biggest mistake. They should have taken his mental condition into consideration and revoked all his access.

While Dr. Jeyn, Tahl and Brea were conferring over the results of the latest tests run on the two men, Decker ordered the ship's computer system to report he and Ashrock were locked in his room. Then he ordered the computer to ignore all their movements, as the two men walked out of Medical. The fourteen dracs proved quite useful, acting as lookouts and creating distractions for crew who might run across the two men sneaking from one shadow and doorway to another. Until they got to the shuttle bay.

The dracs popped in and out all over the ship, gathering up supplies. Clothes. Food. Camping gear. And every piece of personal weaponry that wouldn't set off alarms by vanishing from the armory. Decker didn't have override capability for that system because there was no override.

Then the two men piled all their stolen supplies into the shuttle used for emergency maneuvers and rescue missions. It was a mammoth of a machine, with a cargo hold made for construction equipment. Decker also loaded a thermal excavator.

Those deconstructing the sequence of events calculated the supplies were about halfway packed when M'kar went to talk to her father. When he didn't respond, she used her clearance as a department head and discovered the sound shield. Logic and experience with Decker's legendary nasty tricks prompted her to ask the ship's system what else he had been doing with his top-level access. Thyal was in Engineering by this time, helping Jasper with the drac-proof fence. M'kar contacted him through their link, rather than through the ship's system, just in case Decker had a keyword-triggered tap in the communication system. So he would know when anyone was talking about him. He had done that before, during a ship-wide competition.

Jasper got Thyal into the ship's system and settled that worry. They contacted Veylen and opened up a three-way link between them as they worked around Decker's commands. Then they got the sickroom door open and found everyone gone.

"He's been kind of simple in all this," Jasper observed. "The guy is usually a lot sneakier when we're playing the strategy section of Brain Blast."

"It could be the effect of bescere," Veylan said.

"But what good does it do us?" M'kar asked.

"He thought of the main part, but left out all the strings attached to it," Jasper said. "For instance …" He chuckled. "He told the security system not to tell us where they are, but did he tell it not to tell us where they *aren't*? Did he tell the system not to tell us where all the dracs went?"

Thyal laughed first. M'kar ran, listening to instinct, and sent Barroo to carefully spy for her. She was almost to the shuttle bay when the three men narrowed down the fugitives' location. The images she got from Barroo and from Ha'ess, who had overheard Granny plotting with the teacher dracs, were of flaming holes in the ground and burning away entire jungles, until they revealed a warren of tunnels.

In keeping with the misfit luck of the *Defender*, chances were good Granny had indeed found the numenjax, and determined that she needed to burn away the vines, maybe heat up the tunnels where they were sleeping, before they would awake.

Decker had ordered the doors leading into the shuttle bay and the equipment lockers locked. M'kar took the maintenance access tubes again. The tubes had no doors on them, meaning they couldn't be locked.

They did, however, have emergency measures that included releasing foam sealant that hardened in the presence of vacuum or fire or gases inimical to Human life. M'kar admitted during the debriefing, she didn't think about that possibility until she was halfway down the first tube. She begged Enlo several times that Decker was too busy to convince the emergency controls there was a fire in the tubes.

However, the tubes had dracs for sentinels. When M'kar slid out of one, she was hit with a stunner rod before she could turn around and see who was firing at her.

One unpleasant side-effect of their link meant Thyal shared the sensation of being stunned. Jasper hit the emergency medical alert when Thyal spasmed and nearly threw himself out of his hoverchair. Infrenx went into panic mode and wouldn't let the medics gets near Thyal. Jasper had to call Brea and Tahl and ask them to send their dracs to calm Infrenx before anyone could touch him. Genys heard everything because she was talking with Jasper at the time. She swore on the foundations of the Motherhouse that she was never again leaving her ship during a mission. That oath was recorded. No amount of wheedling later could persuade her superiors to edit that particular promise out of the official mission records.

During the ruckus, Ashrock and Decker obeyed Granny and threw an unconscious M'kar into the shuttle. They nearly rammed their way out of the ship before emergency overrides undid the block that Veylan had put in the system, in an attempt to cancel Decker's commands. Then the shuttle headed out and set off on a course firing on the remaining weather satellites still circling Castitarus.

Veylen sent a second shuttle to try to deactivate the remaining satellites and tow as many as they could into the *Defender*'s bays. Perhaps that action would lure Decker and Ashrock back into the ship. At the very least, they would save some satellites to dismantle and figure out some of the Draxonans' planetary sabotage.

During the short lull, Genys notified the Senate of what had happened. If watching the shuttle wobble in its haphazard orbit of Castitarus, shooting satellites, while waiting for M'kar to wake up and contact Thyal could be called a lull.

By the time M'kar recovered from the stunning, two satellites had been blown to space junk. Chercha and the five most powerful matriarchs of the Senate had arrived in the guesthouse. Genys, Maora and Treinna got to work revealing in as orderly a fashion as possible their discoveries and theories, and what was happening right that moment somewhere overhead. They left the communication channel open, and the translator turned on, as a gesture of good will.

Later, several members of the Alliance Congress and Fleet Command noted that the matriarchs' fascination with the advanced technology did a great deal toward alleviating tension and what could have been righteous fury.

~~~~~

Nausea, cramps, and a sensation like sparks sizzling through her brain warned M'kar she had been stunned. Thanks to inept
~~~~~

trainees and a few unpleasant encounters with overzealous security personnel on unfriendly planets, she had experience. She also knew better than to curl into a ball and press her hands to her head to keep it from exploding. Lying perfectly still was the only way to avoid worse side-effects, while she waited for her brain to reboot and her senses to start functioning clearly.

How bad is it? Thyal's mental voice was a whisper, but it still felt like sand rubbed into sunburned skin. *Sorry. Got a reverb of that.*

Sorry back at you. She repressed a sigh, and nearly smiled when she discovered the mental link seemed to send a cooling sensation through all her scorched nerves. *Did you do that?*

No. Another benefit of our link?

Sharing my stun wasn't. Sorry again.

I have always been a little curious what it was like to be stunned. Now I can stop wondering. I'm going to tell the others you're awake.

When he returned, he shared with her the situation on the ship, on Castitarus, and the progress of the shuttle in destroying satellites. Decker neared the third satellite. The *Defender*'s retrieval shuttle had managed to snag three already by the simple tactic of hitting them with repulson beams and knocking them out of orbit, into the path of a swarm of maintenance drones. Decker didn't seem to notice his targets were vanishing.

What happens when he figures it out? M'kar had to ask.

~~~~~

Meanwhile, on Castitarus, the matriarchs present in the guesthouse voted to adjourn to their chamber and send for all the members of the Senate. They asked the *Defender*'s representatives to set up the communication gear so they could all hear the events as they transpired. There was plenty of time for discussion during the sporadic reporting on satellites destroyed or salvaged, and carefully reworded reports of what M'kar told Thyal. Knowing everything audible would be recorded for the official records, Genys and Veylen maintained private communication by sending Battleaxe and Ha'ess back and forth between the ship and planet with written notes. The first note warned Veylen to avoid anything that would give away the psionic link between M'kar and Thyal.

While waiting for more news, the Senate had deep discussions about lost knowledge and hidden knowledge. Genys reported later, it looked like Castitarus was becoming aware of just how
~~~~~

much damage they had done to themselves over the generations since the battle with the sister world. Not everything could be blamed on the Draxonans' schemes.

M'kar pretended to be stunned as long as possible, but Barroo heard her mind and popped into the shuttle, crooning and cuddling up next to her. He was very upset to discover she was tied hand and foot. Ashrock came and retrieved her from the cargo section of the shuttle, left her bound, and carried her to the passenger compartment. Now she could see what was going on. Decker focused on finding all the satellites and blowing them out of the sky. Ashrock was sloppily apologetic. He explained that they needed her help to run the equipment and coordinate the dracs when they got to Castitarus, because Granny would be busy.

Busy with what, they didn't know. Granny wasn't revealing to her puppets more than a few steps ahead in the grand scheme.

Ashrock brought her water, which she needed desperately, and fed her pieces of a chewy, moist cake that was heavy on dried fruits and strong spices. The first few bites were enjoyable, but then the sweetness grew almost overpowering. The grainy, chewy texture became irritating. The cake seemed to swell up in her throat, so she had a hard time swallowing. The dracs perched all around them in the compartment and watched Ashrock feed her. They wanted that cake.

You're getting fuzzy, Thyal said.

No, I'm feeling kind of good.

Should you be feeling this good, so quickly?

I don't ... well, now that I think about it ... Better than ... She took a deep breath and turned her head away when Ashrock held another morsel of the cake up to her lips. "I'm choking, Po'pa."

"Please, *mi'sho'ki?*" Ashrock grinned and nodded and pushed the morsel against her lips. "You need this. Eat if for me?"

Oh, ga'oosh'ka'ta. Is my own father drugging me? He has to be. I'm having a hard time thinking. Thyal, help?

Let me try something ...

Chapter Seventeen

M'kar gagged. Her throat closed up and she coughed and spat out the chewed bits she had been trying to swallow. Later, she was proud of her aim, because several large chunks hit Ashrock square on his nose. Just like when she had been a baby and didn't like what he was feeding her.

Did it work? Thyal asked when she had caught her breath.

You made me hurl? How?

The fuzzy sensation has opened up your mind to outside influence. That's the simplified explanation. I will try to shield you, but please do not eat any more and make my job harder.

I'll try.

M'kar coughed more. When Ashrock held the water bottle to her lips, she rinsed the bits of the cake from between her teeth, and pretended to cough and gag more, spitting it out on the deck of the shuttle. She inhaled unintentionally and coughed for real. When the coughing ended, a weight settled on her knees. M'kar raised her head and looked into the swirling purple-streaked eyes of Granny.

Just what I theorized, Thyal said.

The sound of his voice in her head jolted M'kar into awareness that she had been drifting, swirling down into the purple depths.

Granny gave a satisfied chirp, leaped up off her knees, and toward the cockpit.

Probably going back to mind-zapping Decker. How? No, I know how. That cake. Granny brought it up, fed it to my father, and probably Decker. Then she dug her claws in and she's running the show, and she was trying to run me, too.

She thinks she is, Thyal responded.

M'kar looked down and realized while she had been drifting, her father had untied her hands and feet.

Now what do we do?

Play along. Find out what she wants. She needs you for something.

Scheming old biddy is in for a big, nasty surprise very soon.

Decker let out a stream of security-foul and Granny echoed him. The other dracs flew up to the cockpit, so M'kar was afraid for a few seconds Decker would lose control of the shuttle. Whatever Thyal was doing to shield her, it allowed some link to remain with Granny, because she understood what upset them.

There were no more satellites. Granny knew there were fifteen more satellites, and Decker had destroyed six of them. Where were the others?

How does she know how many remained to be shot out of orbit?

Thyal was silent for a few moments, while Decker and Ashrock and Granny seemed to be arguing about what to do. That was bizarre enough, M'kar wondered if she had swallowed more of the mind-control cake than she thought.

The shuttle angled downward. M'kar caught her breath at the sudden dropping sensation. She gripped the armrests of the seat, pressed her feet against the deck, and fought the sudden fear she would fall and keep falling, straight through the planet.

Falling isn't so bad, Thyal offered. *It's the sudden stop.*

I'm going to slap you so hard when I see you, you won't need a ship to get home to Le'anka.

Promises, promises. He laughed.

M'kar couldn't get to the cockpit to see the coordinates, but she could guess. It was hard not to guess what the plan was, when Decker and Ashrock both settled back in their seats and chuckled in between repetitive chants of, "Wake up the Big Ones. Make it hot and wake up the Big Ones."

Veylen confirmed her theory, when Thyal shared it with him and Jasper. Engineering seemed to be the new, temporary bridge.

Two centuries ago, the Valley of the Moon on the island of Fire Rock had been the largest volcanic plain on the planet. It was the logical retreat for the numenjax when the planetary temperature started dropping. Folklore agreed the tunnels currently filled with the invasive vines had been the dwelling places of the numenjax. When the cold interval came to Castitarus, they retreated to the Valley of the Moon to sleep, protected by the warmth of the volcanic vents and chambers. Then, when the planet's orbit took it out of the cold interval and the planetary temperature rose again, the numenjax ventured out to the other continents and contacted the Humans once more.

The planetary temperature was rising, but only a fraction of a percentage so far. Granny didn't have enough patience. Decker and

Ashrock were taking the excavators to clear out the vine-filled tunnels and wake the numenjax, whether they were ready to wake up or not.

We are in huge trouble, if they start burning all those vines. Imagine metric tons of that ash, getting into the atmosphere. We're talking planetary winter, along with a strong enough concentration to put half the planet to sleep. Permanently.

Jasper put aside the drac-proof fence project to assemble equipment to contain all the dust and ash that would result. Veylen called up security personnel, men and women in isolation suits, and filled the three remaining shuttles, which left immediately to land before too much damage had been done.

However, the stolen shuttle was close to landing. M'kar saw a sprawling, crater-pocked landscape out the forward viewscreen. Right now the entire planet lay between Fire Rock and where the *Defender* hung in orbit. There was no telling what kind of damage Decker and Ashrock could do in the two hours between the first shuttle landing and when the other shuttles landed and crew could secure the scene. M'kar had no delusions about the kind of control she could enforce on fourteen stubborn dracs, especially when the mind-controlling cake she had eaten could interfere.

She gasped at the first bang, followed by a long skidding sensation as Decker brought the shuttle in for a fast landing. Shuttles weren't made to roll to a stop. They were made to settle vertically into place. Just more proof of how much Granny was in control, and how loopy Decker remained. Baroo crooned and dug his talons into the front of her uniform. The shuttle skidded east-northeast, facing into the rising sun. It hit hard, digging into the ground that gave and seemed to cushion the shuttle so it didn't bounce upward again like M'kar expected. Debris flew up to cover the forward viewscreen. She braced as the shuttle dropped again, bounced up, dropped, skidded, bounced up, and oddly seemed to be dragging on something.

Vines. We're plowing through meters of vines covering the ground.

Ashrock slumped forward in the co-pilot's seat. Decker snarled and fought with the controls, and when Granny swooped in to get a closer look, he swore and batted her away.

Looks like she's losing control. Too late to do us any good?

Maybe Granny has let go of him for now, Thyal responded. *There was a ... a buzzing, a discordant humming in the mental atmosphere, but it has let up for now.*

Ashrock groaned and raised one massive, shaking hand to his head as the shuttle's skid decreased in momentum. He opened one eye and turned to look at Decker. A few muttered Nisandrian curses, some of which M'kar had never heard before, escaped his lips.

"I hoped this was all a bad dream," Ashrock rasped. Then he swore and scrabbled at the belt release. *"Mi'sho'ki?"*

"Change bad dream to nightmare, Po'pa." M'kar hit the release for her belt and got to her feet. The shuttle gave one last lurch and turned sideways a few degrees. She kept her feet and stumbled through the passenger compartment to the cockpit.

"Kid, you are in so much trouble," Decker growled, as a whimpering Spitfire dropped into his lap and clung to the front of his jacket.

"Are both of you back?" M'kar asked. "Any idea what Granny is up to?"

Decker let out another stream of security-foul, which she translated as: Not a clue.

"We have company." Ashrock raised a shaking arm to point out the forward viewscreen.

A large company of people riding on horses and driving wagons appeared, coming around a high ridge in the landscape. M'kar estimated it was maybe two hundred meters away. That was far too close for her taste, considering how much speed the shuttle still carried when it hit the ground. Aniskara had told her no people were allowed on Fire Rock other than the sentinels who camped on the shore. So who were these people?

Granny chirped happily, then popped out. Followed by all the other dracs, except Barroo. He stayed with M'kar, clinging to the front of her jacket.

"Want to tell me what's up?" Decker demanded.

"I think Granny knows them." Ashrock gestured at the swirling cloud of dracs that settled down among the group approaching them, riding on their shoulders.

"Well, that answers a couple questions. This is where Granny and the other dracs have been vanishing to, probably where they got the mind-control cake," M'kar said.

"Yeah, and I'm gonna get my hands on Granny and wring her skinny neck for making me eat that stuff," Decker grumbled. He pressed his fists against his head. "I still feel like I'm lopsided to everything. How did we break free?"

You didn't, Thyal said.

"Huh?" He turned around, so fast he nearly knocked himself out of the pilot's seat. "Who said -- Thyal? How'd he get down here? I remember killing the channel to the ship ..." He moaned again, and this time pressed the heels of his hands to his eyes.

"Thyal isn't here, physically. He's looking in through me. I'm guessing the mind-control drug in the cake is keeping your minds open. If dracs can turn you into puppets, a Le'ankan Master should be able to find some of the strings."

A much better analogy than I was trying to come up with, Thyal said. *A word of warning. Granny still has your strings in her paws, so if you resist any commands she gives you, she might try to yank you free. Distance does seem to make my control somewhat tenuous.*

"Okay, so play along, mess up whatever Granny has us do, and delay until rescue shows up?"

Essentially.

"Got any other surprises we should know about?" Decker's voice was a grumble, but a malicious spark touched his eyes now. He looked down at Spitfire. "You are in so much trouble. Start making up for the trouble you caused by not telling Granny we're starting to think for ourselves, you got me?"

Spitfire let out a sad little chirp, then snuggled closer against him.

He is just gooey putty in her paws.

"She wants us to come out." Ashrock winced and pressed one scarred knuckle against the black spiral tattoo on his left temple. "Our allies are here."

"What do you know about them? Did she tell you anything?" M'kar asked.

"Yeah, these folks dropped their whole sob story on me, when I was a prisoner," Decker said. "Kind of interesting, but the old biddy put a gag order on me when they crammed that stuff down my throat and sent me back to get your dad and steal the shuttle."

He explained as they opened the hatch and climbed out and walked, slowly, to meet the oncoming riders and people driving wagons. These people were led by Dehbor and her daughter Sajan, scholars, low-level members of the Archivists Guild. They were descendants of people who had come from Draxonis during the last opening of the Chute. They had opposed the plans to destroy the numenjax and take over Castitarus. They had tried to sabotage the thermal taps that drained energy to lower the planet's temperature. They were stranded when the plot began to disintegrate and the enemies of the numenjax fled.

They had been working all these decades to counter the effects of two different plants that had been genetically engineered to make the numenjax hibernate, and to make their minds malleable to control. The dracs had been bred to control the numenjax, in the service of their masters on Draxonis.

The main ingredient of the cake used to impose the dracs' will on Decker and Ashrock had been used for generations to cloud the minds and rewrite the memories of the regular patrols on the shore of Fire Rock. It was also a component in the medicine they used to protect their men from bescere. No one ever realized a thriving settlement lived there, trying to reverse what their ancestors had done and find a way to awaken the numenjax. Dehbor and Sajan and other women took turns infiltrating Castitaran society, obtaining supplies and recruits and digging into the archives for information to help their quest.

"You ought to see the archeological work they've done, the tunnels they've cleared of the vines. There's a whole network of tunnels all over the planet, giving the numenjax access to people with psionic gifts, who serve as their voices to the ordinary people. All those tunnels have to be cleared out because the vines impose hibernation even when the planetary temperature has risen."

M'kar refrained from commenting that Decker certainly sounded impressed by these people who had held him prisoner.

"We greet you in the name of the numenjax." The speaker stayed mounted on her chestnut horse while the mixed group of men and women around her dismounted. She looked like she was the oldest, her long face framed with wisps of silver hair escaping what looked like a long scarf wrapped like a turban.

The men in the group didn't show the slightly childish expressions or occasionally blank gazes that M'kar had encountered elsewhere on the planet. They also looked older than most men she had seen on Castitarus. Likely proof what Decker had been told was the truth.

Did you get everything Decker said?

And passed it on to Genys and Veylen, Thyal responded. *They leave it to you to decide if these people can be trusted. Playing for time, Veylen said, might be more successful if you cooperated. Your discretion.*

Oh, just great ... M'kar pulled her shoulders back and stepped up so she was between Decker and her father, and the welcoming party. "I understand your goal is to get rid of all the vines, to aid in waking the numenjax. I don't know how much you know of planetary physics and weather cycles, but destroying the satellites won't raise the planetary temperature in just a few days or even a moon-cycle. Not fast enough to suit Granny," she added, gesturing with a jerk of her chin at the silver drac, who came to land on the woman's shoulder. "Scholar Dehbor?"

"Correct. She and her children brought you here to burn away the vines. We have spent generations fighting the growth, trying to work our way down to the dens where the numenjax sleep, but the vines grow faster than we can chop them apart and carry them away. They are resistant to all but the hottest fires, and the fuel we need is hard to obtain. Your machines will do in a few hours what we were unable to do in several generations."

"Problem. The ash you get from burning the vines is the base component of the sleeping powder the security forces use." M'kar thought a quick prayer for guidance and wisdom. "We scanned the tunnels under this island and calculated the amount of ash that would be produced. The physical damage from that much drugged ash would last for years."

"No one will be drugged." The young woman who spoke held the reins of Dehbor's horse. She looked enough like her, M'kar guessed she was Sajan, her daughter. "High enough temperatures render the ash impotent. The dangerous component lies in the sap that bubbles out of the vine at ignition. If the temperature is not high enough, the fine powder that remains is the soporific. As my mother said, we don't have the fuel to keep the fires going until the vines are completely destroyed. They grow back before we can get more fuel to continue the burning."

"So that's all you want from us?" Decker said. "Housecleaning?"

"No ... the old one says you have people among you who are gifted, able to hear the numanjax speak. We need your help finding those who retain that gift. They must be ready to hear the numenjax when they wake, and restore the benevolent society our ancestors tried to destroy," Dehbor said.

"I'm guessing you're one of those people, since you can hear Granny?" M'kar said.

"Yes, but I and mine must in all honor disqualify ourselves."

"Because your ancestors were egotistical morons?" Decker spat. "Why should you be punished? Seems to me, you've been making up for it for years. Other than you taking me prisoner and shoving that crap down my throat to let the old biddy inside my head, I gotta admit, I've got no gripe with you."

"You are too kind." Sajan made a half-bow to him. A smirk twisted her lips as she straightened up.

M'kar swore she saw a spark pass between her and Decker. Either they liked each other, or the complete opposite had happened while he was a prisoner, and it wouldn't be resolved until they had a chance to beat the snot out of each other.

"Is ..." Decker glanced upward and gestured with a jerk of his head. "Think they're getting all that?"

Yes, and the consensus for now is to proceed as you see fit, Thyal responded. *You don't have to speak aloud. Just think to me.*

Decker grinned. *How about we rile the old biddy and let them know we're back in the pilot's seat?* His mental voice was rich with laughter in M'kar's head. *I'm ready to help these folks. Kind of, what do you call it, cathartic? Kind of cathartic doing some heavy-duty burning. What are the chances the paper-pushers overrule the captain's go-ahead and court-martial all of us for interfering with a society that's functional, even if it's pretty warped functioning?*

"Excuse us, Scholar Dehbor," M'kar said. "Do you have much experience with the substance that opens up minds for drac control? Enough to experience psionic communication? We've been conferring, although it probably looks like we're experiencing some mental problems ..." She took a deep breath. "Enlo, I trust your hand in this, guide me ... Scholar Dehbor, we have permission from our captain to proceed as we deem proper, and we wish to help you. Without the influence of Granny and dracs under her command, who are going to be in so much trouble when we get back to the ship."

Granny lifted up from Dehbor's shoulder and blew raspberries at M'kar. Barroo trilled defiance, then wrapped himself even more securely around her neck and shoulders. Granny and most of the teacher dracs vanished.

M'kar went with Dehbor and Sajan to the opening of the tunnel, guarded by the ridge the riders had come around. She wanted to see the tunnels they had managed to clear out over the years. Decker and Ashrock oversaw the unloading of the thermal excavator. After taking a few minutes to do a general physical scan of her father, to make sure he wasn't suffering anything worse than a headache, she permitted the first dose of the restorative Sajan offered. She put a medical monitor on her father, just because of all the fluctuations and extremes he had gone through lately.

Can we trust them? she asked Thyal, as she rode in silence with the women.

We must. Friendship and alliance have to start somewhere. So far, Genys says the Senate is too stunned by what we have passed on to them to protest. They might decide to complain later that we overstepped ourselves, but all of them have stated at one time or another that they would welcome the return of the numenjax. We have a chance of doing that for them.

Yes, but the reality might be very different from their images and ideas passed down through folklore.

True. He chuckled. *We will make a philosopher of you yet.*

That's the cruelest thing you've ever said to me.

The sound of his laughter in her head eased the residual ache from the mind-control cake, cooling and smoothing all the scorched and rough places.

The exiles had taken some pains to hide their presence and the opening of the tunnel and all the clearing and burning they had done through the years. Despite the mind-fogging properties of the dust they used on security patrols, they weren't taking any chances. M'kar made a mental note to get official names, for the cake and dust and the people themselves. Just the thought of all the reports she would have to complete brought that headache back.

Then she walked through the camouflaged opening of the tunnel and into a passageway that could only have been formed by technology far more sophisticated than what Castitarus possessed.

It was glossy-smooth, except where images carved with deep strokes drew the gaze further into the passageway, until it curved out of sight to the right. The passageway seemed perfectly circular, except for where the flat, smooth floor intersected it in the bottom quarter of the circle. The lighting came from oil lamps set up on stands every two or three meters on both sides of the passage.

Dehbor and Sajan stayed back in the doorway, saying nothing as M'kar stepped up to the first images. Barroo nearly fell off her shoulder, from leaning so far forward to see. He cheeped an apology and jumped off, to hover next to her. She walked a few steps down the wall on the right, then moved back to the doorway and walked down the wall on the left, studying, letting the images carved there give her the narrative of this world.

"Scholar Dehbor, would you mind if I sent for equipment from my ship? My captain needs to see this, our linguist and sociologists need to see this."

"How long will it take for this equipment to come?" Sajan said, after exchanging glances with her mother. "We had hoped to burn away the vines from several turns of the tunnel before nightfall."

"Not long at all." M'kar decided to prime the pump with some trust. "We have shuttles coming, but at a word from me, no one will attack. However, we have a faster way." She held out her arm and Barroo came in to land. When he had the image clear in his head of what she wanted, he trilled and popped out. Then she gave Thyal a list of what to send down to her.

The two women let out sighs of wonder when twenty minutes later, Barroo, Boomer, Ha'ess and Infrenx popped in together, holding the straps of a duffel full of equipment. In minutes, M'kar had the communication pack set up and opened a link with the ship and with Genys in the Senate chambers. She handed recorder wands to the four dracs, hung small, powerful lights around their necks, and set them flying down the passageway, recording everything they saw.

While the dracs worked, she took care of making introductions between the exiles' leaders, Veylan and Thyal on the ship, and Genys, Treinna and Maora in the Senate. Dehbor asked if her superior, Sophria, head of the Archivists Guild, was in the Senate. When the woman acknowledged her presence, Dehbor asked permission to speak with her.

"I must ask your forgiveness and your understanding, for lying to you all these years. The mission I was born into demanded my loyalty. Even above the vows I made to you and to the preservation of knowledge and the rebuilding of what was destroyed through bescere and the loss of the numenjax. My ancestors were responsible, even if they turned away from that road. They were unable to prevent the injustice perpetrated against Castitarus. Please believe me, we worked from the shadows because we knew our enemies had also been stranded on Castitarus when the sky well closed, and they would continue their ancestors' mission of destroying the numenjax, even as we worked to undo it. The only mercy I ask is that you place all the punishment on my head, because all the others of our people who served in the guild continued the deception on my orders. I will submit myself to the discipline of the council --"

"Have you said quite enough, Dee?" a scratchy alto voice cut in. The woman chuckled. "Give us some credit for common sense. The Alliance people have been stunning us with all sorts of theories and information and offering us incredible riches of knowledge. We've been figuring out a few things for ourselves. Yes, you are in trouble, but not as much as you fear. The heritage you have tried to return to us should go a long way toward reducing any punishment that others might want to levy on you."

A few murmurs came through the pickup in the Senate chambers.

"Let's save that for later, much later, when this whole storm has passed, all right?" Sophria concluded.

"The dracs have come to the end of the cleared part of the tunnel," M'kar announced. "Sending through the compilation. The computer will delay as it tries to assemble all the pieces, so we have one coherent, continuous image." She stepped over to the flexible screen she had unrolled and set up in a stand while Dehbor was talking. It was three meters wide and two high, and responded to the commands tapped into her tablet. The first images came up, starting at the front of the cave. She grinned.

"Tell me you see what I'm seeing," she said, after five minutes of silence in which she could feel everyone holding their breaths, on the ship and in the Senate, and the excited racing of their hearts.

"If you see dragons and a whole bunch of weird script carved into the walls, then yeah, we see the same thing," Decker said, startling them all. He and Ashrock stood in the cave opening. Her father grinned and made triumph signs.

The three of them went down the passageway to see what the excavators had to deal with. Behind them, multiple voices rang out with questions and Dehbor and Sajan hurried to answer.

The passageway was a massive spiral going down through the rock, more than wide enough to accommodate the thermal excavator. The exiles had managed to clear out and keep clear three turns. M'kar shuddered a little when she came face to face with the barrier of vines. Green and purple-tinged growth speared through a wall of blackened vines. She swore after standing still for several minutes, she could see and hear the new growth pushing through. No wonder the vines were so pernicious. The rapid growth had to be genetically engineered, along with the resistance to all but the highest temperatures.

When they returned to the opening of the passageway, they found Dehbor and Sajan and a dozen other women, fellow scholars, in a frenzy of what seemed like happy argument over interpretations with the women on the other side of the communication pack. Thyal informed her that Genys had sent for the shuttles to come to the Senate and the Archivists Guild hall first, pick up as many scholars as were adventurous enough to take the flight, and bring them to Fire Rock.

The volume and number of voices trying to speak all at once dropped away. Treinna came on the link to inform them Genys and several matriarchs were going to the shuttle, and would be on Fire Rock by evening. They were also bringing camping gear and provisions. Then the link in the Senate chambers shut down, to be moved to the Archivists Guild hall.

"We must thank Praestantaes for the mercy we have received so far, and pray for continued safety and understanding, and ultimately peace," Dehbor said. She led her people out to begin preparations for the invasion of scholars.

Chapter Eighteen

"I swear my ears are still ringing," M'kar remarked, when Treinna re-established communication, this time a personal link with her tablet. She was now in the larger shuttle, heading for Fire Rock.

For the moment, M'kar was by herself. Decker, Ashrock, and most of Dehbor's men had taken the excavator to get to work burning through the blockage of vines. She settled down in front of the screen with her tablet, going through the images with Treinna, looking for similarities and stumbling through a translation. So far, they agreed the words and images were indeed instructions for those approaching the numenjax.

"Are you avoiding the other side of the tunnel, like our archivist friends were?" Treinna said after maybe half an hour.

By this time, the distinctively chalky odor of burning vines had drifted up the passageway. M'kar flinched every time she got a stronger whiff, and reminded herself several times what Dehbor had said about the dangerous qualities of the vine being destroyed by high temperatures. She was grateful Decker and Ashrock were both wearing breathing gear and had insisted on the men working with them wear it too. Ash was still bad for the lungs, even if all the drugs had been burned out of it.

"What are you picking up that I'm not?" M'kar responded, after yanking her thoughts back to the present moment.

"Maybe I'm crazy --"

"We all are. That's the only way to survive all the misfit luck that tangles up our crew."

"There are some references to powerful travelers. Rescuers. Beings -- not people, but beings -- who came here with children. They were startled when they discovered the numenjax here."

"Meaning ..." M'kar glanced up at the dracs, swooping along the walls, visibly delighted to study the images of the "big ones." Only the young dracs, not the teacher dracs or Granny.

"The powerful visitors. The rescuers." Treinna swallowed audibly. "What if this is a reference to the Gatekeepers?"

"The Gatekeepers brought the ancestors of these people here ... right. That doesn't fit with what we know of the Gatekeepers. How many of our instructors at the Academy grumbled over the Gatekeepers leaving the different Human tribes on primitive worlds? Meaning no civilizations. And how many fell into time-wasting discussions about that being evidence that Humans are the only truly sentient and souled beings Enlo created?"

"Too many, and too many times." She sighed. "But that's the thing. Maybe the Gatekeepers came here, and when they realized the numenjax were sentient, they didn't leave the people here."

"Then how did the people get here?"

"There are a few things ... okay, I'm making enough intuitive leaps here to put my brain on spring-shoes for the rest of my career. However long that lasts, if you ever breathe a word of this to anyone."

"I swear silence." M'kar grinned. Treinna couldn't see her, since both their tablets were set on the images they studied.

"What if ... okay, my theory is that the Gatekeepers took the 'children' mentioned in the carvings to Draxonis. Maybe they could open Chutes like we open jump gates. When the Chute opened up again between the worlds, the Draxonans had built up their technology enough to come here. A few passages indicate the ancestors came specifically to the numenjax for help. They were fleeing trouble, maybe a cataclysm."

"And if the things my Mom discovered are true ..." M'kar took a deep breath, while her brain swirled with the implications and put together a few half-formed ideas. "Okay, maybe the people who were oppressing them on Draxonis ... what? They came looking for them the next time the Chute opened?"

"And decided to punish the numenjax for helping them." Treinna shrugged. "Or maybe they wanted to enslave the numenjax, but couldn't. Does that sound crazy?"

"Considering some of the things we've run into?" She scrubbed her face with her open palms. "I'm guessing you wanted to talk this out before you wrote it down?"

"Even the craziest stuff needs to be recorded, just in case something totally bizarre happens and Fleet wants to know how come somebody didn't at least think of the possibility. If we had thought of it, we would have tried to prevent it."

~~~~~

When the shuttles arrived and the new arrivals set up a camp, they moved the display screen outside and placed it in the largest tent. The scholars needed shelter where they could argue and interpret and search the hundreds of kilos of tablets and scrolls and bound volumes they had brought with them. The extraction equipment Jasper sent down helped to reduce the clouds of ash, but nothing could be done about the noise.

Another tent was designated for negotiations between Dehbor's people and the matriarchs, to exchange information and fill in the missing holes in history. Genys sometimes thought she understood why Captain Shryne had a reputation for bulling her way through problems that some critics always claimed diplomacy could have handled with less damage and need for reparations. The problem was that diplomacy multiplied the time and patience required, as opposed to slapping everyone silent, sending them to their rooms without supper, then making them sit together until they learned to cooperate.

"Maybe I'm being a little Shryne-ish," she admitted to Maora and Treinna and M'kar, when they took some time away from the never-ending meetings to file some reports. "I'm putting all our careers on the line, giving help and making decisions without playing 'Mommy may I' with Congress, the Academy, and Fleet."

She admitted only to herself, and to Battleaxe, she was either hormonal or just frazzled and irritated by the stupidity and selfishness and scheming and arrogance of the ancestors who started all these problems. She needed to thumb her nose at authorities in general just to work off some steam.

The long hours of talking did yield some details necessary for their reports. The exiles had fed the mind-control cake to the Maniterri and sent them up to destroy the satellites. While getting rid of the satellites and letting the weather patterns return to normal would eventually awaken the numenjax, that might take years. The genetically engineered vines thrived in cool and damp, so while return of drier, warmer weather would have slowed their growth, that would take years as well.

Genys didn't blame the people of this world for not having much patience left, after all they had gone through. Especially the ones who had some idea of what had caused all the problems.
~~~~~

The mind-controlling cake was a variant of a substance used to detect people with psionic ability, and help them hear the numenjax, to act as their liaisons with ordinary Humans. The unrefined sap in large quantities granted mind control, while the processed product, when administered by the numenjax, was safe and used for the benefit of all.

The Draxonans had indeed bred the dracs to try to control the numenjax, the people of Castitarus, or both. The plan was to have the dracs ready to invade and take over the planet, which they intended to be in total chaos within a few years of the initial invasion. Except the nanites destroyed the technology of Draxonis before they could implement the second phase of their plan.

Dehbor's people had no idea who had created the nanites, mostly because they didn't know what nanites were. Nothing was mentioned in their ancestors' extensive records. The people of Castitarus certainly didn't possess the scientific knowledge or the technology to do it. The generation that had made the voyage through the Chute to ask for sanctuary with the numenjax had destroyed their higher levels of technology and science, to ensure their descendants would never repeat their generation's mistakes. Dehbor could only speculate that Draxonan history had repeated. A faction arose that created nanites to destroy its enemies, lost control of them, and killed their civilization.

All speculations were put on hold when news came that the excavators had burned down to the bottom of the spiral and reached level ground. The tunnel opened into a vaulted chamber nearly five meters tall, domed and smooth and full of more engravings in the walls. The excavator was having a harder time with the last of the vines because they were embedded in the one flat wall of the domed room, which resisted burning.

"That doesn't make any sense, if you think about it," M'kar said, when the report came to the surface where she, Treinna, Genys and Maora were working. "Weren't the vines taken from here because they could turn solid rock into farmland? How come, if the vines have been growing down there for centuries, there's still rock?"

"And how come we didn't wonder about the tunnels the vines have been filling up all this time?" Maora asked, and fluttered her eyelashes in fake innocence and wonder.

The four women laughed, somewhat wearily.

"Maybe what we consider rock, isn't?" Treinna said. "Maybe it's something synthetic, so the vines can't eat through it?"

"Well, there are insects on Nisandros that build their homes of pebbles, glued together with saliva that has an organic polymer in it," M'kar offered.

"Oh, that's a nice mental image. Tunnels lines with what, numenjax spit?" Genys said.

The communication pack flashed. Later, M'kar said they should have expected an interruption like that, because they had let themselves relax.

"Captain?" Vilson was head of the team running the excavator and attached sensors. "We've cleared away everything we can, nothing more to burn. Shut down maybe twenty minutes ago, taking readings. Now we're getting a thermal spike."

"I'm on my way. Get everyone else and everything out of there, just in case." Genys leaped up from the bench where she had been working on her tablet. For a moment her legs wobbled and M'kar nearly blurted a recommendation she stay there and let them handle it. She knew better. Their captain needed to be there to handle any crisis that might slap her crew.

Decker and several Security personnel joined them. Their pace slowed as they headed down the spiral. They had to move to the side of the passageway to let the excavator trundle past.

They were only three turns from reaching the bottom when Granny and all the teacher dracs burst into the passageway ahead of them. They shrieked and spun through the air, hitting the walls and making everyone go to their knees with their arms shielding their heads. The dracs' eyes spun red and yellow with fury, and a few streaks of greenish fear. Granny hovered in front of M'kar, mouth open and tongue extending, spitting with rage, trembling so her wings stiffened up and she dropped several times. Every time M'kar tried to make contact with her mind, and reached to keep the elderly silver drac from hitting the floor, Granny caught her breath and rose upward again and spun away. Then came back. The pulses of rage in her mind made M'kar's brain sore, so she gave up trying after the fourth scorching moment of psionic contact.

Barroo huddled down on M'kar's shoulder and wrapped his tail so tightly around her throat she almost couldn't breathe. He whimpered and crooned soothingly. His mental touch was cool in comparison with Granny's. The images her drac broadcasted were blurry with fear and confusion, but they clarified as a sense of anger, on M'kar's behalf, battled the other impressions.

"Does anyone else get an image of all of us jumping off the planet and back on the ship and getting out of here?" Decker snarled. "Fast enough to leave tread marks in the atmosphere?"

"Yes," Treinna said. "Granny is furious over something, and she wants to leave now."

"Really?" Genys straightened up. She patted Battleaxe, urging her drac to sit up straight on her shoulder. She glared at Granny and jammed both fists into her hips. "Well with all the trouble you've caused on this mission, if you want to get out of here, then I'm going down to see what you don't want us to see!"

M'kar held her breath as Genys stomped down the passageway.

Granny went silent, hovering unsteadily, and some of the reds and blacks in her eyes were replaced with yellows and greens. She was stunned, maybe confused. Was it possible Genys had frightened her?

"What she said," Decker growled. He cradled Spitfire, who hid her face against his chest and didn't look at Granny as he stomped after Genys. Treinna and Maora followed.

"People are more likely to say yes if you ask instead of order." M'kar had no idea how much of that Granny understood. Patting Barroo once more, and with a gentle tug on his tail to loosen his hold on her neck, she stood up and headed down the passageway. Not quite running, because it was hard to run when she was bracing for another aerial attack.

Granny and the ship's twelve teacher dracs didn't come after them. Listening to gut instinct, M'kar contacted Thyal and told him what had just happened. He put Infrenx on alert. Later, she reported the thirteen dracs had come back to the ship and were curled up in their various perches on the rec deck. Very quiet.

Vilson stood up from the sensor array, the only equipment that had been left in the vaulted room, just as M'kar joined the rest. "I don't really know what's happening, other than thermal activity. Either our equipment is hinked, or I'd swear that wall is thinning."

"Well, this place isn't called Fire Rock for no reason," Decker said with a shrug. "Volcanos, anyone?"

"There's no way, even with all that interference, the sensors on the ship and the shuttle wouldn't have caught *some* volcanic activity. Everything we've been collecting since we got into orbit indicates the volcanos are sleeping," Maora said.

"Then what's that?" He pointed at a spot in the wall level with their shoulders.

"The heat isn't high enough to melt rock," Vilson said, waving a sensor wand at the glowing spot.

"Didn't you say maybe that isn't rock?" Genys murmured.

Later, they wondered why they didn't run. Common sense would have had them running, but perhaps they had all gone over the point of "enough" and they just wanted answers, not more questions. So they stood there -- granted, with about ten meters between them and the glowing spot, that grew wider with every breath -- and waited.

M'kar thought about lava bubbling up and melting through. Yet this glowing of the rock wasn't the steady, ominous red of melting rock, growing brighter, turning orange and then yellow and then white before exploding outward toward them. This glow moved in streaks of gold and white and even hints of blue. The energy here wasn't entirely heat.

Greetings. How refreshing to find a mind containing such a musical resonance.

Many voices filled M'kar's mind, sent her to her knees, and made her deaf to everyone around her. It was an entire orchestra of waterfalls and avalanches and thunder and wind.

Thyal? was all she could manage. M'kar couldn't catch her breath. She was aware of Barroo clutching at her, felt the vibrations of his crooning, but couldn't hear them.

I hear them, he said. *Greetings to you in return. Can you hear me?*

Ah, of course. You can hear and respond because you are more than one small mind standing alone. We are never alone, and that is our blessing and our burden. Tell us, if you can, how long have we been sleeping?

Are you the numenjax?

Hmm, fascinating. We perceive you are a stranger to this world. There is much warping and shadowing of understanding. No, and yes. That is the name the children gave us. We are not entirely the dragons you imagine, yet that is indeed close enough to suit. Here is what we are.

M'kar gasped and sank back, clutching Barroo, aware of the others gathered around her, holding her upright. The image burning through her mind filled her head with a music she only partially comprehended. The being was wreathed in flame. It combined all the features of the drawings of numenjax, merged into one creature. Colorful streaks in a covering that was partially scales, partially feathers. Blue shading into purple into crimson into amber into emerald. Eyes ringed the wedge-shaped head sitting atop a long, graceful neck both swanlike and serpentine.

The Infrenx? Thyal, have we found the Infrenx?

No, children, the voice said, rippling with laughter and regret and something that oddly struck her as pleasure, satisfaction. *We know the Infrenx, and they are as much above us in the service of Enlo as the travelers were above you small mortals who are blessed with such incredible, creation-shaking potential.*

You know Enlo? Thyal asked.

We are not speaking with words, as you comprehend them. You hear us in the words you understand. We know the One who is Many and All, and we believe we are nearly wise enough to devote ourselves to the One's wisdom and to service. That is why when the travelers came here, we offered to help the children in their care. When the children's descendants begged for our help, we could not say no. A sense of laughter washed through M'kar, energizing her, making her feel she was finally breathing clearly for the first time in her life. *Step back for a little, children. Your friends cannot hear us through their terror for you. Encourage them and assure them they will not be consumed. Then return, and we will learn from each other.*

"I'm okay." M'kar's voice sounded rough and weak through the pounding in her ears, and it grated in her throat. Everybody's voices sounded rough and weak and sour, compared to the music that slowly receded from her soul. She was grateful for Genys and Treinna bracing her. When she looked back, as their group retreated from the room, the swirling of colors in the barrier had grown brighter, faster, richer, like a tapestry weaving itself through the stone.

Brea came hurtling down the spiral. Boomer soared over her head. Barroo leaped up and with Moonrise, Spitfire, and Battleaxe let out chirps and squeals and then popped out. Vilson had stayed behind. M'kar imagined him standing there, so fascinated with the readings coming through the sensors, he wouldn't notice until something leaped out of that barrier and gobbled him up.

Don't be ridiculous, child. We have sustenance far more than we need and are not hungry. Granted, the angry ones did something to the root source, souring it, but there is still nutrition aplenty. The voice let out a musical chuckle that eased the last of the weary aches spilling through M'kar from her head downward. *It is quite safe for you to come back. Bring your friend who hears so splendidly. Physical proximity does help.*

"Yeah, it does," she murmured.

The others had stopped, less than halfway up the spiral. They guided her to sit down and Brea got to work. She announced M'kar was fine, but she had undergone a brief flash of psionic "stretching" that depleted her physical resources. They protested a little when M'kar insisted on going back down to the room, but didn't fight or try to drag her away.

She dubbed it the audience chamber, and bits of the information the numenjax had spilled into her mind assembled gradually into understanding. The creatures would not come through the barrier, which as they had surmised was not rock. That had protected them, and the interior of the spiral tunnel, from the destructive qualities of the vine.

"We need to get Thyal down here. I think the only reason I can hear them is because I'm not mentally alone. Our crazy bond, I don't know, makes us strong enough to take the bombardment. Because they're not one mind, they're a lot of minds speaking at once. I think we'll be able to take it better if there isn't physical distance between us.

"I think we're going to be out for a while, even worse than when Barroo hatched. This is a mental suckage on a magnitude I can't even begin to guess." She gestured at the swirling colors in the glowing barrier that now filled the flat wall. "The numenjax are finally awake, and they're catching up on what's been happening since they rolled up the mat and closed the door." She sighed, as more of the information put into her head settled into place. "Could someone get me some water? I've got a killer headache coming on."

You think you have a headache? Thyal sounded amused. *Granny knows the numenjax are awake and she is insisting with increasing fury and volume that we leave the planet right now.*

An image came into her head, of the dracs swarming the bridge, pouncing on different duty stations, trying to move controls. Granny hung in the air in front of Veylen, shrieking and scolding. He sat in the command chair, his face calm, and ignored her, though M'kar caught a few flinches as drac spit hit his face.

"Veylen is my hero."

"What is going on up there?" Genys demanded.

In response, her tool wristband flashed and let out a series of chirps with the code for "contact the ship."

Ah, yes. The numenjax collective voice sounded only slightly amused. *The little ones thought they could command us. They were quite upset to learn that not only are we impervious to their demands, but we can control them. The oldest one is, in your very apt parlance, trying to pick up her toys and go home.*

M'kar burst out laughing. It made her head throb, but she didn't care.

~~~~~

While they waited for Thyal to come down from the ship, M'kar shared some of the information spilled into her mind during the short conversation. It had seemed to take some while for her, but according to her companions, she had only been down on her knees, staring, struggling to breathe, for maybe a minute at the most. The numenjax had taken much information from her, from the upper layers of her thoughts and Thyal's thoughts, and confirmed a number of theories.

The vines were originally their curtains, their defensive measure, a barrier during the cold seasons when they hibernated. The vines soaked up nutrients and water from the surrounding rock and soil and fed the numenjax during their regular cycle of hibernation. The soporific quality was a seasonal aspect of the vines. The Draxonans had done some genetic engineering of the vines, so the chemical composition changed, becoming stronger as the colder and wetter conditions endured. The natural lifecycle of the vines should have adjusted to release them from their hibernation, but the planet's temperature had lowered just a few degrees thanks to the weather satellites and geo-thermal taps.

Dr. Jeyn came down with Thyal. M'kar could almost laugh at how her father seemed to shrink in anticipation of her mother's fury. He had nothing to fear. If he hadn't been purging the last of
~~~~~

the mind-control drugs and the hormonal imbalances of bescere from his system, he wouldn't have worried. Jeyn was just so relieved to have him closer to normal, she laughed with tears in her eyes. Then she insisted on overseeing a thorough physical of both M'kar and Ashrock before the next phase of discussion with the numenjax commenced.

When M'kar and Thyal went back down the spiral to the audience room, the first shuttles had arrived with more representatives from the Senate and the leaders of the guilds and clans. Jasper's construction teams were busy assembling semi-permanent shelters on the plain surrounding the tunnel, and clearing away the camouflaging debris from the tunnel itself. Fire Rock would serve as neutral ground for the negotiations and discussions that would follow.

The meeting of minds took less than an hour, with M'kar and Thyal reclining on cushions embedded with medical monitoring equipment. Tahl and a team of medics oversaw their physical wellbeing during that time.

Brea came up with one of her potions to brace M'kar and Thyal for the anticipated strain of the mental link with the numenjax. Afterward, they needed to sleep, to purge the fatigue poisons that had built up during the extended mental contact. They shared the most important information, confirming several theories, before they went to their bunks in a shuttle and initiated healing trances on themselves.

The Gatekeepers had come to Castitarus. When they found the numenjax, they had taken their refugees to another world on the other end of the Chute. Draxonis. When technology advanced beyond the intellectual and mental maturity of the Draxonans and civil wars broke out, the numenjax had given shelter to refugees. Those who put themselves under their guardianship and chose a simpler lifestyle stayed under their care, while others took their ships and went in search of other worlds. Draxonis made contact the next time the Chute opened. They hadn't learned the right lessons from the destruction of war and the generations of rebuilding. Their attitudes hadn't improved. They considered the protective decrees of the numenjax as interference and slavery. They set out to remake Castitarus to suit themselves. Bescere was an unplanned side-effect from altering the vines to cripple the numenjax.

Their reports finished, M'kar and Thyal slept twenty hours, with the seven dracs keeping watch.

~~~~~

The Senate officially requested partnership and eventual membership in the Alliance. Maora and her team, augmented by the *Dandridge*'s sociologists, got to work hammering out the foundation upon which the diplomats would build once their ships arrived. Between regular doses of tear sop and programming the personal defensive shields to filter out the spore that caused bescere, male crew from both ships were able to come down to the planet. Re-education and restructuring of Castitaran society had to begin with teaching the leadership how to deal with mature, self-controlled men who could think and reason and argue with them. Teaching even the most enlightened to interact with men as more than beasts of burden or children to guide by the hand had to start somewhere. The *Dandridge*'s medics took what Tahl's people had learned, and started the intensive education of Castitarus' healers, to begin the fight to wipe out bescere, and initiate the long-term task of cleansing and rebalancing the blood chemistry of the male population. No one was sure yet if the older generation's mental faculties would be regained or rebuilt after so much time hindered by the hormonal imbalances, yet there was some hope for improvement, if not full healing.

The last few missing Maniterri were found. Vitiarre didn't want to leave the small river canyon where they had been dropped when they became too much trouble to handle. He had been ostracized by his former followers, and spent his days and nights muddy, dressed in rags, trying to dig through the mud to find the numenjax. He insisted he would find their den any day now, and when he had tamed a numenjax to serve him, everyone would be sorry. He shrieked and stomped his feet and refused rescue, until Sh'hari shot him with tranquilizer and dragged him into the shuttle.

M'kar and Thyal spent the better part of three days in mental conference with the numenjax, reporting, then sleeping and recovering. Ashrock made himself their defender and bullied them into eating huge meals in between their sessions. Genys let him tease and bully her into what he called "refresher" training in self-defense, Nisandrian-style. Battleaxe constantly flew over their
~~~~~

heads, scolding and taunting them equally. In those relaxed, semi-private times, when they were waiting for M'kar and Thyal to either wake up or emerge from the tunnel, they had plenty of time to talk. She finally had a chance to ask what *mi'sho'ki* meant. She laughed when Ashrock confessed and then begged her not to reveal that she knew. Genys promised, but she knew, and Ashrock had to know, this was one promise she couldn't keep.

At long last, the vessels filled with diplomats, healers, scientists and teachers reached Castitarus. Genys suspected the only being on the ship more relieved than her to be heading back through the Chute to the Alliance and Anwesta, was Granny. She had spent the decs of waiting in orbit sulking and refusing to socialize with anyone. When she vanished for days at a time, she always returned sulking and starving. Her temper didn't improve until they had gone through the Chute from Castitarus to Draxonis.

Everyone generally agreed there was little hope Granny had learned anything from this defeat and disappointment.

~~~~~

"So ..." Genys watched Battleaxe and Barroo and Infrenx playing tag ahead of them in the ship's corridor, banging into each other and the ceiling. She still cringed every time they hit something, even knowing they wouldn't damage any of the equipment embedded in the walls. The Chute leading to Draxonis was behind them and they were headed for Anwesta.

She and M'kar and Thyal were on their way to Dr. Jeyn and Ashrock's quarters. M'kar's father had insisted on creating an elaborate Nisandrian feast to celebrate the successful completion of their mission.

"So what?" M'kar strolled along beside her, arms clasped behind her back.

Thyal's chair floated along on M'kar's other side. Both had worn the same peaceful, weary smiles since the first draining session with the numenajx. Sometimes Genys wondered if M'kar would ever return to her normal wary, sometimes bitterly humorous, always alert disposition.

"So ..."

"Smell that?" M'kar inhaled loudly. "Despite the lack of half the right ingredients ... I don't know how Po'pa does it, but that is shriek beast stew. Prepare to be scorched inside and out, and love
~~~~~

every awful minute of it."

The door of the guest quarters hung open ahead of them. Genys could have sworn a visible cloud of spices spun out into the hall.

"So, *Mi'sho'ki*. Seriously?" She muffled a chuckle when M'kar stopped short and turned her head, suspicion cracking that placid façade at last. "Really? Deadly Dumpling?"

"Po'pa!" M'kar snarled. She gave Genys one look that might have knocked her flat on her back if she wasn't braced for it, then raced the last few meters to the open door.

Genys followed at a normal pace. She and Thyal exchanged grins, and a crash echoed into the passageway.

Life was good on the *Defender*. And never boring.

END

About the Author

On the road to publication, Michelle fell into fandom in college and has 40+ stories in various SF and fantasy universes. She has a bunch of useless degrees in theater, English, film/communication, and writing. Even worse, she has over 100 books and novellas with multiple small presses, in science fiction and fantasy, YA, suspense, women's fiction, and sub-genres of romance.

Her official launch into publishing came with winning first place in the Writers of the Future contest in 1990. She was a finalist in the EPIC Awards competition multiple times, winning with *Lorien* in 2006 and *The Meruk Episodes, I-V,* in 2010, and was a finalist in the Realm Award competition, in conjunction with the Realm Makers convention.

Her training includes the Institute for Children's Literature; proofreading at an advertising agency; and working at a community newspaper. She is a tea snob and freelance edits for a living (MichelleLevigne@gmail.com for info/rates), but only enough to give her time to write. Her newest crime against the literary world is to be co-managing editor at Mt. Zion Ridge Press and running the publishing co-op, Ye Olde Dragon Books. Be afraid … be very afraid.

www.Mlevigne.com
www.MichelleLevigne.blogspot.com
www.YeOldeDragonBooks.com
www.MtZionRidgePress.com
@MichelleLevigne

Look for Michelle's Goodreads groups:
Guardians of Neighborlee
Voyages of the AFV Defender

NEWSLETTER:
Want to learn about upcoming books, book launch parties, inside information, and cover reveals?
Go to Michelle's website or blog to sign up.

Also by Michelle L. Levigne

Guardians of the Time Stream: 4-book Steampunk series
The Match Girls: Humorous inspirational romance series starting with **A Match (Not) Made in Heaven**
Sarai's Journey: A 2-book biblical fiction series
Tabor Heights: 20-book inspirational small town romance series.
Quarry Hall: 11-book women's fiction/suspense series
For Sale: Wedding Dress. Never Used: inspirational romance
Crooked Creek: Fun Fables About Critters and Kids: Children's short stories.
Do Yourself a Favor: Tips and Quips on the Writing Life. A book of writing advice.
Killing His Alter-Ego: contemporary romance/suspense, taking place in fandom.
The Commonwealth Universe: SF series, 25 books and growing
The Hunt: 5-book YA fantasy series
Faxinor: Fantasy series, 4 books and growing
Wildvine: Fantasy series, 14 books when all released
Neighborlee: Humorous fantasy series
Zygradon: 5-book Arthurian fantasy series
AFV Defender: SF adventure series